The Last
Mrs. Summers

The Last
Mrs. Summers

RHYS BOWEN

BERKLEY PRIME CRIME
New York

BERKLEY PRIME CRIME
Published by Berkley
An imprint of Penguin Random House LLC
penguinrandomhouse.com

Library of Congress Cataloging-in-Publication Data

Names: Bowen, Rhys, author.
Title: The last Mrs. Summers / Rhys Bowen.
Description: First edition. | New York: Berkley Prime Crime, 2020. |
Series: A royal spyness mystery; 14
Identifiers: LCCN 2020010992 (print) | LCCN 2020010993 (ebook) |
ISBN 9780451492876 (hardcover) | ISBN 9780440000068 (ebook)
Subjects: GSAFD: Mystery fiction. | Historical fiction.
Classification: LCC PR6052.O848 L375 2020 (print) |
LCC PR6052.O848 (ebook) | DDC 823/.914—dc23
LC record available at https://lccn.loc.gov/2020010992
LC ebook record available at https://lccn.loc.gov/2020010993

Printed in the United States of America
1   3   5   7   9   10   8   6   4   2

Cover art by John Mattos
Cover design by Rita Frangie

This book is dedicated to my Cornish kin, the Vyvyans,
with whom I stay every summer in a manor house very like Trengilly.
It's one of my favorite parts of the world,
and they will recognize several of the names and references in the book.

I also want to thank my wonderful agents,
Meg Ruley and Christina Hogrebe,
and the entire team at Jane Rotrosen,
as well as Michelle Vega and the whole team at Berkley.
Working with you is always such a joy.

And lastly, as always, a sincere thank-you to my husband, John,
who is my first reader, editor, driver, porter and all around companion.
We have had many Cornish adventures together,
including driving along those lanes.

Foreword

I first discovered Daphne du Maurier's *Rebecca* during my teens. It was the first book that really grabbed me on an emotional level, probably the first book I could not put down. So this book is my homage to *Rebecca*. Those familiar with the book will see the references to the original. If you haven't read *Rebecca* yet, I suggest you do so. It's slightly dated now but great reading.

And I'd just like to say a couple of words about one of the themes in the book: that of men taking for granted that women are fair game, that they are there to be sexually abused. This is an uncomfortable theme, but in those days some property owners still looked upon servants as their property. And the fondling and groping of young women and girls was still overlooked and tolerated in some families.

Young women and girls had to look out for one another, but of course we know now that it shouldn't have been that way; the onus shouldn't have been on them to protect themselves from sexual abuse. You'll find one particular character to be repugnant. I apologize in advance!

The Last
Mrs. Summers

$\mathcal{C}$hapter 1

Last night I had a strange dream. I dreamed that I was mistress of an
enormous house. It was so large that I couldn't find my way
around it. I kept running down long dark hallways and opening
doors but nothing looked familiar. Empty rooms. Furniture
covered in dust sheets. I knew that somewhere was a man who
would take care of me, but I had no idea how to find him. I awoke,
sweating, reached out for Darcy and found only a cold empty bed
beside me. I sat up, heart pounding, before I realized that he had
gone away.

By the light of day I analyzed that dream. The strange thing about it
was that it was all true. I had achieved my ultimate desire: I was married to a gorgeous and sexy man, and really was mistress of a big,
empty house called Eynsleigh. I know—it's still mind-boggling to me!
It was mid-October. We had been married for almost three months
and much of that time had been wonderful. Darcy and I had been

to Kenya on our honeymoon—a little more dramatic than I had anticipated. I had enjoyed learning to be mistress of a large house for the first time, arranging Eynsleigh to my own satisfaction and slipping into a comfortable routine with my new husband.

I had encouraged him to turn down a desk job at the Foreign Office, knowing him too well and suspecting he would be bored with inactivity. But now I was coming to regret this as last week he had accepted some sort of assignment from person or persons unknown, and gone off, unable to tell me the nature of this assignment or where he was going. I had accepted, in theory, that this is what life would be like with Darcy. I was pretty sure by now that he did something undercover for the English government but the reality that he might disappear at a moment's notice with no forwarding address was just beginning to sink in.

"You were the one who insisted I didn't take the desk job, Georgie," he reminded me as he packed a tiny suitcase for himself. He wouldn't even let me feel useful by packing for him. "You knew what you were getting into."

I nodded, determined not to cry in front of him. "I understand, but at least you could give me a hint about where you'll be and how long you'll be gone."

He smiled at me then and ran a hand down my cheek. "Like sending you a postcard saying 'Wish you were here' for all my adversaries to see?"

"Will there be adversaries?" I asked, picturing men with guns hiding behind trees.

"There are plenty around the world who do not like Britain and wish us ill," he said, "but don't worry. I'm not going into any real danger. I'll be back before you know it. Don't think about me while I'm gone. Just enjoy yourself."

"How can I enjoy myself if you're not here?" I said, resting my head against him. "I'll miss you every minute."

He turned toward me then and gave me a little kiss on the forehead. "I'll miss you too, but we have to get on with life, don't we? You must learn to keep yourself busy. Do some entertaining."

"Entertaining?" I sounded more horrified than I intended to. "Dinner parties and things? Without you?"

"It's about time we got to know our neighbors," he said, "and you know they are all dying to take a peek at Eynsleigh and meet the lady of the house, who is reputed to be related to the royal family."

"Oh golly," I said. I had resolved to give up such childish exclamations when I married but they still slipped out in moments of extreme stress. "Darcy, you know very well I have no experience at entertaining. I grew up in a remote Scottish castle. We hardly ever entertained. No—make that never entertained, especially after Fig became Duchess of Rannoch. Who'd want more than one day of her company?" (Fig, for those of you who haven't met her, is my sister-in-law. The less said the better.)

"Then this will be good experience." Darcy looked up from folding a white shirt to give me an encouraging grin. "Nothing fancy. I'm not suggesting you have a costume ball or anything. Maybe a couple of ladies to tea or luncheon. Queenie can manage a luncheon, can't she?"

I nodded. "Maybe," I said dubiously.

He saw my look and went on. "It's always useful to be on good terms with neighbors. We'll become part of the local scene. And you never know when we might need them."

"I suppose so," I muttered while visions of sitting surrounded by formidable ladies at tea parties and my knocking over a cup or dropping a cream cake into somebody's lap swam through my head. I do tend to get a trifle clumsy when I'm nervous.

Darcy put a hand on my shoulder. "You are the mistress of Eynsleigh now, you know. You have to learn how to assume the role. And it will keep you busy so that you don't miss me too much."

"I'll miss you whatever I do," I said. "Do you think you'll be away long?"

"I can't really say." He gave a little frown. "Not too long, I hope."

"In which case I'd just much rather leave the entertaining until we're together, if you don't mind. I'd like reassurance the first time I play at lady of the manor."

He placed his pajamas on top of the other clothes. "Well then, why don't you go up to your family in Scotland? There will be shoots and things, won't there?"

"Do you want to punish me as well as desert me?" I asked, making him chuckle.

"All right. I can see that a week or so with your sister-in-law would be the ultimate punishment. In that case go up to town and stay with Zou Zou. See a show. Let her buy you clothes."

I nodded again, still not wanting my voice to betray me. I took a deep breath before I spoke. "Yes, I could do that. I do adore Zou Zou. Or you know what? I could invite my grandfather down to stay. The *Times* says that the London fogs have begun early this year, and you know he has a bad chest."

"Good idea." Darcy gave me a bright smile and my shoulder a squeeze. "Now I must be off or I won't catch that boat train."

So at least I knew he was going abroad. I was so tempted to ask which boat he was taking. The *Berengaria*? Or the ferry across the channel? Or a tramp steamer to Buenos Aires? It could be any of the above.

"I'll drive you to the station," I said. "I'll have Phipps get out the Bentley."

I constantly surprised myself how easily something like this rolled off my tongue. We had a footman called Phipps. We had a Bentley. We had a house. It seemed like only yesterday that I was camping out in my brother Binky's London residence, living on baked beans and cleaning other people's houses for money. Actually all this current bounty was not technically mine. It belonged to Sir Hubert Anstruther, a dashing mountaineer and explorer, my mother's former husband, or rather one of my mother's former husbands (she had worked her way through rather a lot of men, some of whom she had actually married). Sir Hubert had become very fond of me and wanted to adopt me. The family had not agreed to that—the family being the royal family, since my father was a grandson of Queen Victoria. You see, I'm not quite royal but related to them—too far from the throne to get a royal allowance or a palace or two, but close enough so that I had to abide by their rules. Not any longer, however. I had been permitted to renounce my place in the line of succession when I married Darcy, a Catholic. No Catholics on the throne of England, ever!

I hadn't found out until recently that Sir Hubert had made me his heir and had now invited me to come and live at his lovely house called Eynsleigh while he was off climbing mountains. More than that, he had told me to consider the house as my own and to do what I wanted with it. He had come home for my wedding but now had gone off again, back to Chile to find more peaks to scale. I think this had been prompted by my mother's departure. She had been staying with us all summer, after her own impending marriage to a German industrialist fell through, and I could see that Sir Hubert still had feelings for her. I rather suspected that she might still have feelings for him and hoped that something would come of it. He would make a more suitable husband than Max von Strohheim. I had nothing personally against Max. He clearly adored my mother, but he was also becoming remarkably thick with the Nazis in Germany. I suspected his factories might now be making weapons and tanks rather than motorcars and household items. I had been secretly glad when his father died and, not wanting to upset his puritanical mother, he declared he could no longer marry Mummy, because of her notorious past. But just when Mummy and Sir Hubert were giving each other long, meaningful glances she received a telegram from Max saying he couldn't live without her and to heck with his mother. And off she had rushed, straight back to his arms. I hadn't heard from her for ages. My mother, being completely self-absorbed, only communicated when she needed something.

So now I found myself all alone in a big, beautiful house. Alone with precious little to do. Sir Hubert's former housekeeper, Mrs. Holbrook, had come back at our request and the house now ran like a well-oiled machine. The one thing I had not yet done was to find a new cook. My former maid Queenie, undoubtedly the worst maid in the entire world, had now taken over the cooking. She had proved to be remarkably good at it, but could only manage the plain cooking she was used to. Eventually one does tire of shepherd's pie and toad-in-the-hole. And as Darcy had pointed out, I knew that as chatelaine of a great house I would eventually be expected to entertain. My neighbors had been hinting that they'd love to see Eynsleigh return to its glory days with dinner parties and balls. I pictured a glittering dinner table, women dripping with diamonds and men adorned with medals and then serving them spotted dick (which, in case you don't know, is a suet pudding with currants in it). They would prod it politely, say "Spotted what did you call it?," take a tentative bite . . . no, it was not going to happen. I did need a real cook, but I had hesitated, having had no experience at all in hiring servants.

Was I brave enough to do as Darcy had suggested and start off with a tea party or even a luncheon? Queenie was a dab hand with scones and little cakes. I wasn't so sure about luncheons. I doubted she had even heard of a soufflé and the weather was no longer conducive to ham and salad. Then I came to a conclusion. Tea parties could wait. I'd go and see Zou Zou. She might even know where I could find a cook who wouldn't cost too much. Sir Hubert was paying for the upkeep of the house but I didn't want to use too much of his money and of course had none of my own. Darcy was almost as penniless as I was.

Having come to a decision I found my current maid (a willing village girl called Maisie who had taken over the position from Queenie and was proving a remarkably quick learner—not having lost, scorched, or torn a single item yet) and told her to pack an overnight bag as I was going up to town. I must say it was a relief to know that I would open my suitcase and actually find a matching pair of shoes and enough underclothes after years of Queenie's packing for me. I felt quite excited as I sat in the first-class compartment of the train and we sped past fields of startled cows toward the City. It was an absolutely sparkling day. Instead of being engulfed in fog the outline of the parliament buildings was etched against the purest of blue skies. My spirits soared. A few days of good food with Zou Zou and then taking my grandfather back to Eynsleigh. What could be better? And Darcy would be home before I knew it.

I splurged on a taxi to Eaton Square, where Zou Zou, known to the world as the Princess Zamanska of Poland, lived. I went up the front steps and gave the door a sharp knock. I waited. Nothing happened. This was odd as Zou Zou's French maid, Clotilde, was normally in residence even when her mistress was away. It occurred to me that perhaps I should have telephoned first, but Zou Zou was an impetuous type of person who didn't at all mind one dropping in without warning. I gave the knocker a second, louder, rap.

"The lady's not here, miss," a voice said and I noticed a maid, down on her hands and knees, scrubbing the front step of the next-door house. "She went off in a taxi only yesterday. She had ever so many bags and her maid with her and I heard her tell the taxi driver Victoria Station."

Oh rats, I thought. Zou Zou had gone off to the Continent again. And with ever so many bags it was hardly likely to be a flying visit. I came down the steps feeling rather foolish.

It doesn't matter, I told myself. I'll rescue Granddad, take him down to Eynsleigh and we'll have a lovely time together. We'll take long walks and play cribbage in the evenings. I expect he's feeling lonely too, now that Mrs. Huggins is no more. So I set off resolutely toward the nearest Tube station at Victoria. As I crossed the King's Road I did pause and glance in the direction of my friend Belinda's little mews cottage at the other end of Chesham Street. I gave a little sigh. Belinda had been in Paris for a month, honing her dress designing skills with the best in the business. I missed her. I missed female companionship. To be truthful I even missed Mummy, which was saying a lot as Mummy only liked to talk about herself.

I sighed and walked on. As I came onto Buckingham Palace Road I looked in the direction of the palace and felt another pang of regret. In the past Her Majesty had summoned me to tea with her and given me various little assignments. These ranged from spying on her son the Prince of Wales to recovering a valuable snuffbox or hosting a foreign princess. Actually some of those assignments had been downright embarrassing or even terrifying but it still hurt a little that I might no longer be welcome in royal circles, now that I had officially renounced my place as thirty-fifth in the line of succession.

I pushed the thought aside. I was a married woman with my own household. I had to learn to be grown-up and get on with life. Soon I hoped to be a mother with a family of my own to occupy me. Soon . . . just not yet. I had been married for three months and still no hint of a baby. I had begun to worry whether there might be something wrong with me.

It was still a perfect day when I came out of the station at Upminster Bridge in Essex and walked up the hill toward my grandfather's street. Leaves clung to tree branches and glowed yellow and orange against that blue sky. Some fluttered to the ground and lay in drifts underfoot. I reached the top of the hill and turned onto Glanville Drive. It was a pleasant enough little street of semidetached houses such as one sees in every suburb around London. The front garden at number twenty-two was tiny but immaculate. Most of the summer flowers had died but there were still chrysanthemums around the pocket-handkerchief-sized lawn, and the three gnomes stared at me hopefully as I opened the front gate.

I suppose I should explain briefly for those of you who are confused at my having a grandfather who lived in a semidetached house with gnomes in the front garden, and not in a palace. My father was Queen Victoria's grandson but he had married my mother, a famous actress and the daughter of a London policeman. For that reason I had been kept from meeting my grandfather until I was grown-up. Since then I had made up for lost time and absolutely adored him. I think that he was the one person who loved me unconditionally (apart from Darcy, that is).

I rang the doorbell and prayed that he too wasn't out. At least he was not likely to have gone away anywhere. If he wasn't home it would only be shopping in the high street. I held my breath but then the front door opened and there he was.

"Hello, Granddad," I said.

A big smile spread across his face. "Well, blow me down with a feather," he said. "The last person I expected to see, my love. What are you doing here? Nothing wrong, is there?"

"No, of course not. Everything's perfect. I came to surprise you," I said. "Aren't you going to invite me in?"

He sucked air through his teeth, clearly embarrassed, making me wonder for a second if he had a woman in there. "I'd love to, ducks, but you see I was just . . ."

That's when I noticed that he was dressed in a suit and was wearing polished shoes instead of his slippers. What's more, his hair was slicked down with bay rum.

"Oh dear," I said. "Have I caught you at a bad time?"

"I'm afraid you have, my love," he said. "You see, I'm due at my old police station in Hackney within the hour. I told my old guv that I'd be there and I can't let him down."

"You haven't gone back to work, surely?"

He gave me a challenging look. "What, you think the old geezer is past it, do you?"

"No, of course not," I said hastily. "It's just that you've been retired for some time and . . ."

He put a big hand on my shoulder. "It's all right, ducks. 'old your 'air on. I'm not back on the force. Just doing a bit of volunteer work. My old guv has started a scheme to keep the young folk in the area out of mischief. Get 'em while they are young. That's his philosophy. And he came to me and asked if I'd have time to help him out with it. So of course I jumped at the idea. It's bloomin' boring rattling around in this house all day with nothing to do and no one to talk to."

"You know you are always welcome at Eynsleigh," I said. "I love to have your company and the country air is good for you."

He gave me a sad little smile. "I know, ducks. But it's not my sort of place, is it? Great big house like that, and all them servants. I feel uncomfortable with people waiting on me. I just don't belong." He paused. "Don't get me wrong. I love seeing my granddaughter. It's a real treat. Just not down there. Are you up in the Smoke for long? 'Cos I'll be back this evening. I could bring in some fish and chips."

"I only came up for the day," I lied, hoping he wouldn't notice the small suitcase I was carrying. "I was hoping to take you back with me. Give those lungs of yours some good fresh air."

"Ain't much wrong with the air up here right now, is there?" he asked, smiling up at the blue sky. "Smashing sort of day, isn't it? Makes you want to get out and do some walking. I'm going to set up a football match for the boys. Do them good. There's not much for them to look forward to in that dockland, you know. Most of them are finished with school and there's no jobs to be had for love or money. In the end, crime seems like a good idea to them. That's what my old guv is trying to prevent. Give them some hope and some skills. Put them on the right path."

He took his pocket watch out and glanced surreptitiously at it. "Which means I have to get going. Will you walk with me to the station?"

"Of course I will," I said. "I'm really pleased you have found something worthwhile to do. I know you must have been sad and lonely after Mrs. Huggins died."

He closed the front door behind us and we started walking along Glanville Drive. "You know I didn't think I'd miss her but I did," he said at last. "You get used to somebody, don't you? Expect to have them around. Even if you're listening to the wireless together it's the companionship, isn't it? So I'm glad I'm keeping myself busy. You've got your own life. You and that handsome husband of yours. And pretty soon the patter of tiny feet, eh?" And he dug me in the ribs with a grin.

"I hope so," I said. "But Darcy's away at the moment and like you I'm feeling rather lonely. It's only just beginning to sink in that I'm now mistress of my own house and I have to make a life for myself in the country. But it's hard to know where to start. Darcy suggested I give luncheons or tea parties but the thought terrifies me. You know what some of those county set dowagers are like."

He chuckled then, the chuckle turning to a cough. "Actually I've no idea. Never met one. But take it one step at a time, my love. You'll find your way soon enough. And your own sort of people too. Why don't you invite that friend of yours to stay? Belinda, isn't it? You two were always very thick."

"I would only she's been in Paris for a while now. And Mummy's back in Germany with Max."

That made him give a little grunt. Having lost a son in the Great War he did not approve of Germans. "I think she's making a big mistake there," he said. "That Sir Hubert of yours, smashing chap, if you ask me. And clearly still keen on her. What did she want to go rushing back to that bloomin' Hun again for?"

"I think she likes the money for one thing. Max is awfully rich."

"But at what price, love, eh? Those Germans, they are slipping back to their old ways. All those rallies and that little Hitler bloke shouting and prancing around. I don't like it one bit. I just hope your mum don't find herself on the wrong side if another war happens."

"Oh surely not, Granddad," I said. "Nobody could possibly want war after the last one. Everyone saw what a frightful waste of human life it was."

"Don't count on it, ducks. That Hitler bloke, he's got big ideas. You mark my words. Trouble's coming."

"Golly. I hope you're wrong," I said.

Chapter 2

I felt weighed down by a cloud of doom as I took the train back to Eynsleigh. No Zou Zou, no Belinda, no Queen Mary and no granddad. It really did look as if I'd have to start meeting those neighbors and getting involved in village life. And what Granddad had said about Hitler and Germany weighed on my mind. If there was another war Darcy would be called up to fight. I closed my eyes, not able to bear the thought.

Phipps had dropped me at the station as I had expected to be away for a while. I thought of telephoning Eynsleigh and asking to be picked up, but it was still a glorious day so I decided to walk. Hazelnuts were thick on the trees beside the lane. I made a mental note to come and pick some. Cows and horses peered at me over gates. Sheep regarded me suspiciously and moved away. I came into the village, down the one main street, passing the Queen's Head pub, the baker's, the newsagents, the greengrocer and butcher. Women out doing their shopping nodded to me. One said "Lovely day, isn't it, your ladyship?"

and I agreed that it was. From the village school came the chant of children learning their four times table. "Four fours are sixteen. Five fours are twenty. . . ."

It wasn't such a bad place to be, I told myself. I would learn to get used to life here. I'd join the ladies' guild at the church or help with the Girl Guides or the pony club. Then a few unbidden images formed in my head. Me being asked to iron the church altar cloths, polish the chalices, do the flowers . . . or show the Girl Guides how to tie knots. . . . Golly, I'd be hopeless. But I'd be all right with the pony club. I did know a bit about horses. And I'd learn the names of the children in the village school and invite them to Eynsleigh where Darcy could play Father Christmas. That was the sort of thing the owners of the big house had to do. I had bucked up a lot by the time I passed between the tall stone gateposts, each topped with a lion with its foot on a ball, and started to walk up the drive. The gravel road was lined with plane trees and at the end of it lay the rambling Tudor mansion. Its red brick glowed in the rays of the setting sun and smoke rose from its curly chimneys that were etched against a perfectly duck-egg-blue sky. Rooks cawed as they flew home for the night in a big elm tree. It was a scene of peace and contentment and I gave a little sigh.

"My house," I whispered to myself. "This is my house. My home now."

I started to walk up the drive and suddenly realized how hot and tired I was. The day was warm for October and the small suitcase now suddenly seemed to weigh a ton. I thought about leaving it and sending one of the servants to fetch it for me, but I didn't want to admit any weakness to them so I gritted my teeth and marched on, sweating now under my tweed jacket.

Suddenly I noticed a cloud of dust ahead and saw a vehicle coming toward me. A small low vehicle of some sort. Not a delivery van, then. It was a red sports car and it was approaching fast, sending up a cloud of dust behind it. I had to step hastily out of the way. Who on earth had come to visit driving a car like that? One of Darcy's friends, maybe, disappointed to find he wasn't at home. The car drew level, was about to pass as I stood in the dappled shade of a plane tree, then suddenly screeched to a halt.

The driver leaped out and rushed toward me yelling, "Georgie, darling! It's you! I thought I'd missed you."

Through the cloud of dust the car had stirred up I recognized the flying figure. It was my dear friend Belinda Warburton-Stoke, her sleek black hair hidden under a bright red motoring cap with a jaunty feather on one side and wearing a flame-red cape that flew out as she ran.

"Belinda!" I exclaimed, delighted. "What are you doing here? I thought you were in Paris."

She flung her arms around me, enveloping me in a big hug. "Just got back, darling, and thought I'd come straight down here to surprise you. You can imagine how miffed I felt when your housekeeper said you'd gone up to London for a few days."

"I was hoping to, but nobody was home," I said. "I walked from the station. Thank heavens I didn't stop in the village to get a drink or I'd have missed you."

She released me from the hug and examined me critically. "Yes," she said. "You're looking well. Sex obviously agrees with you, I can see. How is that brute Darcy treating you?"

"He's not a brute, Belinda, as you very well know." I laughed. "Darcy is wonderful, except that he's not here at the moment. He's gone off on some assignment he can't talk about and I'm all alone here. So I'm extra pleased to see you. Turn that spiffy motor of yours around and come and have some tea."

"Hop in," she said. "You can be impressed with my new toy."

I climbed into the passenger seat. "This is yours?" I asked.

"He's an Aston Martin Le Mans. The very latest model!"

"I didn't even know you knew how to drive," I said.

"I did learn on Daddy's estate, years ago," she said, "but I haven't had much chance to practice recently. I don't actually have a license or anything, but it doesn't really matter, does it? I have to confess to being a bit rusty, especially as this beast is quite temperamental when it comes to gears and things."

As if to demonstrate this the gearbox gave an awful grating sound and then the car leaped forward. Belinda managed to change direction after much maneuvering with the accompanying grating of gears.

"I'm sure that can't be good for it," I pointed out.

"He's a good solid British motorcar," she said. "He can stand any amount of abuse." With that we shot up the drive toward the house so fast that my head was thrown against the back of the seat.

"Did you know he can do eighty miles an hour?" Belinda shouted over the roar of the motorcar's engine. "I put him through his paces over the Hog's Back."

"Him? It's definitely a male?"

"Obviously, darling. Can't you feel all that masculine power and testosterone flowing? I've named him Brutus."

I tried not to smirk. "How long have you had it—I mean, him?" I asked.

"Since yesterday. I only got back from Paris two days ago."

"I thought you were planning on staying until the end of the year at least," I shouted back.

"I was, darling, but I got a telegram from the solicitor saying that Granny's will had finally been proved and he needed instructions on what to do with the money. You remember my grandmother had named me in her will, don't you? Lady Knott . . ."

"Not what?" I asked.

She shook her head so that the red feather danced. "Knott, darling. With a *K*. My mother had to grow up being a Knott. Luckily she married someone with a more normal name like Warburton-Stoke."

She paused to give me an indignant look as I laughed. "Anyway, Granny's will has been proved, so I caught the next boat train home and, Georgie, you'll never believe it, but I'm actually quite a rich woman!"

We screeched to a halt outside the front steps, narrowly missing the fountain.

"Hence the spiffy sports car," I said.

She was smiling like a cat with the cream. "I came out of the solicitor's office and spotted it in the showroom on Park Lane, and thought why not? So I went in and bought Brutus on the spot."

I opened my door and climbed out, brushing off the dust that still hovered in a cloud around us. "Come inside and have tea and you can tell me all about it," I said.

I let myself in and was just taking off my jacket in the front hall when Mrs. Holbrook appeared. "Oh, your ladyship," she said, a worried frown on her face. "I didn't hear you come in. We thought you'd gone up to town for a few days."

"Change of plans, Mrs. Holbrook," I said.

"And you didn't telephone for the motorcar. How on earth did you get from the station? A taxi?"

I didn't like to say that I walked. "I met my friend Miss Warburton-Stoke, who gave me a lift. And I've brought her back for tea."

"I'll tell Queenie to make the tea immediately, my lady," she said. "Will your friend be staying the night?"

I looked across at Belinda. "Why don't you?"

Belinda beamed. "Of course. Why not?"

"Then I'll have the end room made up right away, shall I? Did the lady bring her maid with her?"

"The lady is without a personal maid at the moment," Belinda said. "I've been slumming in Paris in a tiny flat up flights and flights of stairs."

"Goodness me." Mrs. Holbrook looked flustered. "Would Miss Warburton-Stoke like a chance to wash and brush up before tea?"

"I think that can wait," Belinda said. "I'm parched and I'm dying to tell Georgie all my news."

Mrs. Holbrook lingered, the worried look still on her face. "I'm not sure what there might be in the way of cakes," she said. "Seeing as how Queenie thought you were going away. But I expect she can whip up some scones quickly and there's the good strawberry jam we made this summer."

"We'll be fine, Mrs. Holbrook," I said. "All we really want is a cuppa and a chance to talk."

Mrs. Holbrook scurried off. "Queenie!" I heard her bellowing. "Get to work. We've got company."

Belinda looked at me suspiciously. "Did she say Queenie? Your former maid? Your absolutely dreadful former maid?"

"The same."

"And she is now your cook? And you haven't been poisoned yet and she hasn't set the kitchen on fire?"

"Once or twice," I admitted, "but she's actually proving to be rather a good cook. Only simple English food, I'm afraid, but she does bake well. And I am supposed to be looking for a proper chef de cuisine. It's just that it seems a little intimidating."

I led Belinda through to the sitting room. She looked around. "You have made this so comfortable," she said. "Those pretty loose covers on the chairs and that divine view over the lake."

"Yes, it is quite nice, isn't it?" I agreed. "Mummy helped me while she was still here and she does have awfully good taste."

Belinda plopped into an armchair. "I can't believe it. My friend Georgie who slept on my couch, who didn't have two halfpennies to rub together, and now all this! Who would have thought that we'd both have fallen on our feet so nicely?"

"We've both been through a lot," I said. Her gaze held mine. We both knew what the lot was that she had been through. The betrayal. The baby she had been forced to give up. Mine had been nothing so dramatic—just the knowledge that I was not wanted in my family home and really hadn't had any means of support until recently. "So tell me," I went on, lifting the conversation out of this gloomy phase, "your grandmother's will. You knew she'd left you money, didn't you? But it was more than you expected?"

"Oh yes. Absolutely oodles of it, darling," Belinda said. "And not just money. Some rather extravagant jewelry, for one thing. Heavy Victorian stuff, nothing I'd wear but some really fine stones that can be reset or sold. Oh, and her house in Bath. A Georgian house in one of the crescents. *Très, très* elegant. And"—she paused, waving an excited finger at me—"a property in Cornwall."

"How amazing," I said. "I thought you told me she had sold her house in Cornwall long ago."

"That's right, so I did," Belinda said. "She had a lovely property near the coast, called Trengilly Manor. I used to spend my summers there, after Daddy married the witch and I was no longer welcome in my own home. I was really despondent when Granny decided that Trengilly had become too much for her and she needed to be near good doctors, good theater and good food and moved to Bath. Then I was sent off to school in Switzerland so it didn't matter awfully much, but I still miss that house. We had such good times there. . . ." Her face had grown quite wistful.

"But now you find she owned another property in Cornwall?"

Belinda nodded. "I was astounded, darling. Why hadn't I known about it? I don't think it's anything impressive like Trengilly was, but it's supposedly in the same part of the world as the old house and it's called White Sails. It may be really nice to have a bolt-hole on a Cornish beach when I need to get away from the world."

She looked around. "So where is everybody? You said Darcy is off somewhere, but your mother and grandfather and Sir Hubert?"

"All deserted me, I'm afraid," I said. "Mummy went back to Max when he sent her a telegram saying he couldn't live without her. That made Sir Hubert decide he needed to go and climb more mountains. And Granddad is whipping the boys of the East End into shape. Everyone has something to do except me. . . ."

We broke off the conversation as Emily, another girl we had recruited from the village to train as a parlormaid, came in wheeling the tea trolley.

"Queenie says she's awful sorry, your ladyship," Emily said, "but she don't have much in the way of cake at the moment. She said she couldn't whip cakes out of thin air." She blushed crimson as she repeated the words.

I looked at the tray that contained cucumber sandwiches, a few chocolate biscuits, some of which were broken, and a rather sad little slice of fruit cake.

This was the part of being lady of the manor that I hated. I wasn't very good at being stern and terrifying. "Would you ask Queenie to come here right away, Emily," I said, trying to keep my face calm and composed.

Belinda shot me an amused look. "Quite a good cook, you said?"

After a few minutes we heard thumping in the corridor outside and Queenie appeared, red-faced as if she'd been running. She adjusted her cap which had fallen over one ear, brushed down a dirty apron and said, "Wotcher, miss. We thought you'd gone off gallivanting in London or I'd have had something for your tea."

"Queenie, what happened to yesterday's sponge cake?" I asked. "I seem to remember there was a big piece left."

Queenie had the grace to blush. "Oh well, seeing as how you'd gone off for a while, we finished it."

"You mean you finished it, I suspect."

She gave an embarrassed little smirk.

I took a deep breath. "Queenie, this isn't good enough," I said. "A house like this should always have a good supply of homemade biscuits, not those odds and ends of chocolate fingers from the village shop. And there should always be some sort of cake in case visitors call unexpectedly. I'm afraid you are becoming rather lazy. Now that you only have one person to cook for apart from the staff let's see a little more effort in the cake department, shall we?"

"Right you are, miss," she said.

"Oh, and, Queenie, Miss Warburton-Stoke will be staying to dinner. I do hope you can rustle up something more appealing than a stodge of some sort."

"I've already made a meat pie," she said.

"That will do splendidly. Your pastry is very good," I said. "Perhaps with a cauliflower au gratin?"

She didn't look too pleased. "Well, miss, you see that pie was supposed to be for our dinner. I'm not sure there's enough to go around."

"Then you'll have to be creative and come up with something else for the staff, won't you?"

"I don't know what," she said, aggressively now. "I ain't some ruddy magician, you know. I can't wave me wand and rustle meals out of thin air. We don't keep a lot of meat in the house when you're not here."

"Then it will have to be bread and dripping, won't it?" I said, giving her a sweet smile. "You'll think of something."

"Bread and dripping? I need to keep up me strength," Queenie said. "It's tiring work all on me tod in a big kitchen like this."

"Then maybe your worries are at an end," I said. "I plan to have Miss Warburton-Stoke help me find a qualified chef."

"What's wrong with my cooking, then?" she demanded.

"Nothing, except it's limited to the foods you know and we will have to start entertaining eventually when Mr. O'Mara comes home."

"You ain't going to get another of them Spaniards, are you? Because if so I'm heading straight back to Darcy's auntie in Ireland. They appreciated me, they did."

"I know that, and I do appreciate you too—most of the time. I just want you to do the job properly. And when we have hired a qualified chef, you should learn from him how to make more elaborate dishes."

"There ain't much wrong with a good old toad-in-the hole or bangers and mash in my opinion," she muttered. "Will that be all, then?"

"How about whipping us up a batch of scones, unless you're also out of flour?"

"Bob's yer uncle, miss," she said, quite happily now and off she went.

Belinda gave me an exasperated look. "Georgie, she's still utterly hopeless," she said. "Wouldn't it be the kindest thing to put her out of her misery right now?"

I had to laugh. "Belinda! She's not too bad most of the time. We've caught her off guard, and she's probably feeling guilty."

Belinda had removed her chic driving cap and shook out her sleek black hair. "You're going to have to get rid of her eventually, you know. You can't have proper visitors here with a cook who talks to you like that."

I sighed. "The problem is that I'm fond of her in a way. And she has been awfully brave in difficult situations. She saved my life, you know. I have come to accept that she will never learn."

"She doesn't want to learn, that's quite obvious. She's completely bolshie. But I must say, I was impressed with the way you spoke to her. Quite like the lady of the manor. You've come a long way since you were shy and bumbling Georgie."

"I still hate doing it," I said. "I'm not naturally bossy." I picked up the teapot and poured two cups. "Anyway, back to Cornwall," I said. "This new property. What do you know about it?"

"Absolutely nothing," Belinda said. "So I thought I ought to go down and take a look for myself. And I wondered if you'd like to come with me. A girl's outing. And adventure. Just like old times, what?"

"Oh rather," I said.

Chapter 3

TUESDAY, OCTOBER 15

On the way to Cornwall. Holding on to my hat. Belinda drives awfully
   fast! Golly, I hope we get there in one piece.

We set off at first light the next day. The journey did not start too
auspiciously as Queenie overslept (no doubt as a result of that large
piece of sponge cake and the remains of the jam roly-poly she made for
dinner) and did not wake us with the customary cup of tea.

When she found out we were about to depart that morning she
looked hurt. "You're buggering off, without me?" she said. "I might
be the cook now but I'm also your maid, ain't I? It's not right that you
go off without a maid. Who else is going to take care of you?"

I found this rather touching. She had been the worst maid in the
history of service but, as I told Belinda, she had also been awfully brave
at times. I found myself smiling. "That's very kind of you, Queenie.
But we are going in Miss Belinda's little sports car and frankly you
wouldn't fit inside. Besides, it's not as if we are attending a house party

where a maid would be in order. We are just going to look at a piece of property."

"Bob's yer uncle, then," she said. "But if you're buggering off, there ain't no point in my making them cakes you wanted, is there?" And she went back to her kitchen before I could reply.

When we went to retrieve the motorcar from the stables we found that yesterday's glorious weather had turned into a more normal October day of blustery rain that peppered windows and swirled up dead leaves. Belinda and Phipps had to wrestle to put up the roof of the sports car and we discovered that it wasn't exactly wind- and rain-proof. We set off, both of us feeling a little grumpy.

"We could wait for better weather, I suppose," Belinda had said.

"It could rain for the whole rest of the month," I pointed out.

She nodded agreement. "Perhaps it will be better in Cornwall. I always remember such glorious weather during my summer holidays there."

"It's all right. I'm used to rain," I said. "Up at Castle Rannoch in Scotland this kind of weather was the norm. All summer too. So depressing. My brother, Binky, is the only one who manages to remain cheerful. I'm so glad I'm far away."

"From your frightful sister-in-law, Fig, you mean?"

"I do. The last time she wrote she suggested it might be fun for them to come down to us for Christmas, since I have now inherited such a large house. Can you imagine Christmas with Fig? Father Christmas would take one look and not come down the chimney."

Belinda laughed. I stopped talking hurriedly and grabbed on to the door as we skidded around a corner. "Perhaps you should slow down a little on these wet roads," I suggested.

"We want to make it by nightfall, don't we?" Belinda said. "There's precious few places to spend the night along the way, not until we get to the coast. And night on Bodmin Moor is not what I'd recommend."

She put her foot down again and we slithered around the next corner, coming dangerously close to the bank. Things improved a little when we picked up the main road to the West Country, except that Belinda felt she had to overtake every lorry she met. We had a few close calls, making me wonder if this trip was such a good idea after all. Then we struck out cross-country again, speeding through Winchester, Salisbury, then into Somerset and finally Devon. Luckily the inclement weather meant that there was not too much traffic, as we were still going awfully fast. We passed through one pretty Devon town after another, with Belinda impatiently negotiating narrow streets. At last she was brought to a halt in Honiton where it was market day and we had to wait while farmers drove herds of sheep or led cows through the streets. We stopped for a late lunch in Exeter, eating a rather good roast lamb in the shadow of Exeter Cathedral. We filled the tank with petrol and set off again. As Belinda had predicted, the rain had lifted a little. It was now a fine drizzle rather than the more dangerous bluster we had endured previously.

Then we forged into bleaker country, skirting the northern edge of Dartmoor with scant signs of civilization.

"I could do with a cup of tea and to stretch my legs, couldn't you?" I suggested after we had been driving through wild and deserted countryside with only a hint of an occasional tin mine or clay digging to tell us that other humans were not too far away.

"Good luck with that," Belinda said. "We haven't passed a house for at least half an hour. Where are we, anyway?"

I had been assigned the job of navigator with a map on my knees. I peered down at it. "We must be close to Bodmin Moor."

"Why does that not cheer me up?" Belinda said. "About the most desolate spot on the planet. Oh, and look, the mist is coming down, right on cue."

And it was. As the road entered a countryside of desolate upland, the light rain turned to mist. We could hardly see the road ahead.

"One of the old smuggling routes." Belinda attempted to sound cheerful. "We'll be fine as long as we don't come across four and twenty ponies trotting through the dark. Remember that poem?"

I nodded. "'Watch the wall, my darling, as the gentlemen go by.'" I chuckled. "They don't still go in for smuggling in Cornwall, do they?"

"Oh, I should think so. It's in the blood. They probably have stopped deliberately wrecking ships by luring them onto the rocks and then plundering them, but who knows? They are a wild bunch down here, you know. Mad Celts."

"Aren't you one of them?" I gave her a challenging glance.

"Not really. My grandfather bought the house in Cornwall when they returned from India when my mother was a child. We're not a Cornish family. So I'm actually perfectly civilized."

"Most of the time," I added.

I think we were keeping up the banter to keep our spirits cheerful. It really was a most dreary place. Occasionally a wheelhouse of a tin mine would rear through the mist like a strange creature, but then we'd be driving through nothingness again, the cold damp mist swirling around us.

"Just how big is this moor?" I asked. "It's not the one with the hound of the Baskervilles, is it?"

"No, that's Dartmoor. We've already done that."

"Well, that's a relief," I said. "I think a giant slavering hound might be the last straw right now in making me want to spend a penny."

"We could stop and you could go beside the road," Belinda suggested.

"Belinda, I certainly couldn't do that."

"There is nobody else for miles, Georgie." She put her foot on the brake and pulled to the side of the road. "There. A bush for you."

Reluctantly I got out and was instantly enveloped in moist, sticky mist. I picked my way over tufts of rough grass.

"Watch out for bogs," Belinda called after me. "Bodmin Moor is famous for its bogs."

"Thanks a lot," I called back. "I had an encounter with a bog on Dartmoor once and I have no wish to repeat it."

"You got stuck in one?"

"No, I watched somebody disappear in one. It was horrid."

"You've lived an interesting life," she called after me. Her voice echoed strangely through the mist. Although I was only a few paces from the motor it was hard to say in which direction it was. I took care of the most urgent matter as quickly as I could and was thankful to find the road again. I got in, brushing moisture from my face. "It's truly miserable out there. I hope all of Cornwall isn't going to be like this?"

"Oh no. Just the moor. You'll see, when we reach the town of Bodmin, we'll be on the other side and all will be fine again. Cornwall is noted for its good weather, remember. The English Riviera."

"Really." I peered into the gloom.

At last the uplands came to an end and we encountered our first house. We stopped for a cup of tea and a bun in the town of Bodmin and then on again.

"Not far now," Belinda said, and true to her word the mist had vanished, leaving that fine rain again. The road passed through small mining towns, each with streets of faceless gray stone houses. I began to wonder what Belinda thought was so magical about this place, but I kept my thoughts to myself. After all, I was with my best friend on an adventure which was certainly better than sitting alone at Eynsleigh and wondering what Queenie would serve for dinner.

We had left any semblance of towns behind. The road had now turned into a lane with stone walls on either side, so narrow that I don't know what we'd have done if we met another car. Even Belinda had to slow down at this point. Over high hedges I just had occasional glimpses of fields. And in the fields were tall chunks of granite.

"What are those for?" I asked.

"Those are standing stones, from Celtic times. Cornwall is full of them," Belinda said. "Older than Stonehenge. I think they used to have human sacrifices."

"Charming. Now I feel really welcome."

Belinda laughed. "We are near the coast now," she said. "I remember this part."

She slowed. "What does that signpost say?"

I stared out of the window. "Saint Tudy and Saint Mabyn in one direction, Saint Breock and Saint Issey in the other. Those surely aren't real saints," I said, laughing.

"They are Cornish saints," Belinda said. "They were the first Christian monks to come across from Ireland."

"Tudy and Issey were monks?"

She shrugged. "Don't ask me. I'm not an expert. I'm only repeating what I was told."

"So what are we looking for now on the map?"

"Splatt and Rock and Pityme."

"You're making it up."

She laughed. "No, I'm not. They are real places."

"Splatt? People live in a place called Splatt?"

"Not many. Oh, and if Rock doesn't show up on the map, look for Trebetherick or Polzeath."

"Do they not have any normal names here?" I asked.

"Those two are Cornish. Another language, you know. Like Welsh."

"Do they speak another language here?"

"Not anymore. Only the very old people can remember Cornish. It has pretty much died out, I'm afraid."

"I'm not. I have enough trouble with French," I said.

We paused at another signpost. The light was now fast fading and it was hard to read. "Oh, that's right. Polzeath, straight ahead," Belinda said. "We're going in the right direction. Now we are very close. I wonder if we should stop and get some supplies if we pass a village shop that is still open."

"It's almost dark. Perhaps we should locate the house first," I replied. "We can always come back and eat a meal at the nearest pub tonight."

"Good idea." She negotiated a particularly sharp bend as the lane passed under a stand of trees, and drips rained onto us, thudding on the soft top roof. On the other side we emerged to a glimpse of shining water.

"The sea at last," I said, uttering a little prayer of thanks that we had arrived safely.

"Not technically. It's the Camel Estuary."

"Camel?" I asked. "They have camels in Cornwall?"

"No, darling. It's the name of a river and it must be high tide," she said, "because at low tide this is almost all sandbars. But the end really is in sight now. Trengilly is just down on the shore. And from my recollection there is only one big house beyond Polzeath and then it's just grass and rocks. White Sails must be on the other side of the headland."

The road now climbed above the river estuary into which great waves from the Atlantic were rolling. On either side of us was nothing but bleak grass and heather. The rain had picked up again, blowing straight at us from the Atlantic Ocean. The windscreen wipers were working furiously.

"Bloody hell," Belinda muttered we went around a sharp bend, rather too fast and rather close to the edge of what was now definitely the Atlantic Ocean and not an estuary. Yes, I know a lady does not swear, but there are extenuating circumstances and almost going over a cliff is one of them. She gave me a nervous grin. "I hope the house has good heating, don't you? I'm ready for a bath and a nice hot cup of tea. Do you think there is a resident servant? Wouldn't that be nice?"

"Very nice," I said. "But not very likely that your grandmother would have kept a servant in a house you didn't even know about. I'm rather hungry too. I hope that pub isn't too far away." I didn't like to admit that I hadn't seen any house since we left the last village behind. A steep upland of bare grass rose ahead of us, topped with a rocky outcropping. The road had become little more than a track.

"This can't be right," Belinda said. "I don't remember this at all. I thought it was supposed to be near Trengilly." She slowed the car to a crawl. "Oh, look. An answer to our prayers, darling. There's someone to ask. Be an angel and find out, will you?"

"You want me to get out into that? I'll be blown away."

"You grew up in Scotland, darling. You've faced much worse. See. He's not being blown away."

Reluctantly I tied a scarf firmly around my head and stepped out into the full force of the gale. A man was leaning on a gate, watching us. He didn't seem to mind getting wet at all. I went over to him.

"Excuse me, but do you know a house called White Sails?"

"Ooo arr," he said, nodding with enthusiasm. He was an older man with a weathered face and a mouth missing several teeth. He was wearing an old sack over his shoulders and a shapeless faded hat on his head. "Fish!"

"No, I don't want fish. I want directions to a house called White Sails." I tried not to sound too exasperated.

"That's right. Err wants fish." He had a really strong burr to his accent and he was grinning at me. Clearly only the village idiot would be out in rain like this.

"White Sails," I said again, trying to be patient. "It's a house on the coast near here. Could you tell us how to get there?"

He was eyeing me up and down as if I was a creature from a distant planet. "Round little rumps," he said with even greater enthusiasm.

"Well, really." I stalked back to the car.

"Disgusting old man." I slammed the car door behind me. "He was leering at me and then he said I had round little rumps. The nerve of it."

Belinda looked at me and then suddenly started laughing.

"It's not funny. You might not mind having men comment on your shape but I certainly do. Especially when I'm cold, wet and hungry."

"He was telling us the way, darling. I've remembered now. The headland is called Little Rumps. We're on the right track."

"Little Rumps," I muttered. "What a stupid name for a headland. Camels and Splatt and now Little Rumps. This really is a very silly place!"

Belinda steered us carefully around the side of the headland. I could feel the motorcar being buffeted by the wind. Below us we could see the waves crashing against the rocky shore. Then the road wound up and over the top, leaving the shore. The rain had abated as quickly as it had begun and the last rays of a setting sun poked between dark clouds over an angry Atlantic Ocean. It was a red sun, painting the landscape as if it were on fire. On the top of the hill, rising from the short cropped grass, was another standing stone and now it glowed bloodred. In that fading light it almost looked like a figure standing there and I shivered.

"This is a spooky sort of place, isn't it?"

"Not normally," Belinda said. "It will look much better by daylight. I only have fond memories, you know. Of course Granny's proper house was down by the estuary, where it's more sheltered and not so bleak as here."

We crested the headland, passing that standing stone, then dropped to the other side to find another bay ahead of us. Suddenly she jammed on the brakes and pointed. "Look. Here we are."

There was a sign on the gate beside the road. It said *White Sails*.

Chapter 4

TUESDAY, OCTOBER 15
AT WHITE SAILS, A COTTAGE IN CORNWALL

Not exactly what I had expected. Belinda is keen to stay and fix it up.
Frankly I think she's being a trifle optimistic. Foul weather. Cold
and damp. I'm missing Darcy.

Belinda pulled onto the grass beside the road. "I see the sign but I
don't see a house, do you?"

"Not at the moment." I opened my door, only to have it nearly
snatched out of my hands by the force of the wind. I grabbed my scarf
as the wind threatened to rip it from my head and tear open my overcoat. I held on to the car as I came around it. I heard Belinda utter a
swear word as her door nearly slammed on her. "Who in their right
mind would build a house here?" she asked. "And where is it, for God's
sake?"

We peered together over the gate.

"Oh, there it is," I said. Through the growing darkness we could see a steep flight of steps going down the hillside. And below them we could make out the roof of a house.

"Extraordinary," Belinda said. "No wonder Granny never mentioned this. She'd never have made the steps with her rheumatism. I wonder why she bought it in the first place. Perhaps it came with Trengilly. Oh well. We're here now. Let's go down and investigate, shall we?"

The gate opened with a creak and we started down the steps. It wasn't easy going, as they were wet and steep and there was no rail. The house was in a little gully, sheltered from the worst of the wind.

"I don't fancy carrying groceries and supplies down here," Belinda called to me. The wind snatched away her words. "I hope someone delivers."

"Are you sure this is the right place?" I shouted back. "It doesn't seem the sort of place your grandmother would want, does it? Somehow I'm pretty sure there is no servant in residence."

The steps turned to the right, crossing a rushing stream by a little bridge, and there below us was the house—well, rather a gray stone cottage with a slate roof. It sat on a rocky platform, nestled into the cliffside, not far above the shoreline and to one side was a natural harbor in the rocks, onto which a stone jetty had been built, protecting it from the worst of the waves.

"Oh, I see," Belinda said. "I understand now. It was probably built as a smuggler's cottage with that convenient little harbor beside it. And more recently it was a fishing cottage. Yes, I do remember somebody mentioning this once. My uncle Francis was staying at the fishing cottage and Granny said not to get our hopes up that he'd ever catch anything because he was bone idle."

"Fish!" I exclaimed. Belinda looked at me inquiringly. "That's what the old man said when I asked him for directions to White Sails. He said, 'Err wants fish.' Maybe that's what the locals call it. The fish house, perhaps."

"Well, at least we made it," Belinda said. "It looks like quite a pretty little place, doesn't it?"

"It does," I agreed, although I wasn't so sure. It was a simple one-story cottage, built of rough Cornish stone. There were white shutters at the windows, but one of them was now hanging loose, flapping in the wind and in danger of flying off at any moment. Bushes had been planted around the house, in the hope, probably, of sheltering it from the worst of the wind. As we came down the last of the steps I tasted the salt of spray. Belinda paused at the front door and fished in her handbag for a key.

"For heaven's sake, don't drop it," I pleaded. "We'd never find it again."

"Don't worry. I'm quite capable," she said. She stepped up to the front door and waved the key at me. It turned in the lock and Belinda opened the door triumphantly. "I suppose it's too much to hope that there is electricity," she said as we both stepped into a damp and musty room. She fished in her handbag again and produced a cigarette lighter. "Lucky that one of us smokes," she said. She flicked it on and held it up, illuminating the room. What we saw did not look too promising. We were standing in a living room with a table and two chairs on one side, a battered old sofa in front of a fireplace on the other. Belinda located an oil lamp on the windowsill and miraculously there was oil in it.

"Do you know how to light one of these things?" She carried it over to the table.

"Not really. We used them when the power went out at Castle Rannoch but we always had servants to light them."

"That's just the problem, isn't it?" Belinda said. "We've never had to stand on our own feet."

"Don't you think it would be wise to go back to the nearest village and stay the night somewhere? We need to eat anyway."

"You're suddenly obsessed with eating," Belinda said. "Are you pregnant?"

"No, I'm not," I snapped at her. "I'm just a normally hungry person. And then we can explore this place properly in the morning."

"That might be a good idea," Belinda agreed. "I wonder where the nearest pub might be? Probably all the way back in Rock. I'm not sure there was a pub in Polzeath."

"What would we find if we kept on going the way we were heading?"

Belinda frowned. "I don't think there is anything for quite a while. This is a deserted stretch of coast as far as I can remember. No, we'll have to go back to get something for dinner. Come on, then. My lighter won't keep going much longer."

We closed the front door, then made our way up the steps again. We were both out of breath by the time we reached the motorcar.

"Those Cornish people must be hardy," I gasped. "This is worse than Castle Rannoch."

"It will all look better in the morning," Belinda said. I could tell she was trying to sound cheerful. "And we'll feel much better after a good hot meal and a glass of something."

Belinda managed to turn the motor around successfully while I said a little prayer, then we negotiated the winding road until we saw the first welcoming lights of human habitation, with, thank goodness, a pub. But there was no sign of life as we pulled up outside the Smuggler's Inn.

"Surely the pub will still be open," I said. "It doesn't look . . ."

But Belinda had gone ahead. She pushed open the heavy oak door. "It's fine," she called. "Come on."

We stepped into a warm and smoky room. Across the ceiling were oak beams, the walls were wood paneled and a fire glowed in the fireplace. Several men sat at a table and a couple more stood beside the bar. Fishermen, I thought, judging by the big waterproof boots and a lingering odor of fish. At least two of them were smoking a pipe and it was hard to make out details through the fug. But at least it was a comforting warmth. I followed Belinda up to the bar.

"Good evening," she said, making all the men abruptly stop their conversations and swivel to look at us, pipes poised in midair, mouths open. "I hope you are still serving food."

The hefty middle-aged woman behind the bar had been deep in conversation with two of the men. She stared at us as if we were alien beings before she folded her arms across her ample bosom and said, "No women allowed in the public bar, I'm afraid. Ladies lounge around the corner." She indicated with a jerk of her head.

Belinda glanced at me in amusement. "Come on, old thing. We're breaking the rules." We came out, back into the blustery night, went around to the side of the pub and entered through a side door to find ourselves on the other side of the same bar, but in a much less pleasant room. There were several leather armchairs with small glass-topped tables and no fire in the fireplace. One anemic light bulb hung from the ceiling. It was about as unwelcoming as any room could be. Belinda strode up to the bar. I followed. The barmaid turned away from the men and came across to us. "Found it all right, then?" she asked. "Now what will it be?"

"What food do you have?" Belinda said. "We'd like a meal, please."

"Oh no. We don't do food here, miss. Only in the summer for the tourists," she said.

"Is there anywhere else nearby?" I asked. My stomach was now growling with hunger.

The woman considered this, then shook her head. Her several chins wobbled. "Nothing closer than Wadebridge, I wouldn't reckon. We only cater to local folks and they get their suppers at home. You'd be better off going around the Camel and into Padstow. They cater to outsiders there so I've heard."

"How far away is that?" I asked.

"Well, if you're driving a motor car you have to go around the estuary, don't you? Until there's a bridge. I reckon it's at least ten miles."

I gave Belinda a despairing glance.

"So you have no food at all you could find for us? We've been driving all day and we're really hungry."

"I've pasties you can have," she said reluctantly. "I always make a couple extra in case my man gets hungry between meals. He's a prodigious healthy appetite has Mr. Trevelean. No doubt I could warm a couple up for you in the oven if you don't mind waiting."

"That would be marvelous," Belinda said. "Thank you so much. And a couple of pints of cider, please."

The woman pulled these effortlessly, putting the big glasses on the bar. "That will be three shillings, my lovey," she said.

Belinda paid her.

"You are visiting these parts, then?" the landlady asked.

"We are. I've just inherited a house near here," Belinda said. "White Sails. Do you know it?"

"Can't say I do," the woman said. "People give their houses all kinds of fancy names these days, don't they?"

"It's on the coast past Little Rumps," Belinda said. "But we'd rather wait until the morning before we take a look at it. Do you happen to have a room for the night?"

"Room for the night?" The woman behind the bar now looked as if we had just asked her if she ran a brothel.

"No rooms here. And you won't find a room closer than Wadebridge, maybe. More likely Padstow. Everything closes when the summer visitors are gone."

"I see," Belinda said. "Well, we'd be grateful for the pasties. If you'd pop them in the oven for a minute."

We carried our glasses over to one of the tables and sat on the cold leather seats.

"Cheerful sort, isn't she?" Belinda muttered to me. "I always remember the Cornish as being much friendlier."

"Perhaps she doesn't approve of women traveling alone," I whispered back. "She thinks we might lure her menfolk."

"What—that lot of old codgers?" Belinda chuckled.

"Well, you do look rather stylish, you know."

"Really? This old thing?" But I could tell Belinda was pleased. "One of my own designs, this cape. Do you like it?"

"I think it's fabulous."

"I was hoping to get an order from Harrods, but now I don't actually need the money. Still, I can't see myself being idle. It's just not in my nature. I nearly went bonkers when I was holed up in Switzerland with nothing to do."

"I agree," I said. "I was becoming so bored alone at Eynsleigh. Darcy wanted me to start entertaining the neighbors but frankly the thought terrifies me. I've never given a tea party in my life."

Belinda laughed. "I can just see you as lady of the manor, holding court over the village, opening garden fetes, judging livestock competitions, sitting on the parish council, leading the Girl Guides."

"Don't." I shuddered. "I'm just beginning to realize that this is now the life I'm stuck with. I'm not sure I'm ready for it. And certainly not sure I'll be any good at it. Can you see me leading the Girl Guides?"

"You'll soon have oodles of babies to amuse you," Belinda said. "I'm sure Darcy hasn't wasted any time in that department."

"I hope so," I said.

Belinda caught my tone and looked up from her glass. "What's the matter? Is something wrong?"

I chewed on my lip. "It's just that we've been married three months and no sign of a baby yet. You're right. Darcy is a very enthusiastic lovemaker so I'm beginning to wonder if something is wrong with me. What if I can't have children?"

Belinda gave an incredulous laugh. "Three months? Darling, that's nothing at all. Goodness, if I'd become pregnant at the drop of a hat, I'd have had a whole brood of children by now. Frankly I was flirting with danger and terribly lucky it only happened once."

"But you said you took precautions?"

"I did, but they are not always reliable, you know. And there were times when one got carried away and was not too careful. And in my defense I have to say that I really believed that chap wanted to marry me. He certainly hinted as much." She sighed. "Anyway, it's all past now and it turned out for the best, didn't it? So no more men for me. I've renounced them entirely from now on. I'm going to become pure and virginal."

I chuckled. "Hardly the latter, at this stage."

"Well, pure anyway. I'll become an incredibly successful business-woman and an adoring godmother to your brood of children."

We both looked up as the woman came in bearing two plates on which resided enormous pasties. I had been rather afraid that a pasty would be a dainty little thing and I'd still be hungry. Instead they filled a whole dinner plate. I took a bite: warm flaky pastry and then a delicious interior of meat, potatoes and root vegetables in a rich gravy.

"This is delicious," I commented, looking up for a second.

"They are good, aren't they? Cornish pasties are one of the things I remember fondly from my childhood. They make them for the miners, you know. To take down the mines for their lunch. That rim of pastry is for the miners to hold with their dirty hands so that they don't actually touch the good part."

"How interesting," I managed to say before I went back to eating.

After a pint of hard cider that was surprisingly strong and the pasty I felt much better. Ready for anything, in fact. Belinda must have felt the same because she said, "Well, now we'd better go back and tackle that oil lamp, I suppose, since there is nowhere to stay and I don't feel like driving all the way into Padstow."

Chapter 5

AT WHITE SAILS.
THE NIGHT OF OCTOBER 15

White Sails is an overly refined name for what is a primitive
fisherman's cottage, and so remote it feels like the middle of
nowhere. I'm not sure I want to stay here but Belinda still seems
quite keen.

We managed to coax a box of matches from the landlady and went back
out into the night. The wind had dropped when we arrived back at
White Sails and we could hear the surf crashing onto rocks far below us.

"I wish we had thought to ask to borrow a torch," Belinda said as we
felt our way down the treacherous steps. She clicked her cigarette lighter
on again and held it up like the lady with the lamp as we found our way
down to the house. Once inside we took the glass top off the oil lamp
and after much discussion (and a few choice words) we got it to light.

"At least it still has oil in it," Belinda said, turning it up so that soft
light flooded the room. She turned to examine our surroundings.
"Oh, and look. There is some firewood beside the stove."

This was now my turn to show expertise. When I had first arrived in London alone, without servants, I had learned to light a fire. I got this one going, to Belinda's squeaks of admiration, and suddenly the room looked much better. We found a candle on a window ledge and carried it through to the rest of the house.

"Please tell me there is a bathroom," Belinda said.

"There's a kitchen with a big sink," I said. I went over to it and turned on the tap. Water came out, ice cold but with a satisfying patter. I turned it off again.

"Oh, and this is the bedroom." Belinda was also exploring.

There was just one bedroom, containing one bed, a large rickety wardrobe and a tall chest of drawers.

"It looks as if we'll have to share the bed tonight, unless you'd rather have the sofa," Belinda said.

"The sofa looks lumpy and not quite long enough," I said. "At least it's a big bed."

"I can see that furniture shopping will be the number one priority." Belinda left the bedroom and went back into the kitchen, carrying the candle. Not wanting to be left alone in the dark I followed her. There was an old wood-burning stove and a sink, but in the larder we made an interesting discovery. "Look. There's some food in here," Belinda said. "A tea caddy and some bread that's not too stale, butter, milk, cheese and a jar of jam. . . . Someone has been here recently."

"I wonder if your solicitor telephoned and had someone stock up on basics for you."

"But he didn't know when I'd be coming down. I only said that I'd want to take a look at the property before I decided whether to keep it or sell it."

"Well then, perhaps one of the locals has been using it to go fishing."

"Or it's possible it was my uncle Francis," Belinda said suddenly. I heard the uncertainty in her voice.

"Does he live down here? You've never talked about him."

"That's because I never liked him. I don't think Granny did much either. He was the black sheep of the family, you know. My mother's younger brother. Much younger. Never settled down, never got a job, always in debt. Gambled, drank, mixed with undesirable people."

"So where is he now?"

"I've no idea. When Granny sold I heard that she settled some money on Uncle Francis but that's the last I heard of him. Probably got through it quickly in Monte Carlo."

"But he didn't inherit any of your grandmother's estate when she died?"

"No. It all came to me. You should see how furious my stepmother was that I was now a rich woman. She suggested I share the bounty after all they'd done for me. The cheek of it! Granny paid for my schooling and the wicked witch made me feel quite unwelcome on the few occasions I came home."

"Just like me and Fig," I said, nodding in sympathy. "But what about your father?"

"Daddy? He's not a bad sort but quite clueless about what's going on around him. He loves his farm and his pigs and prize bulls and would never notice when the witch was horrid to me. Anyway, that's now all in the past. I am independent and have a bright future ahead."

She said this more to convince herself than me, I thought.

"We still haven't found the bathroom," I pointed out. "I don't fancy going out into the storm to pee."

"Well, it's not here, is it?" Belinda sounded frustrated. "The inhabitants must have a chamber pot somewhere and then chucked it out of the window and into the sea."

"Don't even entertain such a disgusting thought," I said. We were both giggling to mask our uneasiness with this situation.

We searched some more until we found a door we hadn't noticed before, in the kitchen wall. It opened onto a flight of steps descending into darkness.

"Goodness, how scary," Belinda said. "I wonder what can be down there. Surely not the bathroom?"

Belinda held up the candle, looking like something from a gothic novel, and we went down the steps, one at a time. I have to confess I let Belinda go first. Below was a stone basement with another large sink. The smell of fish still lingered. In one corner was a rusted tin bathtub, and in another a toilet. Goodness knows where that drained to!

"Not exactly much privacy," I pointed out.

"Not much privacy? Is that all you can say? Georgie, it's awful! Can you imagine coming down here in the night?" Belinda sounded horrified. "Forget what I said about furniture being the number one priority. The first task is a proper bathroom."

"Are you sure this place is worth all the effort?" I asked. "It's terribly remote. Would you really want to be here alone?"

"I'm not sure," she said. "I like the idea, but . . . let's sleep on it. I always say things look better in the morning."

We took turns in using the facilities while the other stood guard at the top of the stairs.

"Do you think we should lock the front door, just in case?" I asked as we started to get ready for bed.

"Who is possibly going to bother us out here?" Belinda said. "But maybe you're right. We are far from any help, aren't we?"

She turned the big iron key in the latch. "Satisfied?" she asked. I was.

"I don't feel like turning off that oil lamp, if you don't mind," Belinda said.

"I agree. And wake me up if you need to go down to the lavatory."

"I rather wish I hadn't had that pint of cider now," Belinda said.

"Me too."

We climbed into the bed. The mattress was lumpy and the springs squeaked every time one of us moved.

"I wouldn't recommend this for a romantic hideaway," I said, making Belinda laugh.

"Oh crikey, can you imagine!"

We both lay there laughing, as one does when very nervous.

"I'm freezing. How about you?" Belinda asked.

"I certainly am. The blankets feel damp, don't they?"

"I could put my cape over us. And your overcoat." She got up and started to drape them over the bedding.

"Remind me whose mad idea this was," I said.

"At least you are not having to give tea parties and feel lonely and bored," she said.

"You're quite right. It is an adventure. I must remind myself of that—especially if I have to get up in the night."

"Wake me and I'll hold a candle for you," Belinda said.

The extra layers started to warm us up. The wind had died down and all one could hear was the distant thump of waves on the rocks below. Gradually I drifted off to sleep. I awoke to pitch darkness. The oil in the lamp must have finally given out. I lay, staring at nothing, wondering what might have woken me. Then I heard it again . . . the slightest sound. Was it the creak of a door?

Only the wind, I told myself. I knew from experience at Castle Rannoch that old houses were full of noises as they creaked and sighed and shifted. I turned over and tried to go back to sleep. I had almost drifted off when I felt the covers being thrown back and someone climbed into the bed beside me. The bedsprings creaked ominously. Silly Belinda, I thought. She's been to the loo by herself. How considerate of her not to have woken me up.

Then I realized this person was getting into the bed on my left side. Belinda had been lying on my right. I reached out a hand and felt the warmth of her body. Then who on earth? It's Darcy, I thought. Darcy coming to surprise me. He had done the same sort of thing before, arriving unexpectedly in the middle of the night, creeping into bed beside me. That was when I remembered that Darcy would have no idea I'd be here. I hadn't given the address to Mrs. Holbrook.

I was instantly wide awake and sat bolt upright. "Belinda! Wake up. There's someone in our bed."

This had an immediate effect. The intruder leaped away, exclaiming, "What in God's name?"

"What's happening? What is it?" Belinda murmured sleepily. I could see why she had had so many problem encounters with men if it took more than this to wake her up!

My heart was thudding so fast I could hardly breathe. A cigarette lighter was switched on, revealing a disheveled young man with dark, unruly curls not unlike Darcy's staring at us as if we were ghosts. He was wearing a big fisherman's jersey, his trousers were rolled up above bare legs and he was holding that lighter out in front of him as if to keep us at bay.

The only comforting thought was that he looked as alarmed at seeing us as I was at finding him climbing into my bed beside me.

"Who the devil are you?" he demanded. "What are you doing here?"

Belinda had regained consciousness. "I am Belinda Warburton-Stoke and this is my property. So more to the point would be what are *you* doing here?"

"The place has been empty for years," he said. "I've been using it when I come back late from a fishing trip. Good little harbor to put into when the sea gets up." He stopped, thought for a moment and then said, "Did you say you were Belinda? Lady Knott's granddaughter?"

"That's right. My grandmother has died and I have inherited her property," Belinda said, still sounding like I did when I was under extreme duress and could hear myself giving an imitation of my great-grandmother Queen Victoria.

"Your old granny was quite fond of me," the intruder said. "She used to let me use this place."

"Did she really? Well, I'm afraid those days are over. Kindly leave immediately."

He came a little closer, holding up the lighter over us. "But I remember you," he said. "You used to come down here for the summers, didn't you? There was that whole group of kids. I used to join you when I wasn't needed to help my dad. I'm Jago. Remember me?"

"Jago?" She stared at him. "But you were a skinny boy, rather shy around the rest of us. And didn't you have blond hair in those days?"

"That's right. From being out in the sun so much. I might have grown and filled out a bit since then." And he laughed. Again I was struck by the resemblance to Darcy. That self-assured, almost cocky laughter. He was really rather handsome.

"And I seem to remember you were quite a pale and skinny little girl yourself at the time. You had freckles and your hair also wasn't quite as dark."

"Maybe so." Belinda snapped the words, confirming what I had always suspected—she dyed her hair black. "So you're still living down here and fishing for a living?"

"Well, the fishing is more like a sideline," he said. "But, yes, I'm still down here."

"Well, I suppose I can't turn you out in the middle of the night," Belinda said. "You can sleep on the sofa but I don't want this to happen again."

"Very well, your ladyship," he said primly.

"I'm not a lady. Only a miss," she said.

"Not married yet?"

"That's rather an impertinent question to ask a stranger. Are you?"

"Haven't found the right girl yet," he said.

"And I have been too busy furthering my career." Belinda still sounded haughty and huffy. "My friend beside me is both a lady and married."

"Well, bully for her," he exclaimed with an amused grin in my direction. "So are you coming down here to live now?"

"I'm not sure of my plans yet," Belinda said. "My first one is for a good night's uninterrupted sleep after a long day's driving."

He cleared his throat as if the encounter had been making him as nervous as we were. "Very well, Miss Belinda. I appreciate the offer of your sofa because I don't like to leave my boat unguarded. But I'll not trouble you any longer and wish you a good night's rest."

He and his cigarette lighter disappeared into the living room and we heard the sofa creaking as he made himself comfortable.

"Well, I promised you adventure, didn't I? You can't say this is boring," Belinda whispered to me. "Jago—what was his last name? I can't remember. He was one of the local boys who hung around with us in the summer. We had a group of kids who played together, mostly summer visitors but a couple of local children too."

"Was his father a fisherman?" I asked.

"I don't think so. Anyway, he's certainly grown a lot since then."

"He's quite handsome, don't you think? He looks a lot like Darcy."

"Really? I hadn't noticed. I was too annoyed." She moved closer and whispered in my ear. "Actually you know what he was doing, don't you? Did he smell of fish to you?"

"Not exactly. He smelled maybe salty. Of the sea?"

"So he wasn't fishing at all, Georgie. He was smuggling!"

Chapter 6

More excitement! An intruder in the middle of the night. And what's
more, he knew Belinda. Goodness, won't I have a lot to tell Darcy!

When we awoke the next morning there was no sign of our intruder
or of any boat in the little harbor below. He might almost have been
a ghost or even a bad dream brought on by too much pasty, except a
large hunk of the bread and cheese was now missing from the larder!

"I must say the fellow has a nerve," Belinda said. "I wonder what
he was smuggling? Cigarettes and booze from the Continent, I
shouldn't wonder. Liquor has always been the smugglers' favorite."
Then she frowned. "I just hope it isn't something worse."

"Like drugs, you mean? Cocaine and things?"

"Or even weapons."

"Weapons?" I had to laugh at that. "What would the weapons be
for? We are not exactly a race of anarchists."

"There is good money to be had in the sale of weapons," Belinda said, "and we do have extremists in the country, don't we? Oswald Mosley and his gang of thugs. And some communists. And IRA activists. I expect he'd find a ready market if he chose. I just hope he hasn't stashed anything in this house."

"How did he get in, that's what I want to know," I said. "You locked the door."

"That's right. I did," Belinda said. "Come on, let's go and check."

The front door was still locked. The windows all intact.

Belinda gave me a puzzled look. "He can't have come down the chimney. Let's take a look in the cellar."

We went down those steps again. Now, by daylight, we noticed a small window, high up in the wall, that threw anemic light onto the stone floor.

"He didn't climb in through that, anyway," Belinda commented. "He had broad shoulders, didn't he?"

"So you noticed that much, did you?" I teased. "I thought this was the woman who had renounced men forever and was going to remain pure and virginal."

"That doesn't stop me from admiring the human form, purely on an artistic level," she said, making me laugh.

Further inspection of the cellar revealed the answer to our visitor's midnight entrance. What we had taken to be an alcove in the wall partly concealed by an old oilskin coat hanging on a peg was actually a flight of narrow steps going down, with a glimmer of light at the bottom. "A smuggler's stair. See, I told you," Belinda said. "That is why this cottage was built. They'd sneak into the little harbor where nobody could see them and bring the goods up through the rock. I wonder if he's stashed anything away down here."

We went down the stairs cautiously as they were uneven, steep and slippery. They ended in a shallow cave among the rocks with sea spray lapping at the bottom of them.

"I wouldn't enjoy coming in this way, would you?" I said. "It looks downright dangerous. But I can't see anywhere he might have hidden smuggled goods."

"Probably left the goods in the boat overnight," Belinda said. "Come on. Let's have breakfast. I'm starving, aren't you?"

We went up again. I got the stove going, made toast and tea over it and sat at the table in the window, looking out over a broad expanse of bay. Belinda had been right. There was no habitation to be seen in that direction, only grass-topped cliffs.

"So what is the plan for today?" I asked. "You surely don't want to stay here any longer, do you?"

"I certainly don't want to sleep another night in that bed nor have to use that loo in the cellar," she said. "But I'm not ready to give up on the cottage yet. Besides, we've come all this way. You don't want to rush straight back to Eynsleigh, do you?"

"No, of course not," I agreed. "I just don't fancy the bed or the loo either."

"Oh definitely not," Belinda said. "Especially as we have no way of preventing further night visitors."

"You make it sound as if we might have a whole parade of them."

"You never know. There is not much work in this part of Cornwall. The whole community might be in on the smuggling. This might be their headquarters."

This seemed a little far-fetched to me, but I was glad that Belinda was as keen to change our place of abode as I was.

"We're bound to find a place to stay somewhere," she said. "If there are no hotels, then I'm sure a local person would rent out a spare room. Then I'd like to find a handyman and see what suggestions he might have about putting in a proper bathroom—oh, and a good solid door to that staircase. One we can lock."

I nodded. "And maybe an estate agent, in case you want to sell it."

Belinda gazed out of the window. "It's a lovely view, isn't it?" she said. "Look how blue the ocean is today. And the seagulls flying. It would be the perfect place to get away from the hubbub of London life."

"Do you want to get away?" I asked with concern. "Belinda, I don't want to feel that you are giving up on life. You always were the ultimate social butterfly. You loved parties. You used to have so much fun."

Belinda stared past me, out to the scene beyond our window. "Maybe it's a case of once bitten, twice shy," she said. "I took so many risks in those days. I'm lucky I came out relatively unscathed."

"But you want to get married one day, don't you?" I asked.

She shrugged. "Who would have me? I'm damaged goods, Georgie."

"Surely not. Nobody knew about the baby."

"Even if they didn't, I was Belinda, the party girl. The one you had fun with but not the one you introduced to your parents."

"You'll find the right man, I promise you." I reached across and squeezed her hand.

"I hope so. Things may be different when word gets out about my inheritance. There are still owners of stately homes who would love an infusion of cash." Before I could say anything she went on, "But I'm in no hurry, Georgie. I want to make a name for myself in the fashion world to rival Chanel."

"A modest goal," I replied, making her laugh.

Belinda carried her plate and cup over to the sink. "I tell you one thing," she said, "I'm not about to take a cold bath down in that cellar. Let's go and find a comfortable bed and a good bathroom. Then we can think about spiffing this place up. It will be a fun challenge, won't it?"

"Oh definitely," I agreed, although secretly I thought that we were looking at an enormous project. We warmed water over the fire for a quick wash and then we set off. Now I was able to see the surroundings in the daylight and to appreciate fully where we had come. The scenery was indeed spectacular. To our right was nothing but granite cliffs above a wide bay. There were no beaches and waves rolled in from the Atlantic to break on the rocks below. Out at sea was a small rocky island over which the spray was breaking while seagulls whirled. Not a friendly sort of coastline, I thought. I could understand how wreckers did good business here.

Now that the weather was sparkling clear Belinda insisted on putting Brutus's top down. "It's why I bought a sports car, darling," she said. "The wind in our hair."

"May I remind you that it's October and it's rather a cold wind," I pointed out.

"Oh, Georgie, don't be such a wet blanket. You were raised at Castle Rannoch. You're used to Highland gales, surely."

"Yes, but it doesn't mean that I enjoyed them," I said.

"You'll thank me for this," she said as the top folded flat and was latched down. She started the engine, had a couple of attempts at getting the motor into gear and then we shot forward. "You see," she shouted. "Invigorating."

I noticed she wasn't wearing her stylish driving cap, but the sort of scarf one wears for horse trials. I had been foolish enough to put on my felt beret and had to hold on to it for dear life. We rounded the headland with the standing stone looking down on us. In the light of day it looked like a large lump of upright granite, nothing more sinister. Ahead of us was the Camel Estuary gleaming in the sun. The tide was now partially out and the water flowed between sandbars. On our right a high brick wall ran along the road. Behind it was a stand of Scots pines and in the middle an impressive wrought iron gateway with a gravel drive leading away down the hill. I hadn't noticed this the night before, but then I had been too intent in making sure Belinda didn't drive us over a cliff.

"Is that your grandmother's former house?" I asked.

"No, hers will be coming up in a little while," Belinda answered. "Nothing as impressive as this. That's a place called Trewoma Hall. The local stately home. I was taken there once for a garden party but

I don't think I ever went inside much. The situation is quite lovely—on the cliffs with a view over the estuary and the ocean."

"Who lives there?"

"One of the important Cornish families own it. Trefusis is their name. They own a lot of land in this part of the world, and fishing rights and goodness knows what else. Very wealthy. Their daughter, Jonquil, was one of my playmates when we were small." She paused and made a face. "I was about to say one of my friends, but that wouldn't have exactly been correct. She was superior to me in every way."

"Superior to you? Your own grandmother was a lady, wasn't she? Your father is not exactly a peasant."

"Well, let's just say that she thought herself superior to me. She was two or three years older, for one thing. Very sophisticated. Frankly I was in awe of her. A little scared of her. She went to Roedean that, as you know, likes to think of itself as the premier girl's school in England. And she'd traveled all over the world with her father who owned land in Barbados and Argentina and God knows where else. What's more, she was gorgeous. She had the most striking blond hair that she wore in this sleek chignon that I could never have managed. Never a hair out of place, Georgie, even when we went on one of our mad escapades."

"What sort of mad escapades?"

She grinned. "Oh, you know the sort of thing that adolescents get up to. Bonfires on the beach, exploring old smuggler's caves, making rafts that sank in the current. In spite of Jonquil we actually had a lot of fun."

"Does the family still live there?"

"I'd imagine so." Belinda peered through the gates. "They have done since the fourteen hundreds."

"And what about your chum Jonquil?"

"I've no idea. I didn't keep in touch with any of those people. I expect she married somebody equally rich and wonderful. Probably has two perfect children by now."

"Did she have any brothers?"

"No, an only child."

"So who will inherit?"

Belinda gave an exasperated laugh. "Georgie, how would I know? Certainly not me. Why this interest?"

"I'm always interested in inheritance, I suppose, since it's so important to my own family."

"Well, yes, it would be," she agreed. "Your dear cousin David, the Prince of Wales, who will probably ruin the monarchy in a couple of years."

"Don't say that." I gave an involuntary shiver. "I do hope he'll do the right thing when his father dies. And I hope his father will live until he's ninety-nine."

"Not much hope of that, is there? He's been quite ill."

"Yes, he has. He didn't look at all well when I last saw him."

"When was that?"

"Before I went on my honeymoon to Kenya. I haven't seen them since. I don't suppose I shall any longer, since I had to renounce my place in the line of succession when I married Darcy."

"That's probably a relief, isn't it? No more dos at Buck House?"

"In a way it is. I didn't think I'd miss it, but I've grown quite fond of Queen Mary and I shall miss my chats with her, even if I was always terrified of knocking over a priceless vase or spilling my tea on the Persian carpet."

Belinda laughed. "But she always made you do awkward and embarrassing things for her, like spying on your cousin."

"She did, that's true. Oh well. Perhaps I'm well away from the whole royal scene. Dealing with smugglers in the middle of the night is much more fun."

We had left the impressive gates and continued to follow the estuary. We passed a cluster of cottages and the Smuggler's Inn pub of the night before. Belinda identified this as the village of Polzeath. It boasted one small shop and two women stood outside it, baskets over their arms. They looked up as we passed, as if seeing a stranger was a novelty. After we had left the houses we moved into a gentler scene where the landscape was sheltered from the Atlantic gales. There were more trees here—I remembered this part of the road where the trees had dripped on us and provided a dark tunnel the night before.

"Oh look. Here we are," Belinda said with excitement in her voice. "Trengilly. This was Granny's house."

She pulled up at a gateway made of two granite posts, each carved with a Celtic cross. The wrought iron gates were closed, held secure by a big padlock. The driveway was lined with yew trees, bent by a constant west wind, and beyond it I could see only part of a gray stone manor house.

"So who lives there now?" I asked.

"I don't really know. I understood that it was someone from the City, a financier of some sort, who bought it but wasn't going to be there most of the time. Granny thought it was an awful waste but of course she had to sell to the highest bidder. We can find out if anyone is in residence. Perhaps there is a caretaker who can show us around. I'd like you to see it. It was such a great house with grounds going down to the river and a little dock. That was where we used to launch our ill-fated rafts." She laughed at the memory.

"So why is everything beginning with 'Tre' around here?" I asked. "Trewoma, Trengilly?"

" 'By Tre, Pol and Pen, ye shall know the Cornishmen,'" Belinda quoted. "The Cornish language. I think 'Pen' means 'head' but I'm not sure what 'Pol' and 'Tre' mean. There are certainly a lot of them."

Shortly after leaving Trengilly Manor we came into the village of Rock. This looked more like a proper village with a church, a row of shops and a pub called the Trefusis Arms.

"See, what did I tell you?" Belinda said. "They own this part of Cornwall."

We left the car outside the churchyard and went into the newsagent's, which was also the post office and also sold everything from fishing tackle to sweets. When asked about a possible place to stay the pleasant-faced woman behind the counter frowned. "I can't think of anywhere right around here, my lovies. Old Bob at the pub stopped letting out rooms when his wife died. I reckon the only place with fancy hotels would be Newquay and most of them close for the winter, don't they?"

"It doesn't have to be fancy," Belinda said. "I'd like to be close enough to the property I've just inherited so that I can supervise any renovations."

"And what property would that be?" The woman looked really interested now. A good topic for local gossip, obviously.

"It's called White Sails. The cottage on the rocks, the other side of Little Rumps."

"That used to belong to Trengilly, didn't it? Old Lady Knott's place?"

"That's right. She was my grandmother. I've inherited her estate."

The woman's face broke into a broad smile. "I knew there was something familiar about you. What was your name again?"

"Belinda. Belinda Warburton-Stoke."

"That's right. Miss Belinda. You used to come in here when you were a little nipper and you stayed with your granny. I remember your mum too. You have her look, you know."

"Do I?" Belinda looked pleased. "Yes, now I remember coming in here with my pocket money to buy sweets."

"That was a good while ago now, wasn't it, my lovey?" the woman said. "I certainly miss those days. Your granny was a lovely lady. So refined and polite. A bit of a stickler for doing the right thing and for knowing your place, but a decent sort. Those days are gone now. And the new lot—well, it's different, isn't it? I mean—" She broke off suddenly, looking up. A wary look had come over her face.

I turned to see that a woman had entered the shop.

"Did a package arrive for me, Mrs. Briggs?" the woman asked. She was about our age, solidly built with a round flat face, an upturned button of a nose and upwardly slanted eyes. I took in immediately that she was expensively dressed, wearing a mink stole, and her haircut was stylish, although her accent was decidedly from the West Country.

"I'm afraid it didn't, Mrs. Summers," the shopkeeper replied stiffly.

"So annoying," the woman snapped. "They promised me it would be here by today."

"If it comes by a later delivery I'll have the boy bring it up to the house, shall I?" Mrs. Briggs asked.

"Thank you. I'd appreciate it. Oh, and while I'm here, a packet of Players please."

Belinda glanced at me and we decided there was no point in lingering. "Come on, Georgie. We might as well drive into Wadebridge and see if there is anything there. And failing that, Padstow," Belinda said.

We had reached the door when a voice behind us said, "Wait a minute. I know you. Aren't you Belinda?"

Belinda turned to look at the woman as she came toward us. "Rosie?" she asked in surprise.

Chapter 7

Great excitement last night! Strange man in our bed. Now we
  desperately need a more comfortable place to stay. I imagine that
  will be our quest for the day!

"Rosie?" Belinda repeated. "Mrs. Barnes's daughter?"

"The very same," the young woman replied. "I haven't seen you
since your grandma sold the place. That must have been what—twelve
years ago now?"

"At least," Belinda said. "So you are still living in the area? I heard
your mother moved away. Didn't she open up a café in Bath?"

"She did. Your grandma gave her a nice parting gift that set her
up. She's doing quite comfortably, thank you."

"But you stayed on here?"

"As a matter of fact I went up to London and worked there for a
while. But now I'm back, I'm pleased to say. I live at Trewoma Hall."

"As what?" Belinda asked. I don't think it was meant to be rude but it did sound that way. Rose's white moon face flushed red. "As mistress of the house. I'm married to Tony Summers."

It was Belinda's turn to look confused. "Tony Summers? You're married to Tony Summers?"

Now Rose's look had turned to a triumphant smile. "That surprises you, does it? Little Rosie Barnes."

"But I had no idea Tony came back to this part of the world." Belinda still sounded flustered. "And Trewoma Hall? How did you wind up there? Are you renting it from the Trefusis family?"

"No. We own it," Rose said. There was a sort of forced bravado about the way she tossed her head.

"They sold to you?"

Rose shook her head now. "No. It wasn't like that. I don't suppose you ever heard that Jonquil's parents were killed in an aeroplane crash in the West Indies? Well, Jonquil inherited the property. Tony married Jonquil and unfortunately Jonquil died after only a year of marriage."

"I'm sorry to hear that. Was it an illness?"

"An accident. She fell off the cliffs," Rosie said. "A part of the cliff crumbled away and she fell."

"How tragic," Belinda said. "If anyone loved life it was Jonquil, wasn't it?"

"You're right. She took all kinds of risks—she used to love playing polo, hunting, and surfing in the big waves, but in the end it was her own home that killed her."

"So Tony inherited Trewoma?" Belinda asked.

Rose nodded. "There were no more Trefusis members. Tony inherited."

"Lucky for him. Lucky for you," Belinda said. "How did you two meet again?"

"In London, amazingly. I had taken a secretarial course and was working as a secretary for a solicitor in London. Sharing digs with some girls in Camden Town. Rather run-down sort of place. I had treated myself to a day in the West End and I met Tony walking through

Hyde Park. Can you believe the coincidence? I think he was still coming to terms with the loss of his wife and he was glad to see a friendly face. We had dinner together. And we corresponded for a while, and then one thing led to another."

"I'm very happy for you," Belinda said. Her voice sounded as if she wasn't happy at all. "I expect your mother is very proud too."

"She is. I've invited her to come and live with us but she likes her own life. She enjoys the freedom after all those years." She paused. "So what brings you back here now? On a bit of a holiday, are you?"

"No, I came to see a piece of property that my grandmother left me."

"I was sorry to hear that your grandmother finally died. My mum wrote and told me," Rose said. "Too bad she sold Trengilly or we could have been neighbors."

"She's left me a nice house in Bath," Belinda said, "and a cottage called White Sails. Do you know it?"

"The old fishing shack?" Rosie chuckled. "I don't suppose you'd want to hang on to that. Perched on the edge of the cliff, isn't it? About to fall down at any moment. I'd be thinking of Jonquil all the time I was there."

She seemed to be aware of me for the first time. "I'm sorry. I don't think I know your friend."

"Oh, forgive me. Where are my manners," Belinda said. She still sounded flustered. "Rose Summers, this is my good friend Lady Georgiana. Used to be Rannoch, but is now Mrs. O'Mara."

Rose extended a chubby hand on which were several rings. "Pleased to meet you," she said. Then she paused, staring at me. "But I've seen your picture, haven't I? It was in the *Tattler* this summer. Your wedding. The king and queen attended and the little princesses were bridesmaids, weren't they?"

"They were," I agreed. "I was scared stiff with all those royals present."

"But you're related to them, aren't you?"

"Yes. The king is my father's first cousin. That makes me once removed, I believe."

"Fancy that." Rose looked really impressed. "And you and Miss Belinda are friends, then?"

"We have been since we were at school together in Switzerland."

"Isn't that nice? You must come to Trewoma for tea while you're here. I'd love to show you around. Are you staying nearby?"

"We're not sure yet," Belinda said. "We only arrived last night and obviously can't stay at White Sails the way it is at the moment. No proper bathroom, for one thing. But there don't seem to be any rooms for rent at this time of year. Is there still a ferry across to Padstow? I wonder if we'd find a hotel or boarding house over there."

"Then you must come and stay with us," Rose exclaimed. "Tony would love to meet you again after all this time and I'd welcome the company. It can feel rather gloomy stuck away in a big house like Trewoma."

"Oh no," Belinda said, rather too hastily, I thought. "We couldn't possibly put you out."

"It would be no trouble. We've a pack of servants with not enough to do and certainly enough bedrooms to host an army. Do come." She put her hand on Belinda's arm. "I absolutely insist. Let me go on home ahead of you and make sure that rooms are made up for you."

"That really is awfully kind of you," Belinda said.

"What else would I do for an old friend?" Rose said. "We'll have some good chats about old times, won't we?"

"Oh, definitely," Belinda said. "We are most grateful, Rose. We'll follow along in a while, then, shall we? I want to show Georgie the harbor and the ferry."

"You know where to find us, I take it?" And Rose laughed as she walked toward a shiny new Daimler motorcar parked across the street.

Belinda waited until Rose had driven off, then she turned back to me. There was a look on her face that I couldn't read.

"That was jolly kind of her, wasn't it?" I said. "Now we'll have a decent bathroom and a bed that doesn't squeak."

I stopped, seeing her face. She was angry, but more than that. She was confused too.

"What's the matter?" I asked.

"Old friends, indeed," she snapped. "Do you know who she was? She was my grandmother's cook's daughter. She lived with an aunt for most of the year but she used to come to stay with us in the summers. She was a pathetic creature, really. She hung around and wanted to be part of our group. We usually let her although Jonquil could be quite scathing about her. She wasn't at all athletic like the rest of us, you see. If it came to climbing rocks, she had to be rescued. She couldn't ride, so she didn't join us if we went out on our ponies. And she wasn't even that grateful when we included her. A bit of a sneak, you know. She spied on me. Read my diary. Told tales."

"Well, I suppose everyone improves after childhood. I was shy and awkward when I first met you," I commented.

"Yes, but she was the cook's daughter."

"Belinda, that's horribly snobbish of you. You should be pleased that she's improved her status in life and made a good marriage."

"I suppose I would be if I hadn't disliked her so much before. But that's not the only fly in the ointment here. The main problem is Tony Summers."

"He was one of your group down here?"

She nodded. "He was the group's leader. He and Jonquil. We were all in awe of both of them and followed them around. His father was something in the City. Banking or investing. Incredibly rich. Tony went to Eton. They rented a place down here every summer and Tony would come with his mother while his father stayed in London. He was very handsome even then. And so cocky, so self-assured. All the girls had a crush on him. I certainly did, but he didn't ever notice me. I was two years younger and rather gangly and awkward at that age."

"So why are you reluctant to see him again?" I asked.

Belinda chewed on her lip, something she did only in moments of great anxiety. "Because a few years ago I bumped into him in London. We were both gambling at Crockfords. We had a drink together. It turned out his father had lost his fortune in the great crash of twenty-nine. Tony was articled to a chartered accountant and hated it. Bored to tears. Anyway, there was this instant spark between us and . . . and we had this wild little fling." She paused. "That was before the time we went to Hollywood and I met . . . you know."

I nodded. I did know. She had fallen in love and been betrayed there.

"Tony would have been a good match for you, even without all his money," I said. "Why didn't it last?"

"Because we'd been together for a couple of weeks when he let it slip out that he was engaged. I didn't realize at the time but it must have been to Jonquil. Anyway, I told him that I wasn't going to go on seeing him if he was engaged to another woman." She paused, as if the memory was painful.

"You did the right thing," I said.

"I suppose so. But afterward I asked myself if he might have broken off the engagement and married me instead if I'd kept on seeing him."

"You really liked him, then?"

"It was the residual effect of that adolescent crush, I expect. But we did have fun together. I can't believe he married Rose. What did he see in her? She must be the least exciting person in the universe. Utterly boring."

"You don't know that. She may have improved since you knew her. And anyway, she provided him with a shoulder to cry on after he lost his wife. Presumably he was in love with Jonquil?"

"Maybe." Belinda shrugged, staring out past me to where a small passenger ferry was chugging to the jetty. "Maybe he saw a good opportunity by marrying a rich heiress," she said. "He always was a risk-taker. Not exactly the reliable type, as he proved by not telling me about his engagement for two weeks that we spent mostly in bed."

"Oh dear," I said. "So this stay at Trewoma will be doubly awkward for you?"

Belinda gave an exasperated smile. "You can say that again!"

Chapter 8

OCTOBER 16

HEADING FOR TREWOMA HALL, CORNWALL

A change of fortune at last. No more sleeping on the lumpy, creaky bed
with the chamber of horrors in the cellar. We'll be in great comfort
for the rest of our stay but unfortunately Belinda is not too happy
about it. Oh dear. I hope it will be all right!

"We don't have to stay long," I said as we walked back to Belinda's
motor. "We can always claim we're needed back in London."

"Except that I'd really like to be close by to supervise the work on
the cottage," Belinda said. "For that the position is ideal. I'll just have
to be grown-up about it, to be cool but civil to Tony and polite to
Rose. Mrs. Summers." She shook her head. "Can you imagine anyone
less suited to being mistress of Trewoma?"

"You may be surprised," I said. "She had the gumption to go up
to London and become a secretary. She didn't just marry the nearest
fisherman down here. And she certainly dresses well." I wagged a

finger as an idea struck me. "You can design a wardrobe for her. As a thank-you for her hospitality. She'll be thrilled and impressed."

"I suppose I could." Belinda toyed with the idea. "Oh well. She wants time to prepare the staff for our invasion. We'd better take that stroll down to the harbor," she continued as I fell into step beside her. "I wonder how she handles staff in a big house like that. They must all know she was a cook's daughter. I bet that doesn't go down well."

"Poor Rose," I said. "I'm beginning to feel sorry for her."

"Sorry for her? My dear, she's just landed the plum. The nicest house for miles around *and* Tony Summers. What more could one want?"

"You're jealous. That's why you're so miffed," I teased.

She nodded. "You're right. Absolutely green with envy!"

"Except you wouldn't want to be stuck down here all the time, would you? I've just found that being mistress of a great house can be boring and lonely. You always were such a party girl."

"Not anymore, darling." She sighed. "Remember. Pure and virginal. In fact the convent is the only future that may be right for me."

I looked at her face and saw it twitch into a smile. "You're pulling my leg again. Anyway, it's like falling off a horse. You have to get right back on again. It should be like that for you and men. You had a bad experience. Now you can start dating some good eggs."

"If there are any that haven't been snapped up by people like Rosie Barnes!" she said and stomped ahead of me.

We came down to the estuary. The little ferry had disgorged its passengers and was now chugging back to Padstow on the other side. Padstow, I could see from here, looked like the traditional Cornish harbor town with houses clinging to the hillside above a harbor wall. This side had no proper sheltered cove, only a jetty. Most of the boats were moored out in the channel and were now sitting on the sandy bottom, the tide having receded. Beside the jetty there was a tackle shop, displaying everything from marine engines to buckets, spades and shrimping nets for young holidaymakers. I didn't think there would be much call for those at this time of year.

"Not exactly a lot to see, is there?" Belinda said. "The whole place is deserted."

"It is October," I pointed out. "And when you think of the weather yesterday it would hardly entice anyone down here. Would you say those are fishing boats or only pleasure craft?"

Belinda examined them. "Oh, I think the fishing boats would be on the other side at Padstow," she said. "Good little harbor there. It wouldn't be much good trying to make your living as a fisherman if your boat was stuck on a sandbar half the time."

"How big a start should we give Rose?" I asked. The breeze was now picking up and was quite cold here facing the open sea. "Should we see if there is somewhere to get a cup of tea or coffee first?"

Belinda hesitated. "Anything to put it off a little longer," she said. "I so wish we hadn't agreed to do this. But there wasn't really any way out of it, was there? She wouldn't take no for an answer."

"Buck up, old thing. It might be quite fun." I put a hand on her shoulder. "Good food and a good bed, anyway."

"I don't think I could define time spent with Rose as fun," she said, shrugging off my hand. "And I'm worried about Tony. What if Rose is not proving satisfactory in the marital department and he wants to resume where we left off?"

"I'll stick to you like glue, if you like," I said. "But you should give poor Rose the benefit of the doubt. And if it's too uncomfortable, we'll find our excuse to leave."

Belinda nodded. She had been staring down the estuary in the direction of Trewoma. Now she turned back to the tackle shop. "They might know where we could find a cup of tea," she said.

As she was about to go in a man was coming out, his arms laden with several packages. He almost bumped into her.

"Oh, I'm frightfully sorry," he said. Then he squinted, frowned and exclaimed. "My God, it's Belinda. What in God's name are you doing here?"

"Uncle Francis!" Belinda cried. "I had no idea you were in this part of the world."

"Oh yes, rather. Lying low for a while, don't you know."

Now I had a chance to examine him I could see the resemblance. He had Belinda's dark eyes and straight nose but his features were now marred by bags under those eyes and sagging jowls. He wore a jaunty yachting cap and sported a pencil-thin mustache in the manner of Clark Gable. I could see he might have been handsome once, but had lived too much of a good life for too long.

"So where are you living?" she asked. "Have you bought a place down here?"

"Not exactly a place, my dear child. Having not inherited a fortune like you, but a mere pittance to keep me off the streets. Unfortunately I was not the favored one. My dear mama did not trust my judgment when it came to money. I am left an allowance, pocket money, like a child. So I have bought a boat. Nice little craft. Forty footer. Big enough to live on and I've got her moored across the way in Padstow. I go up and down the coast as the mood takes me. Even across the Channel when I feel daring. Fancy free, that is me."

He had a light and high-pitched voice for his size. He was smiling as he spoke, but I noticed his eyes darted around, as if he was scared of being noticed.

"More to the point, what are you doing here?" he asked. "There's nothing for you in this part of the world, is there? Not now Trengilly is long gone."

"Actually part of my inheritance was a fishing cottage called White Sails," Belinda said.

"That old ruin? My darling child, you are welcome to it. I don't know what you'd do with it. It's good for nothing except smuggling brandy."

"You're right. It is pretty ghastly," she said.

"You're not staying there, are you?" he asked.

"Last night. That was enough. But we've been invited to stay at Trewoma. Rather more civilized, don't you think?"

"Trewoma. My, my, that's moving up in the world. Although the new owner is not my favorite person."

"Tony Summers, you mean? You know him?"

"Summers. Yes, that's the name. I can't say I know him. Certainly know of him. He owns the mooring rights on this stretch of river. He's raising the prices. Charging a fortune. And the crab and lobster rights too. A fellow can't even catch himself a decent lobster without running afoul of that blighter Summers and the local law." He wagged a chubby finger at her. "You might just point out to him that local chappies like me are struggling to pay his rents while he lives in luxury. He'll pay for it when the communists take over."

Belinda laughed. "Are they about to take over? And don't tell me you are a communist? I seem to remember you were always fond of the good things of life."

"I'd willingly change my tune to see that blighter Summers get his just deserts," he snapped. "In fact if you'd like to put some rat poison in his tea while you're there, I'd be very grateful. Do it for your old uncle, eh?"

"What an awful thing to say," Belinda said.

He gave a high-pitched giggle. "Just a joke, you know. Anyway, must fly. Have to see a man about a dog before I catch the ferry back to Padstow with this lot. I have to repaint her bottom sometime. Toodle-oo. We must meet up at a pub while you are here. Catch up on the good old days at Trengilly, what?"

He didn't wait for an answer but strode in the direction of the jetty.

Belinda turned to me. "Sorry if I didn't introduce you but I can't stand the man. I never could. I never trusted him even when I was a child. He was one of those uncles who liked to sit you on his knee and let his hands wander while all the time pretending he's playing a game with you."

"How awful," I said.

She nodded. "Luckily in those days he was rarely home. He always had some sort of get-rich-quick scheme he was promoting or would find someone to take him to the Continent. Granny despaired of him. She'd say, 'That boy will be the ruin of me yet.' But I wonder why he chose to come back here again. I don't see him enjoying a pint with local fishermen. Of course, if there is still smuggling going on, then that would be more his style."

She started to walk away. "Come on. I think we've dallied long enough. We can head to the next unpleasant encounter at Trewoma."

Chapter 9

OCTOBER 16

A HOUSE CALLED TREWOMA, CORNWALL

I'm not sure this is going to be an improvement on White Sails.
Belinda isn't at all keen, but we are stuck with it now, whether we like it or not. I have to confess I'm dying to meet Tony and see what he is like.

We returned to Belinda's motorcar and to my relief she agreed it might be a good idea to put the top back up before we were rained on. After we had managed this we set off back up the estuary toward the headland. Neither of us spoke for a while. The tide was coming in as great waves rushed up the estuary to swallow the sandbars. The boats that had lain pitifully on their sides were now bobbing in water again.

We had left the last houses behind. Ahead of us was nothing but grassy headland on one side and a rocky shoreline going out to the point on the other. As the road started to climb we got the full force of the wind coming straight at us.

"I'm glad we put the top up or my beret would have been long gone," I said.

"It's certainly blustery enough, isn't it? It's hard to hold the steering wheel and not get blown over the edge. It's a wonder Jonquil wasn't actually blown off the cliff top. I wonder what she was doing there in the first place."

"It does seem strange," I replied. "I mean, she had lived in that house all her life. She must have known it would be dangerous to go near the edge of the cliffs."

"Perhaps something happened down below," Belinda suggested. "A boat ran aground or she heard a cry for help from someone cut off by the tide. She went to the edge to look over and it gave way."

"Possible." I nodded. "How sad for Tony Summers. Only married to her for a year."

"At least he inherited a large estate," Belinda pointed out. "Rather convenient when his own family fortunes had waned."

I glanced at her sharply, wondering what she might be suggesting, but her eyes were focused on the road ahead.

"Ah, here we are," she said. "And Rose has left the gates open for us. How thoughtful."

Again I couldn't tell whether she meant what she was saying or was being sarcastic. We drove through the gates. The drive turned a corner so that it was impossible to see the house ahead of us. Instead it wound into a small wood so that we were passing through another avenue of trees that interlaced above our heads. In the summer it would have been a canopy of green, but at this time of year and with the sort of gales coming from the ocean most of the leaves had already fallen and it was bare branches that were entangled above us while a yellow and brown carpet lay underfoot and covered the driveway. It felt rather strange, like bony fingers reaching out over us and I was glad when we finally emerged from the trees. As we came out of the wood the drive turned again and this time was lined with tall bushes. I'm not exactly an expert on horticulture but I think they were all rhododendrons, of course not flowering right now but they were big enough that they hid any view beyond.

Suddenly a figure stepped out between the bushes. Belinda gasped and slammed on the brakes. It was lucky that the driveway was winding so that she was not traveling at her usual speed or she would have hit him. I recognized him instantly as the old man I had questioned the day before and had given me a toothless grin when he said "Round Little Rumps." He stood now in the middle of the driveway, staring at us with that not-quite-all-there expression on his face. He came up to the car and leaned over Belinda.

"I know you," he said. "You were the ones who were askin' about the fishing place, weren't you? Didn't you find it?"

"Oh yes, we found it perfectly, thank you." Belinda's voice was ultrapolite. He was leaning in a little too closely.

"Her weren't no sort of place for young ladies like yourselves, was her, now?"

"A little run-down," Belinda admitted.

"See, I knew. I knew as soon as I tells 'ee. I says to myself, Harry, you big duffer, you should have told the young mistress that it weren't the right sort of place for them. So now you're visiting here instead, are you?"

"Yes. Mrs. Summers has invited us."

He wagged a finger in Belinda's face. "This is your sort of place, all right, although it's not how it used to be. Not like when the old master was alive. He were a grand gentleman, he were. And his lady too. And the young one what had the fall. But now she's taken over, ain't she? And all the old servants gone. Got rid of Gladys, didn't she? And Margie? And even Will, who was so good with the horses. All gone." He paused, staring off into the distance. I could tell that Belinda was dying to drive on, but he had one hand on the side window of the car. "The old master, he used to give me odd jobs too, you know. A proper gentleman, he were. Now they don't want me around no more. She don't want me around. I don't know why. I ain't said nothing. But

I know what I saw, all right." He paused again, staring at something we couldn't see. "But I expect you'll be all right," he said, "Strangers like you. No, you'll be just fine." And with that he turned and stomped back into the bushes again.

"I wonder what he meant about expecting we'd be all right?" I shivered.

"Obviously the village idiot," Belinda said. She put her foot on the accelerator and we shot forward. Another bend and suddenly the driveway opened up and there was the house ahead of us. Unlike the plain Cornish stone of Belinda's grandmother's home this was an extravagant building. It might have started as a simple manor but had been added to by successive generations. There were towers on both corners, and gables and a broad flight of steps leading up to the front door. All in all a little Gothic and over-the-top.

"It's a bloody great monstrosity, isn't it?" Belinda said. "You take the simple lines of Cornish stone and ruin the place. Those Victorians should never have been allowed to build anything."

I nodded agreement.

We crossed a gravel forecourt with an ornamental pond and Belinda brought the car to a stop. As we pulled up beneath these steps a footman in livery came out to open the car door for me.

"Welcome to Trewoma, my lady," he said. "May I take your bags?"

He assisted me from the car seat and then opened the boot to take out our modest suitcases.

"Clearly he has been told that you are the important one and I am not worth bothering with," Belinda muttered. She adjusted her cape and put her hand to her scarf as the wind threatened it. "Ah well." She looked at me and took a deep breath. "Here goes, then."

I had to smile. "You make it sound as if we were entering a lion's den."

"Far worse than that, darling. Still, one can endure anything for a couple of days. I have even been known to be civil to my stepmother over the Christmas holiday."

"I have learned to be civil to Fig for much longer than that," I said. "I'm sure it builds character."

"I don't know if I want my character built," Belinda said.

"Besides, you have to give your Rosie the benefit of the doubt," I went on. "She may have been an awful child because she felt unwanted and insecure. Now she's mistress of her own house she may be absolutely charming."

Belinda frowned at me. "When did you become such a sage? Has marriage really turned you into a sensible and mature person?"

"Implying boring as well? I hope not. But being with my grandfather has been a good influence on me. He always sees the best in people and never hastens to a judgment."

"You're right," Belinda said as she picked her way daintily up the steps in her delicate kid shoes. "He's a wonderful person. So was my grandmother, in her way. She was more correct and very hot on good manners and that sort of thing, but she was fond of me. The only person who was after my mother died."

I followed her up the steps, pondering on this. Earlier in our relationship I had come to Belinda with my problems. I had relied on her as being older and wiser and certainly more worldly. Now it seemed our relationship had changed. I was the one with a stable life and she needed me. Interesting.

I had no more time to weigh these facts as we reached the front door and stepped into a vast dark wood-paneled foyer. On one side a curved staircase ascended to a balcony. An enormous wooden chandelier hung above the stairs. The floor was composed of black and white marble squares. On the walls various hunting trophies, ranging from stags to buffalo, stared down at us. It was one of the most gloomy entrances I had ever seen and I'd grown up at Castle Rannoch, which ranks extremely high on the gloom scale.

I didn't notice the woman standing beside a tall potted palm until she spoke.

"Welcome to Trewoma, my lady and Miss Warburton-Stoke. I am

Mrs. Mannering, the housekeeper. I hope your stay here will be a pleasant one. James will take your coats," she said and the footman now stepped forward to assist me off with my overcoat and then took Belinda's cape.

"I remember your grandmother with great respect, Miss Warburton-Stoke. A true lady. Sorely missed," the housekeeper went on as the footman whisked our garments away. She turned to me. "And I understand that you are Lady Georgiana Rannoch, sister to the duke and cousin to the king. It is a great honor to have you at our house, my lady."

"Thank you, it's most kind of you," I said. "But I'm actually now married and a simple Mrs. O'Mara."

"A lady is always a lady, is she not?" the housekeeper said. "If you would come this way, I believe Mrs. Summers is awaiting you in the morning room."

She was almost a caricature of a perfect housekeeper. She had an old but unlined and expressionless face. Her hair was set into a perfect cap of gray waves. She wore a black dress with a white collar, the combination of which removed all the color from her face, giving the impression of a skull floating above blackness.

She led us across the foyer; down a long, dark paneled hallway; round a couple of corners; and opened a door ahead of her. We stepped into a delightfully warm room with tall arched windows that looked out onto manicured lawns and a view of the headlands beyond. Armchairs and sofas were arranged around a massive marble fireplace in which a log fire was blazing. Rose had been sitting in one of the armchairs but she sprang up as we came in.

"Oh splendid. You found us. So what do you think? Isn't this a lovely room? It's my favorite in the house. I expect that's because it's not too big and overwhelming. Shall we have some coffee first or would you like to see your rooms?"

"I expect the young ladies would like to attend to their hair, after having been out in the wind," Mrs. Mannering said. "Would you like me to take them to their rooms, madam?"

"Oh no. That won't be necessary. I can do it. Why don't you arrange for some coffee and some of Cook's gingerbread for us?"

"Very good, madam." The voice was flat.

"You've put them in the west wing, I hope?"

"No, madam," the housekeeper replied, her voice still calm and expressionless. "I have put them in the east wing. In the pink room and the lavender room."

I was watching Rose's face. It was flushed with annoyance and embarrassment. "But I expressly told you . . . I wanted them to have the good view across the headlands."

"The young ladies are from London and therefore not used to our brisk climate. The rooms I selected are smaller and therefore easier to heat. I am sure they will appreciate that when they awake and have to dress in the morning."

"I suppose you are right." Rose clearly wanted to say something different but she was not going to fight in front of visitors. I thought that wise of her. From what I had seen of the housekeeper it would have been a losing battle.

"I take it the young ladies did not bring a maid with them," Mrs. Mannering said. "I will assign young Elsie to unpack and take care of their clothes. She seems to be coming along nicely in her training. Willing to learn." As we went to walk away she added, "And please do show the young ladies that there are oil lamps in each of the bedrooms, just in case we lose power, which happens all too frequently in our part of the world during storms."

"Yes, Mrs. Mannering." Rose couldn't hide the annoyance in her voice. I had to admit it did sound as if the housekeeper was the one giving the orders.

Rose led us out of the room, back down that long hallway and up the stairs. A balcony ran across linking the two wings. Rose hesitated, looking to the right, then turned to the left and strode angrily in that direction. When we approached that wing she glanced back to see the hallway below us was empty before she muttered to us, "That woman is going to drive me mad. I give her an order and she goes and does exactly what she wants to anyway. I really wanted you to enjoy the view from the west wing. It is quite spectacular. But she doesn't like using those rooms because those were Jonquil's when she a girl."

"She came with the house, then?" Belinda said. "She was here when Jonquil was a child?"

"Oh yes. She's been here for donkey's years. Who knows how old she is? I suspect she's actually a witch and is probably several hundred years old and takes some kind of rejuvenating potion." She gave a nervous little chuckle, and I noticed she glanced over her shoulder in case she could be overheard. "She looked after Jonquil when she was a little girl. Adored her. She thought the sun shone out of Jonquil's head. Miss Jonquil was such a pretty child, such a good horsewoman, so clever, played the piano so well. Talk about rubbing it in that I am none of those things."

We had entered a long hallway with windows along one side, looking down onto a formal garden between the two wings.

"The trouble is," she went on, "that she is so blooming efficient. The house runs like clockwork. Everything is in its place, everything shines and gleams. She comes to me every morning with the menus for the day and they are always perfect. There is nothing for me to change or add. She seems to know exactly what Tony would like to eat at a certain time. It's uncanny."

She stopped outside one of the first doors to our left. "Wait. Is this the pink room? I can never remember." She opened the door, peered inside then went in. "Ah yes. See. What did I tell you? Bed made up, fire in the hearth, fresh flowers on the dresser, even though it's October. From the greenhouse, of course. Everything perfect."

"Having just had to deal with a crew of hopeless staff I'd be grateful if I were you," I said.

Rose sighed. "I know I should be grateful, but it leaves nothing for me to do except rattle around this big place all day. Tony is busy with running things—we have a large farm farther inland as well as the estate here and the properties abroad. So he's completely busy and happy and I have nothing to keep me occupied."

"I know just what it's like," I said. "I'm going through the same sort of thing. I've inherited this big house and there is very little for me to do when my husband is away. It's lonely, isn't it? Darcy was urging me to entertain—give luncheons and tea parties and get involved in the local society but it's hard to take that first step."

"It's all right for you," Rose said. "You're a real lady, aren't you. Anyone would be happy to come to your parties or to have you involved in their local charities. But me—everyone knows I was the cook's daughter. They are polite enough to my face but I know what they are saying behind my back. Besides, we're rather remote here. It's mostly fishing families. It's too bad that nobody actually lives at Trengilly anymore."

"We heard it's someone from London? A banker or something?" Belinda looked inquiringly at Rose.

"I'm not exactly sure. It's mostly rumors floating around. Some say he's Greek, others that he's a Jewish financier. Stinking rich, wherever he comes from. Tony thinks he's up to no good. Shady money. He's had the whole interior redecorated. I believe he's only been down a couple of times. He brings a house party with him and all his food and drink. The locals aren't very pleased about that. They get nothing out of it. Not a good way to endear oneself. But he probably doesn't care."

"If he's in banking, presumably Tony knows him?" I said. "Didn't you say his father was in something like that?"

"Until he lost it all," she replied. "Tony's parents upped and moved to Italy. They live quite simply in Florence these days. I've only met them once. I suggested to Tony that we go for a visit this winter, but he seems so occupied with all the business of the estate." She looked at Belinda. "He'll be so surprised when he sees you're here, Belinda. I'm sure he won't recognize you. You are so glamorous these days."

"Thank you," Belinda said. "One tries."

"Belinda is starting her own fashion house," I said. "She's been working in Paris."

"Fancy that." This sounded like something Queenie would have said. The wistful servant trying to picture something beyond her comprehension.

"Oh, I see my bag's already been brought up," Belinda said. "So is it all right if I take this room? Or do you want it, Georgie?"

"No, please take it. I really don't mind where I sleep," I said.

"That other one is just as nice," Rose said. "I'll show you."

My room was next door to Belinda's. It wasn't really my choice of room—a little too like Castle Rannoch to ever be cozy. The walls were wood paneled, the furniture also dark and heavy, but it was decorated with lilac curtains and pillows on a window seat. There was also a fire burning in the grate which added to the friendliness. The view was mainly across the grounds with that rhododendron wilderness and the wood beyond, but one could glimpse the estuary winding inland from the far right.

"This will suit me perfectly," I said. "It really is so kind of you to take us in like this."

Rose flushed. "Well, Belinda's old grandma was always good to my mum. And she gave her a nice legacy that has set her up with her own café. So I'm grateful. And besides that, I'm happy to have the company, especially an old friend."

"The bathrooms are all the way at the other end of the hall, I'm afraid," Rose said. "I don't know why she chose these two rooms for you. I suppose she had her reasons."

"Don't worry. The rooms are perfect," Belinda said. "And I'm sure we're both used to walking miles to a bathroom, aren't we, Georgie?"

Rose waited while we arranged our hair and Belinda reapplied her bright red lipstick. I still hadn't learned the habit of making up my face on a regular basis. Then Rose led us back along the upstairs corridor. At the top of the stairs she paused. "I really should show you what you are missing," she said. "Come on. You have to see the west wing."

We followed her back to the balcony and crossed the foyer to an identical corridor. Toward the end she opened a door. Sunshine streamed into a lovely room, with a spectacular view of the estuary and the Atlantic beyond. It held a bed made up with white lace pillows. White lace curtains hung at the windows. There was a set of blue enamel-backed brushes on a white dressing table in front of one of the windows. Along one wall was a bookcase containing leather-bound volumes. A series of china dolls sat on the shelf above. There were even a pair of slippers placed beside the bed and a robe draped over it.

"Is this your room now?" I asked.

Rose shook her head. "No, it's Jonquil's," she said. "Nobody uses it. Mrs. Mannering keeps it exactly as it always was. And her nursery on the other side. I keep hoping we'll be able to use the nursery one day."

She gave me a nervous little smile. I understood. She came out of the room and opened the adjoining door. This was a child's perfect nursery, a white-canopied crib, a rocking horse in the window, a doll's house and a sturdy wooden cart big enough for a child to sit in but now full of various dolls and animals, all going for a ride. The room looked lived in, as if the child who owned it was only outside playing and would come running back with red cheeks to tell her dolls about her adventures. I went over and looked out of the window.

"So is your bedroom on this side of the house?" Belinda asked.

"No. After Jonquil died Tony decided he didn't want this view any longer. It looks down on the cliff where she fell. So our bedroom is at the far end of the corridor where your rooms are."

"Oh. I see," Belinda said. "He didn't actually see her fall, did he?"

"Let's not talk about it anymore," Rose said. There was something in her face that I couldn't read. A wariness. Almost a fear as if she was treading on dangerous ground.

"Why, there you are, Mrs. Summers." The voice in the doorway made us jump. Rose sprang around guiltily as Mrs. Mannering stood, arms folded across her chest, disapproval written all over her face. "I hope the young ladies are satisfied with the rooms I have prepared for them."

"We certainly are," I said. "Mrs. Summers wanted to show us the view from this part of the house."

"Indeed."

"Jonquil must have loved this room when she was growing up," Belinda said.

"Miss Jonquil loved everything. She loved life. 'I can't wait to be up and out there, Manny,' she'd say to me every morning when I came to brush her hair. One hundred strokes every day. She had hair like spun gold, didn't she? I used to tell her she was Rapunzel and one day her hair would be so long that she could lower it from her window. But do you know what she said? She said, 'I think it might hurt if a prince climbed up it, don't you?' Such a witty child, always."

"I think we've seen all we need to," Rose interrupted. "Is coffee ready?"

"That was why I came to find you, madam," Mrs. Mannering said. "Coffee is served in the morning room."

As we headed along the hallway I heard the sound of a key being turned in the lock behind us. Mrs. Mannering followed us down the stairs. Just as we reached the bottom of the stairs the front door opened, sending in a great blast of wind and swirling leaves. The man who stood framed against the light was tall, broad shouldered with striking blond hair and a tanned face. Cornwall seems to be full of handsome men, I thought.

"Oh good, Tony, you've come home," Rose said. "We have guests, darling. Two old friends coming to stay. Isn't that wonderful?"

Tony Summers crossed the foyer toward us. He was wearing a Harris Tweed jacket and riding boots. "You didn't tell me anyone was coming, Rose, or I'd have spruced myself up first," he said. He came toward us, hand extended. "How do you do? I'm Tony—" He broke off as recognition dawned. "My God," he said. "Belinda!"

$\mathcal{C}$hapter 10

Golly, I really wish we hadn't bumped into Rose Summers. It already
feels uncomfortable staying here, even though we are being well
looked after. Mrs. Mannering is too perfect. I'm so glad she's not
my housekeeper.

"Hello, Tony," Belinda said in a remarkably even voice. "How lovely
to see you again."

"You recognized her," Rose said. "I'm impressed. She certainly
didn't look like that when she used to stay at her grandma's and we
used to launch those rafts from their dock."

"No, I'd say she's improved since then," Tony said. His voice had
that smooth, almost lazy quality of the Eton educated and I noticed
how his gaze lingered on Belinda. "So what brings you to this part of
the world?"

"I've come down for a few days with my friend Lady Georgiana,"

Belinda said. "We wanted to inspect a property I'd been left, but it turned out to be White Sails."

"White Sails?" he asked.

"The old fishing cottage," Rose interjected. "You know. After you go around Little Rumps."

For some reason hearing this again made me grin like a schoolgirl. I'd really have to learn to look grown-up and sophisticated now that I was married.

"Oh yes." Tony nodded. "With that strange little harbor. Hardly the sort of place for a city girl like you, I'd have thought. Will you sell it?"

"I haven't decided yet," Belinda said. "We obviously can't stay in it the way it is. It would need considerable remodeling, but it might be nice to have a cottage in Cornwall to retreat to occasionally."

"Yes. That might be nice."

I was watching the way he looked at her. He was clearly hinting it might be nice to have her as a near neighbor. "So do I take it you'll be staying with us?"

"I invited them," Rose said. "I hope that's all right?"

"It's your house too," he said. "And I'm always delighted to have guests, particularly attractive ones. You must let me give you a tour of the estate. And the home farm. They are coming along splendidly. We've a herd of Jersey cows and you must taste the clotted cream. I'm trying to find a way to export it to London."

"Coffee is ready in the morning room, Tony," Rose said. "Shall we go through before it gets cold?"

"If I know Mrs. Mannering she will make sure it is piping hot." Tony paused, testing it with a nod of satisfaction. "Isn't she a marvel? This place runs like clockwork," he echoed exactly what Rose had said previously. "And you wait until you try the food." He turned back to us and brought his fingers to his lips in a sign of appreciation. "I'm so glad she didn't leave after Jonquil—" He broke off and I saw a spasm of pain cross his face. He really loved her, I thought.

After coffee Tony fetched the estate car and drove us to the home farm. Rose insisted on coming with us which made the journey rather cramped. "I haven't seen the cows in ages," Rose said. "The calves must be quite grown-up by now."

"Oh come on, Rose. You can see the cows anytime you want," Tony said.

"But you never invite me to go with you," she said calmly.

"I don't have to invite you. You are my wife."

I could feel the tension as we got into the vehicle. She doesn't want to chance his being alone with Belinda, I thought. We drove past a stable yard. "We've a few good mounts if you care to go for a ride," Tony said. "I'm busy today but tomorrow I could come with you. Early morning gallop."

"They won't want to get up at the hour you do, Tony," Rose said in a peeved voice.

"Just because you can't ride and won't learn, don't think that everyone else hates horses."

"I don't hate horses. I just don't see the point of being bumped around on a hard saddle when you have a perfectly good motorcar to take you."

"If you're here long enough, I expect we could find a hunt," Tony said.

"I'm afraid we didn't bring our riding clothes," Belinda said. "And besides, we are only here for a day or two."

"Oh, but you must stay longer than that. What's the rush?"

"I need to get back to my house," I said before Belinda could answer. "I promised my husband I'd hire a new cook while he was away."

"What does your husband do?" Tony asked. "Or is he a fellow aristocrat and does nothing much?"

"He's a spy," I replied.

Tony laughed. "No, really?"

"He goes abroad a lot on various commissions," I said, "but he is a fellow aristocrat. And we have just acquired a big estate to run."

"Good for you. It takes a lot of work, doesn't it? As I have been finding out since I came here."

"We don't have a home farm, just the estate, but the grounds are quite big and have been neglected for a while."

We drove in through a white-painted gate and up to a field of cream-colored cows. They were adorable with their big dark eyes and long lashes.

"I'm not sure I'm cut out to be a farmer," Tony said as we complimented him. "It's been a good challenge to get the herd up and running, but doing this every day, for the rest of my life when there is a big world out there? We have properties in Barbados, you know. Sugarcane. That might be fun."

"I'm not sure I'd like Barbados," Rose said from the backseat. "It's awfully hot, isn't it? And all the servants would be natives."

"Oh, Rose, you are so horribly provincial," Tony said. "Travel broadens the mind, you know. Belinda knows that, don't you?"

I was glad Belinda had put me between her and Tony on the seat as I saw him sneak glances in her direction. Poor old Rose in the backseat, I thought.

⚜

TONY JOINED US for luncheon in a dining room down yet another corridor. I began to feel I might lose my way if left to wander unescorted in this house. The dining table could easily have seated thirty and we four sat at one end of it. I couldn't help thinking how lonely it would be if just Rose and Tony sat there. Perhaps they had a less formal room when no guests were present. Then I remembered that we always ate in such a room at home in Scotland. It's what aristocrats do. The lunch itself was a gammon steak with parsley sauce followed by a blackberry and apple crumble. Both delicious.

"Would you like a little rest?" Rose asked. "I usually have one."

"No, I think I'm going to see if we can get a closer look at Trengilly," Belinda said. "Now I know there is nobody in residence, I think we might be able to get into the grounds along the shoreline and up the rocks." She paused. "You don't think he has watchdogs or anything, do you?"

"Not that I've heard," Rose said.

"At least we'll be able to peek in through the windows and Georgie can see a taste of what it was like."

"I bet you won't even recognize it," Rose said. "I hear it's frightfully modern now."

We found our way back to the foyer, rescued our coats and set off. The day had clouded over, as so often happens after a fine start. "Let's hope it doesn't rain before we can see the house," Belinda said.

"Do you think it's okay, sneaking in like this? I didn't like the look of that great padlock on the front gates."

"We're not going to burgle the place, only to take a look at it," Belinda said. "If there is a watchman, I'll tell him who I am and he'll understand."

We parked the motorcar beside the road and took a footpath down to a small beach. Now that the tide was almost in, there was only a couple of feet of sand and these were threatened to be swallowed up any moment. Belinda strode out ahead with the confidence of one who knows her way and started to climb the rocks at the end of the beach. I followed, wishing I had put on more sensible shoes. My old Scottish brogues would have been ideal. We made our way along the shoreline, working our way around rocky outcroppings until a jetty appeared ahead of us.

"Aha. Here we are." Belinda sounded triumphant.

She clambered up ahead of me. I followed and we found ourselves standing on a grassy bluff. Ahead of us was the house with a new conservatory added at the back. To one side was a former kitchen garden and apple orchard. To the other a new tennis court.

"My, my," Belinda said. "We used to play tennis by putting up a net and painting lines on the grass. I wonder what they've done with the stables. He surely doesn't bother to keep horses if he's only here occasionally."

"Perhaps he's converted them to garages," I said. "Most people do these days. Although I'm looking forward to getting a couple of horses for Darcy and me. I'd like to ride with the local hunt."

"That's what I really miss about living in town," Belinda said. "So far so good. Come on. Let's take a look at the house, shall we?"

I noticed that she didn't walk straight up the lawn but rather hugged the trees to one side until we were quite close. "That's the drawing room at this end," she said. "And then a little sitting room, the library and the morning room facing east. The dining room was at the front."

She sprinted across the last stretch of grass, which had been impeccably mown, and went up to the nearest window.

"Oh rats," she exclaimed. "The curtains are all closed That is really unfair. There must be one that is open a little. I think I can see in. Goodness, what an awful color scheme. And look at that furniture. Granny would turn in her grave. Come and see this, Georgie."

Suddenly I heard footsteps on the gravel. "Wait, there's someone coming." I tugged at Belinda's coat sleeve.

Belinda looked up. A man was walking toward us. "It's all right," she said. "It's only Jago. I wonder what he's doing here? Up to no good, I'll bet. Let's see him try and talk his way out of this."

"Hey!" Jago quickened his pace. "What are you doing here?"

"Hello, Jago," Belinda said. "We meet again, it seems. I used to live here, remember. And more to the point, what are you doing here?"

"I work here. And you are trespassing."

"You work here? Really?"

"Yes. Really. Now I must ask you to leave."

"Oh come on, Jago. Don't be a spoilsport," Belinda said. "I only want to let Georgie get a glimpse of my old house."

"She's had a glimpse," Jago said. "Now I'm afraid you should go.

The owner is rather paranoid about anyone on the property. How did you get in anyway?"

"Along the rocks, like we used to," Belinda said.

Jago rolled his eyes. "Aren't you a little old for such things these days? The tide comes in quickly, you know. You'll find yourself cut off."

"We can manage it perfectly well, thank you."

"Only if you head back right away." He paused, then sighed. "Very well. I suppose I should take pity on you and let you out through the gate. I wouldn't like two bodies to be on my conscience."

He set off at a brisk pace around the building. We had to break into a trot to keep up with him. "I'm sorry," Belinda said. "I don't want to get you in trouble."

"It's all right. There is nobody here but me," Jago answered. "But you're lucky. The owner is thinking of installing some of his art collection. Some pretty valuable paintings from his villa in the South of France. And he's suggesting we keep watchdogs."

We came around to the front of the house. Here there were charming formal gardens. Lines of rosebushes were neatly pruned back for the winter. Holly bushes were already showing some red berries, but otherwise there was no color at this time of year.

"You should see it when the lilac is out on those bushes in the spring," Belinda said to me. "And the daffodils all over the woods."

"It's a treat, isn't it?" Jago looked back at her and smiled agreement.

"The gardens still look good," Belinda said. "Does he not have gardeners living on the premises?"

"No. They don't live in. We have a team coming once a week in the winter. There's not that much to do. And no resident housekeeper either."

"And you keep an eye on the place, do you?"

"That sort of thing," he said. He struck out through the woodland at the front of the estate, and then instead of going to the big iron gates, he went up to the wall and opened a small door, half concealed by ivy.

"I never knew this existed," Belinda said.

"It didn't. The boss had it put in, so that the main gate doesn't have to be opened when people like me go in and out." He stood back to let us through. "Look, I'm sorry I can't show you the house but . . ."

"Of course. I understand. You have your orders," Belinda said. She turned back to him. "Thank you, Jago. It seems you're a man of many talents."

"You don't know half of them," he replied with a flirtatious glance. I felt an odd pang of jealousy, or was it regret. I was now a married woman. There would be no more flirting in my life. Then I remembered the goings-on among the British aristocrats in Kenya. They didn't seem to care that they were married. Goodness, I'd never want to live like that. I should be happy I had such a wonderful husband.

"Well, that was a turn up for the books, wasn't it?" Belinda said as we heard the gate closing behind us and we started to walk away. "I wonder if he really does work there or if he was also on the property illegally? He certainly was anxious to get rid of us, wasn't he?"

"He's probably a groundskeeper, or watchman, and trying to do his job," I said.

"Or he's using the property to store items he's smuggled?" Belinda said. "It's convenient that there's a dock. Perhaps he keeps his stash in the outbuildings."

"Belinda, why are you so sure he's a smuggler?" I asked.

"Why else would someone creep into White Sails in the middle of the night?" Belinda shook her head in exasperation. "And why would we miraculously find him here the next day? And you know what? I wouldn't be at all surprised if my uncle Francis was in on it too. 'See a man about a dog.' That's what he said. I remember that was his expression when he was up to something shady and wanted to keep it from my grandmother."

"Anyway, it's none of our business," I said. "I've seen the house from the outside and it is lovely and being well looked after, so you should be happy. And now I suppose we should get back and face the music."

"Oh dear." Belinda sighed. "I'm in no rush to get back to Trewoma, are you?"

"I can't say that I am," I agreed.

"So you feel it too, do you? The tension. And a strange atmosphere. Rose is clearly ill at ease."

"Well, wouldn't you be with a housekeeper like that hovering all the time and disregarding your orders? I wonder Rose doesn't sack her and get in someone more friendly."

"Doesn't dare, I suppose. I'm beginning to have more sympathy for poor Rose. It can't be easy when everyone knows you were the cook's daughter."

"And apparently everyone adored Jonquil, including Tony," I pointed out.

Belinda nodded. "We won't stay long, I promise. As soon as I've decided what needs to be done with White Sails we're off. I know." She grabbed my arm. "Let's go back to the cottage now and take another look. Let's see if it's feasible to put in a bathroom."

"And electricity," I added. "It's scary in the night when lamps go out."

"It was. I'm beginning more and more to think it might be best just to put it up for sale and walk away. But then I keep thinking it's my last link to Cornwall. My mother grew up here. I had happy childhood memories."

"You have come into money, Belinda. Buy yourself another cottage—one with all modern conveniences."

Belinda laughed. We drove off, speeding past the entrance to Trewoma, just in case anyone was looking, and continued on around the headland to White Sails. Waves were breaking over the little rocky island, sending up impressive sheets of spray. Seagulls circled, screeching. As we left the motorcar and opened the gate I could see the value of that little harbor. Waves splashed against the harbor wall, but inside the water was sheltered and calm. I was surprised to see a boat tied up against the wall.

"Look," I said to Belinda. "Is that Jago's? It wasn't there this morning."

"It can't be. He's at Trengilly. Although we didn't see his boat at the jetty there, did we?" She gave me a knowing look. "Interesting. Perhaps this is part of the smuggling chain—someone come to pick up the smuggled goods."

"I don't know where Jago could have stashed them," I said. "We didn't see any sign this morning, did we?"

"Maybe in the cave down below? Although that might be risky because I think it gets flooded at high tide." She gave my shoulder a pat. "Come on. Let's go and see if we have an intruder. Perhaps they have been using this cottage for years with impunity. We'll soon put a stop to that."

"Belinda, if they are smugglers . . ." I began. "Well, they might be dangerous. We should go carefully."

"Nonsense," Belinda said. "The sooner they know they are not wanted here, the better."

I watched her stalking resolutely down the steps ahead of me and had to admire her bravado. Why did I always have to think of what could go wrong with every situation while she never seemed to? Perhaps it was because my old nanny always brought me up to be careful. "Watch where you are going. Don't be too hasty." Those were the sort of things she always said. And of course I had recently found myself in several dangerous situations. I knew that some people could be violent and desperate and could even kill.

We reached the cottage. Belinda did not hesitate. She turned the key and we stepped into the living room that still felt pleasantly warm with the lingering ashes of the fire. It also smelled of this morning's toast and of something else: cigarette smoke. I looked at Belinda.

"Someone's here," I whispered.

She nodded, went over to the fire and picked up the poker. "Right. Let's investigate," she said. She pushed the bedroom door slowly open. Nothing.

"Must be down in the cellar," she mouthed to me and started down the stairs. Halfway down she froze and motioned for me to freeze too. I heard the tinkle of water and saw to my embarrassment that a man was standing in the far corner, peeing into the lavatory. She gave me an inquiring glance, looking first at the poker, then at him. I got her message. Hit him while he is otherwise occupied. I shook my head furiously and began to retreat silently up the stairs. She followed suit, waited a respectable amount of time and then called out in a loud voice, "Is somebody down there? Show yourself instantly or I'll have you up for trespassing."

We heard scrambling and a voice saying, "Belinda? Is that you? It's only me. Uncle Francis."

He came into view, staring up at us, looking horribly embarrassed.

"What are you doing here?" Belinda asked. It seemed as if the last few hours had been a repetition of that phrase. Everybody was surprised to see everybody else in this part of the world.

"I had the boat out so I thought I'd just take a look at the old place, remind myself whether it was as ghastly as I remembered it."

"How did you get in?" Belinda asked.

"Oh, you know. The way we always used to," he said, looking even more embarrassed now. "Through the cave. There are steps in the wall."

"You do know that's trespassing, don't you?" Belinda said. "Now, if you would please come up and leave by the front door?"

He came up the steps, eyeing her with suspicion. "You can put down that poker. I'm not a burglar," he said.

"Only because there is nothing worth stealing," she said.

"What an awful thing to say to your old uncle, who is so fond of you."

"Uncle Francis, I know perfectly well that you would strip the rings from your dying grandmother's fingers. Now please go down to your boat and sail into the sunset."

"Well, I must say," he answered huffily. "There's family spirit for you. Your old uncle pays you a friendly visit and you cast him out into the storm without even the offer of a cup of tea."

"I'm afraid we don't have time for a cup of tea," Belinda said. "We came to have another look and see if it might be possible to put in a proper bathroom—one with some privacy," she added, giving him a knowing glance. "But we have to get back to Trewoma or they will wonder what has become of us."

Uncle Francis leaned against the mantelpiece and took out his cigarette case. He extracted a cigarette, put it in his mouth and lit it without offering one to us. He took a long drag then asked, "So how is it? As extravagant as one hears? And lord of the manor, that blighter Summers? You know him, presumably?"

"From our youth," Belinda said carefully. "We all used to play together as children."

"Did you? He lived around here? I don't remember him."

"They rented a place in the summer. His father was a big shot in the City."

"I must have been away at the time," he said. "So he was a childhood friend. How convenient."

"His wife too," Belinda said.

"He married the Trefusis girl, did he? Of course I've been out of the county for too long but one heard rumors."

"Yes, he married Jonquil, but unfortunately she died. Now he's married to another person from my childhood, Rose Barnes."

"Barnes?" Uncle Francis frowned. "The name rings a bell."

"Granny's old cook's daughter."

"Rosie Barnes? My God. The cook's daughter is now mistress of Trewoma and I, a peer of the realm, am reduced to sleeping in a small sailing boat? What is the world coming to?"

Belinda laughed. "You were the one who was advocating communism this morning. Equality for all, remember."

Uncle Francis stood looking around him. "Nice little spot this. Sheltered, private. But you wouldn't really want to keep it, would you?"

Belinda laughed. "You are suggesting that I give it to my aged uncle, is that right?"

"It wouldn't hurt you to. You did get the house in Bath and the money and jewelry after all. A mere crumb to a struggling relative would be a noble gesture."

"You've had your share, Uncle Francis. I believe Granny settled a good amount on you when she sold Trengilly."

"I told you, dear child. Most of it in the form of an allowance, doled out in spoonsful by a stingy and critical bank manager. Never enough to really enjoy myself or to get ahead."

"You could find yourself a job," Belinda said.

"At my age?"

"You are not that old. You can't be more than fifty."

"But I'm a peer of the realm. Our sort don't take jobs. We own things. We ride to hounds. We give orders. I should be living at Trengilly. I should be lord of the manor here, not that upstart Summers and his cook wife."

"Life is hard, Uncle Francis," Belinda said. "I'm afraid you'll just have to get used to it. And we must be going. So out with you, please." She gave him a shove and moved to open the front door. When we were all outside she turned the key in the lock.

"You are an ungrateful, heartless wench, you know that," he said. "One day you'll regret this." And he stomped down the stone steps cut into the cliff face toward his boat.

I began the climb up to the motorcar. Belinda followed. Neither of us spoke until we had regained the road.

"Oh dear," she said, panting a little because there were a lot of steps. "I feel awful. Do you think I should let him have the cottage? I mean, I did inherit everything and he's living on a boat."

"You just said that he squandered his money. And he fondled you when you were a child."

"Yes, but he is family. And I don't really need the cottage, do I?"

"It's up to you, Belinda. But I don't think you owe him anything."

We climbed into the motor, and Belinda started the engine. "You're right. I'm too softhearted. And I'm sure if he had this place he'd use it for his nefarious schemes."

As we drove along the headland we watched the boat putting out to sea. Against the backdrop of the Atlantic it did look awfully small.

Chapter 11

OCTOBER 16
TREWOMA, CORNWALL

Back at Trewoma after a rather unpleasant encounter at White Sails.
  Golly, I hope this evening is not going to be too tense.

We returned to find my belongings unpacked, my toiletries arranged on the dressing table and my slippers beside the bed, just like Jonquil's had been in her room. I got the feeling that Mrs. Mannering had supervised and presumably snooped at what I had brought with me. She wouldn't get much joy from my things, except for the photo of Darcy and me on our honeymoon.

We came downstairs and after a couple of wrong turns that led to the kitchens and then the library we were rescued by a maid who informed us that the mistress was taking tea in the long gallery and escorted us there. It really was a most confusing house! Rose was sitting in a room that must have been the original hall in medieval times where family life went on. It was a vast room overlooking the ocean with heavy tapestries of battles hanging on the walls and dark velvet curtains at the windows. On one side was a minstrel gallery and in the middle was a hearth big enough to roast an ox. Not what I would call a friendly room.

But it was a scrumptious tea with clotted cream and strawberry jam to go with the warm scones and a variety of tiny meringues, éclairs and iced cakes. I watched Rose tuck in with relish. I wondered whether this was wise, given that I had been told Tony had a roving eye.

We chatted pleasantly enough through tea, then Rose urged us to go for a walk around the grounds. Black clouds had been rushing in from the Atlantic and it didn't look too promising as we stepped out of the front door.

"It's going to rain, Rose," Belinda said. "Better put this off until later."

"Oh, come on, Belinda. Don't be a spoilsport," Rose said. "You know good old Cornish rain. It's only a fine mist usually, isn't it? I'm really keen to show you around. It's still all so new to me too."

And she looked so hopeful that Belinda shrugged and went along. "Oh well. It's only rain," she said. "I suppose it can't kill us."

I, having been raised at Castle Rannoch, was used to rain, snow, sleet and hail so it didn't worry me, but I did wonder why Rose was so awfully keen for us to see the grounds when she had a whole lovely house to show off.

We set off, along the front of the house and across a manicured lawn with a statue of a Greek nymph in the middle of it. A flower bed around the edge was bare at this time of year. Beyond, a rose arbor was also pruned down to barren sticks. It didn't look particularly appetizing and again I wondered why Rose wanted to get us out of the house. Something to do with being away from Mrs. Mannering, I thought.

We had only made it halfway across the lawn when the heavens opened. This was certainly no Cornish mist but a full-blown downpour. In seconds we were drenched with icy water and we had to dash inside again where Mrs. Mannering was waiting to greet us, tut-tutting at our foolishness. So Rose gave us a tour of the reception rooms instead. These were certainly impressive. We admired the white grand piano and full-sized harp in the music room, the walls lined with leather-bound books in the dark and somber library and the family portraits in the drawing room. Former owners of Trewoma, those who had established plantations in far-flung corners of the globe, had brought back interesting objects and these were displayed in every nook. In the library there was a glass case of spectacular butterflies; a stuffed king cobra poised to strike and looking horribly realistic; brightly colored stuffed birds; evil-looking masks on walls as well as many strange weapons: swords, daggers and cutlasses.

"What on earth is this?" Belinda asked, pausing in front of a sword adorned with what looked like strings of human teeth.

"Oh that?" Rose made a face. "It's a headhunter's sword from Borneo. Those are the teeth of his victims. Isn't it horrible? We've also got some shrunken heads somewhere. But come and see the pretty little conservatory at the end of the hall. That has nothing disgusting in it and it's lovely to sit there on sunny days."

The conservatory was delightful, filled with white wicker furniture and tall green plants. "There were also some orchids," Rose said. "But I'm afraid I don't have a green thumb. I tried taking care of them and I killed them. Mrs. Mannering was angry, I know. But I wanted to do something useful. It's strange having nothing to do expect be waited on."

"I know how you feel," I said. "You should get a dog. Several dogs. They always make a house feel more like home and they are great companions."

"I'm afraid of dogs," Rose said. "I was bitten once as a child, by your grandmother's dog, Belinda."

"What, old Spingo? He was the only dog I remember and he was harmless."

Rose shook her head. "Well, he bit me," she said.

"Dogs always know who is afraid," I said. "They sense fear and that makes them nervous."

"Tony keeps saying he wants dogs," Rose said. "Jonquil had a couple but they were put down when she died."

"How horrid—who did that?" I asked, being incredibly fond of the dogs I'd grown up with.

"I don't know. I wasn't anywhere around here in those days," Rose said. "I was up in London, remember."

"Of course."

As we spoke I had been admiring the view. The conservatory faced the back grounds with a view over the cliffs to the ocean beyond. It must have been spectacular on sunny days. Today, however, the rain peppered against the glass and angry waves raced up the river. It could have been a lovely house in many ways but everywhere felt so cold, the corridors so long and dark, and I found I was looking over my shoulder.

"Is Trewoma supposed to be haunted?" I blurted out the words before I decided they weren't exactly tactful. After all, Rose had to live there.

Rose nodded. "There's a haunted room upstairs. Over the porch. A young woman's ghost visits anyone who isn't a family member. Needless to say I haven't ever slept in there. Tony did once, for a dare, when he was married to Jonquil but he said the ghost didn't bother him because he was married to a family member, which was just as good."

We finished our tour then went up to change for dinner. Mrs. Mannering appeared from nowhere as we were going up the stairs. "Since I can only offer you one maid to help with your attire perhaps I could assist the other young lady," she said.

"Oh, Mrs. Mannering, that won't be necessary," Belinda said. "Lady Georgiana and I are quite capable of dressing ourselves and as you can see, my haircut just requires a quick brush."

"Very well, Miss Warburton-Stoke, but I will send up Elsie anyway. You may need assistance with hooking your evening gown."

"I'm afraid we didn't bring evening gowns," Belinda said. "We had not planned on staying with anyone, just visiting a piece of property."

Mrs. Mannering stared at Belinda for a moment as if not bringing an evening gown was a mortal sin, then said, "Maybe one of Miss Jonquil's gowns would fit you. You have a wonderfully slim figure, just like she did. And you too, my lady."

"Oh, we couldn't possibly . . ." I said, but she waved the rest of my protest away.

"Who else would wear them? Such lovely gowns and they lie languishing in her wardrobe. I'll select a couple and bring them to you."

And off she went. I gave Belinda a worried look. "I don't like doing this at all. How can we get out of it?"

"I don't think we can. How awkward."

The housekeeper returned carrying two long gowns over her arm. Belinda's was emerald green in a Grecian style, mine was pale blue. Mrs. Mannering insisted on staying to instruct the maid as we were dressed in them. They were both exquisite but I was holding my breath as we came downstairs. Tony and Rose were waiting for us with drinks in the long gallery. They looked up as we came in.

"Oh, what lovely dresses," Rose started to say, but Tony was staring at us as if he couldn't believe his eyes.

"Isn't that one of Jonquil's gowns?" he demanded.

"They both are," Belinda said. "We explained to Mrs. Mannering that we had not brought evening clothes with us as we were not expecting to stay with anyone and she insisted that we wear two of Jonquil's gowns."

"Well, I must say they fit you both very well," he conceded. "Quite a treat for the eye. You must keep them. They're of no use here."

"Oh, I'm sure Mrs. Mannering wouldn't want us to walk off with them," Belinda said.

"Mrs. Mannering does not have the final word over my departed wife's gowns," Tony said. "If you want them, they are yours. Now what will you have? Sherry?"

We each took a glass of sherry and went over to the fireplace. There was a draft blowing in from the sea, making the tapestries on the wall flap alarmingly, and I definitely felt a little chilly in that evening gown. I began to wish Mrs. Mannering had offered us fur wraps as well. Rose was noticeably silent. Maybe the sight of us in Jonquil's gowns had made her realize what Tony had lost, and that she could never compete with a beautiful dead woman.

"So what did you think of my cows?" Tony asked. He had moved over to the fire and was now standing rather close to Belinda.

"I thought they had lovely eyelashes," she said.

He laughed. "Typical woman. Notices the eyelashes, not the prodigious udders."

"Which is what a man would have noticed," Belinda replied.

I felt the conversation was veering into the realm of flirtation and turned to examine a cluster of silver-framed photographs on a side table. One particularly caught my eye. It was a snapshot of a group of young people, the girls in shorts, their hair tied back. I recognized a young Tony, handsome and self-assured even then. And the striking blond girl must have been Jonquil. She was looking at the camera with arrogant defiance. Rose's moon face peeked from the back of the group, looking shy and uncertain. And perched on the five bar gate . . . "Is this you, Belinda?" I asked.

She came over to see the photograph. Tony followed her.

"Oh my goodness, don't I look awful," she replied. "Talk about skinny. And I'm frowning at the camera." She looked up at Tony. "I've never seen this before. It's a photo of our set. It must have been the last summer before Granny moved. You're there, standing behind the gate, Rose. Oh, and look at Jago. Wasn't he tall? But also skinny."

"I seem to remember he had a bit of a crush on you, Belinda, didn't he?" Rose said.

"I wouldn't call it a crush." Belinda had gone red. "I remember he kissed me once, before I left for school. It wasn't bad either."

"That blighter," Tony said. "Never did like him. He's come back to the area, you know."

"Yes, we ran into him today. He says he's working at Trengilly."

"Yes. He works for the foreign gentleman who bought the place," Rose said.

"Foreign gentleman!" Tony gave a disparaging sniff. "Bit of a crook from what I've heard. The whole thing's suspicious if you ask me."

"Why is that?" I asked.

"I've heard things about where his money comes from. Dubious sources."

Belinda was still examining the photograph. "And who is the pale boy standing behind me?" She looked up, her mouth open in realization. "Oh, it's Colin, isn't it? I'd forgotten all about him. Poor Colin."

"Who was Colin?" I asked. "I haven't heard him mentioned before."

"He was only here that one summer," Tony said. "A summer visitor staying with someone. We always picked up a couple of extras who were just here for a few weeks. Well, Colin latched on to us. We never encouraged him. Boring sort of chap, wasn't he? The brainy type who likes to quote statistics. He went to a grammar school." He grinned as if this was a sin.

"It's not funny, Tony," Rose said suddenly. She had been so quiet I'd almost forgotten she was there. "You and Jonquil loved to tease him."

"It didn't put him off, though, did it? He kept on showing up."

"He wanted to be included, like I did," she said. "How can you talk about him like that, as if nothing had happened?"

Tony turned back to her. "All right. Don't upset yourself. We all felt bad but it was an accident, wasn't it? How were we to know?"

"To know what?" I asked.

"That he couldn't swim," Tony replied.

I looked to Belinda for an explanation. "Jonquil dared us to see if we could cross the river on foot. She said she had done it on her horse and if we timed the tide just right she thought we could do it. So we started off. It was hard going over some of the sandbanks. Soft sand, you know. We kept getting stuck and in the end we decided we should turn back." She took a deep breath. "But the tide was already coming in. We started running. We didn't notice that Colin was having trouble keeping up. He got cut off. When we heard him calling and looked back, he was already up to his knees in water. And we shouted, 'You'll have to swim for it,' and he shouted back, 'I can't swim.'

"Jago and Tony started back toward him, but a wave knocked him off his feet and he thrashed for a bit and then . . ." She paused and took another deep breath. "And then we didn't see him anymore. He was gone. We looked and looked but they didn't find his body until the next day on the other shore."

"When you think about it, it was rather idiotic of him to embark on something like that, knowing he couldn't swim," Tony said. "After all, it was crossing a river, for God's sake."

"He so desperately wanted to be included, and he trusted us, Tony," Rose said. "You and Jonquil always seemed so confident. If you remember I didn't even come with you, because I thought you were taking too big a risk."

"You were always scared to do anything dangerous, Rose," he said. "But I would have stopped him if I'd known he couldn't swim. I mean, who comes down to Cornwall for the summer and doesn't learn to swim? It's all about beaches, isn't it?" He paused, gave an uneasy laugh, then added, "Actually Jonquil confessed afterward that she knew he couldn't swim."

There was an awkward silence, then Tony added, "That was Jonquil all over, wasn't it? It added to the risk. She loved playing with fire."

A clatter on the table behind us made us turn around. Mrs. Mannering had knocked over a bronze oriental statue. She righted it hastily. "I came in to see if the fire needs making up, sir," she said. "Dinner will be served in ten minutes."

※

AFTER THAT UNSETTLING episode, dinner passed remarkably smoothly. There was pleasant chatter around the table, mostly dwelling on Belinda's recent time in Paris and what Madame Chanel was like, also my visit to Kenya and the habits of various wild animals. I had to describe my dangerous encounters, including the lion outside my tent and the elephant that stepped out in front of our car. They were duly impressed. The food that evening was outstanding. I could see why Tony insisted on keeping Mrs. Mannering if she arranged such meals. We started with a clear consommé with croutons followed by lobster salad. Then leg of pork with crackling and sage and onion stuffing, chocolate mousse with clotted cream and finally anchovy toast. It was accompanied by excellent wines and I felt quite relaxed and happy by the time the meal ended.

Rose suggested we ladies go through for coffee while Tony enjoyed his cigar.

"I think I'll forego the cigar this evening and come with you," he said. "It's not often I have the privilege of witty company. We're rather out of the way down here. I keep telling Rose it's high time we checked out the property in Barbados. If it's not being run well, I may just sell it and buy a house in London."

"Think of the upkeep," Rose said. "You'd need to have servants there."

"Just a pied-à-terre, like Belinda's mews cottage," he said.

Rose looked at him sharply. "How did you know that Belinda has a mews cottage?"

Tony looked amused. "She mentioned it earlier, or Georgiana mentioned it. Did you say it was in Mayfair, Belinda?"

"In Knightsbridge."

"Ah yes. I understand they are becoming quite popular these days. When you think that they used to stable horses there." He laughed again and the subject moved on to Barbados and what we knew of the Caribbean.

We settled into armchairs by the fire and one of the maids handed us coffee. Rose sipped hers, then looked up. "That's interesting, it doesn't taste bitter this evening." She gave a little laugh. "I've never really learned to like coffee. Not having grown up with it, I suppose."

"Well, at least you're trying it, which is one step in the right direction," Tony said.

I was glad when Belinda announced that she was tired, having not had much sleep the night before, and would everyone excuse her if she went up. I took my cue and followed her. At the top of the stairs she let out a sigh of relief. "I don't think I could have taken much more, Georgie. What was Tony thinking, hinting that he had been to my mews? And reviving all that awful time with Colin."

"How very sad," I said. "You must have felt terrible."

"The strange thing was that one didn't. We were kids at the time, you know. It was just 'poor old Colin' and then we forgot about him."

"What about his parents? His family?"

"I really don't remember. I know they went home, instead of having a funeral service here, and the police interviewed us and told us we had behaved stupidly trying to outrun the tide. And then I went off to school in Switzerland and never thought about it again."

As we reached the balcony at the top of the stairs Mrs. Mannering was waiting, appearing out of nowhere with that uncanny skill of hers. "I'll send up Elsie right away, Miss Warburton-Stoke," she said. "And I will personally assist you with your gown, Lady Georgiana."

"You shouldn't have waited up, Mrs. Mannering. I'm sure we could have managed to unhook each other." I glanced at Belinda.

"It's my job, my lady. I have never failed to do what was required of me. Not once in over thirty years." She followed me into my bedroom. I felt quite strange as she lifted the pale silk over my head and I was standing before her in my underwear. I found myself wishing I had worn the slinky Parisian undies that Zou Zou had brought back for my trousseau, instead of my boring daily cotton. Mrs. Mannering laid the dress on my bed. "It suited you perfectly, my lady. Please do keep it. It was made to be worn by a person of quality."

"I really couldn't, Mrs. Mannering," I said. "Besides, it's not yours to give, is it? It belongs to the lady of the household now."

"As if she could ever fit into it," she said with a snort of derision.

"Or play the part, even if it could be altered for her. And the master. He might have come from money, but in my mind money does not equal breeding. I have had to educate both of them about the right way to do things. He seems to have learned well, but I'm afraid she never will." She scooped up the dress. "I will wrap this in tissue paper for you. And maybe you might want to look and see if there are any more of Miss Jonquil's things that might suit. I fear they will all be donated to a charity one day. So far I have kept everything as it was, keeping her memory alive. But there will come a time when that woman learns to assert herself and . . ."

She broke off as the floorboards creaked and someone was walking down the hallway.

"Is everything all right?" Rose's voice came through my door. "Anything that you need?"

"I am taking care of the young lady, Mrs. Summers," the housekeeper said in a calm voice. "You can go to bed. I'll lock up and make sure everything is in order."

She gave me a look almost of triumph as she swept out of the room with my dress in her arms.

Chapter 12

THURSDAY, OCTOBER 17
TREWOMA, CORNWALL

I knew I felt uneasy here. Oh dear. I wish we had never come.

That night I had a nightmare. It might have only been the combination of the lobster, pork and rich dessert, but it seemed very real. In my dream I was in another strange house with long dark corridors. I couldn't see properly where I was going or what lay ahead. I was running, searching for Darcy. I called his name and someone stepped out behind me and put a hand on my shoulder, making me jump out of my skin. I turned to see who it was and a voice said, "You won't find him here. He has gone. This path only leads to destruction." And the person laughed. I couldn't tell if it was a man or a woman.

I awoke to a world of whiteness. The sea fog had come in overnight and hung over us so thickly that I could see only a few yards outside the window. The first trees were already faint gray shapes. I was very relieved when Mrs. Mannering did not appear to help me with my morning toilette. I managed to wash and dress without interference, then came down to find that only Tony was up, sitting at the breakfast table tucking into kidneys and bacon.

"Jolly good spread here for breakfast always," he said. "Help yourself. I have to get going. I've a man coming about our calves today."

I poured myself some coffee and came to sit at the table. "Do you enjoy being a farmer?" I asked. "It must be a big change from what you were used to."

"I do quite like it," he said. "My father had always expected that I'd go into finance like him, but I never had his knack with figures. But he articled me to an accountant anyway. Boring as hell. This is much more my style. Free to come and go as I please and some nice properties in suitably warm places in the winter. I've been toying with ideas for this house. It's far too big for just the two of us. Maybe a luxury hotel and put in a golf course?" He gave me a grin that suddenly made him look young and unsophisticated. Then he added, "Belinda not up yet? I've been thinking about that cottage of hers— White Sails. I can put her in touch with local builders to see if it can be made habitable. It would be jolly nice if she'd come back to our part of the world occasionally. Liven things up a little around here." He paused, looked around, then added, "One of the disadvantages of being a farmer. The social life is terribly dull."

I wasn't quite sure what I should say to this—warn him that it wasn't a good idea to show interest in Belinda? Instead I went over to the sideboard and helped myself to a plate of smoked haddock and scrambled egg. Tony pushed away his plate and got up.

"Enjoy your day," he said. "I have a date with my cow man."

By the time I had finished Belinda and Rose had arrived and we lingered, talking over cups of tea.

"I thought we'd go for a walk after breakfast," Rose said. "You haven't yet seen the best part of the grounds."

"Not exactly walking weather, is it?" Belinda peered out into the fog. "Besides, I have to do something about finding a builder for the cottage."

"Leave that to Tony," Rose said. "He mentioned last night that he'll set you up with a local builder. Besides, you can't go driving in this weather. You might run into a farm vehicle or even miss the road and drive off a cliff."

Belinda went to say something but then shrugged. "Oh well, I suppose a walk would do us good. Just as long as you don't take us anywhere near the top of those cliffs. I don't want to suffer Jonquil's fate."

Rose shook her head. "Oh no. Trust me. I don't go anywhere near the top of the cliffs. You know me. I always was the timid one. Jonquil used to be so rude about it. So did Tony, for that matter." She gave an embarrassed grin. "So let's get coats and scarves on. There is a part of the grounds I am dying to show you. It's quite unique."

We were just buttoning outdoor coats when Mrs. Mannering appeared. "Surely not going out in this weather, Mrs. Summers?"

"I thought a walk would do us good," Rose said, flushing as she always did when speaking to the housekeeper.

"You'll come back with pneumonia if you're not careful. It's bitter out there."

"We are bundled up and I'm anxious to show the ladies our grounds. We had to abandon our walk yesterday when it started to rain."

Mrs. Mannering was frowning. "Then I had better tell Cook to have a good hot soup ready for luncheon. And I suggest you walk with caution. There are parts of this estate that can be dangerous."

Rose opened the front door, and a cold dampness swirled in. It wasn't the most inviting of days but Rose set out with determination and we had no choice but to follow. Rose led us across a lawn and into a copse of trees. "You wait until you see this," she said. "It's quite surprising."

We could not see more than a few feet ahead of us but suddenly the path plunged downward between steep banks. We were entering a little dell. Bushes rose on either side, higher than our heads. A small stream ran gurgling beside us, dancing over stones as it made its way down the hill. Then we came to plants with giant leaves, two or three feet across, reaching out across the path. There was something unreal, otherworldly, about them and I shrank back when one brushed against me, as if they might well prove to be carnivorous.

"Isn't this amazing?" Rose said and her voice had an odd, echoing quality. "It goes all the way down to the beach. It's so sheltered that exotic plants grow here. A former Trefusis brought back tropical plants from the Caribbean. In the summer there are orchids and flowering vines. It's a bit dreary at this time of year."

"What are these awful-looking things?" I asked as we approached an even bigger plant with almost circular leaves at least three feet wide. It towered over our heads and reached out across the narrow path. I moved past it cautiously.

"I forget their name, but they grow well in Cornwall. It's something like *Gunnera*?"

"Or ask Mrs. Mannering. I'm sure she knows," Belinda said dryly. "She knows everything."

"Doesn't she just." Rose snapped out the words. Then she turned to look back before drawing closer to us. "Look, I know it isn't exactly the kind of weather to go exploring but I wanted to get you away from the house, where we can't be overheard." Again she glanced around nervously, before she said, "You've sensed it, haven't you?"

"Sensed what?" Belinda asked.

"The house. The atmosphere. That feeling of danger. Of doom."

"Oh, come on, Rose," Belinda said. "I admit the house does feel a trifle gloomy, but . . ."

"I've felt it since the moment I moved in," Rose said. "It's as if I've been holding my breath, waiting for doom to strike."

"From where? What are you afraid of?" I asked.

Rose's voice lowered to a whisper. We could hardly hear her over the noise of the stream, spilling over a little waterfall. "Jonquil's death was not an accident," she said. "I believe she was pushed."

"What on earth makes you suspect that?" Belinda said.

Rose leaned until she was only inches away from us. "I went to the spot where she fell. Those cliffs are granite. Solid granite. They don't crumble like chalk or sandstone. And there were marks on the rock that made me think that someone had chipped some chunks away to give the impression that the cliff had crumbled."

"But who would do such a thing?" I asked. "Did Jonquil have enemies?"

Rose grabbed at my sleeve. "I think it was Tony. Tony killed her."

"Why on earth would he do that?"

"Jonquil wasn't exactly the faithful type. She had lovers, you know. And I think she'd fallen out of love with Tony. She probably found he was a bit boring for her taste. You know how she loved excitement. You'd already moved away, Belinda, but the moment she could drive, her parents bought her a fast sports car and she was a menace on the road. She actually killed a child, you know. She claimed the boy darted out after a ball, and that may have been true, but she always drove so fast she couldn't have stopped."

"Where did this happen?" I asked.

"In the village of Rock," Rose said.

"So if you are right that Jonquil was pushed off a cliff, why don't you think it was one of the child's relatives, getting revenge?" I asked. "Why are you so sure it was Tony?"

"This is what I have gleaned from asking people," Rose said. "I think Jonquil wanted a divorce. If that happened, Tony would lose Trewoma. And all the lovely Trefusis money too."

Belinda shook her head. "I can't believe it, Rose. Tony would never do a thing like that, surely?"

"I wouldn't have believed it before, but now I do. I often wondered why he got rid of all the staff after her death. Only Mrs. Mannering stayed on and I think that was because she knew too much. He's afraid of her, just like I am." She walked on a few steps, then turned back to us. "The worst thing is, I think that now he's trying to kill me," she said in a lowered voice.

"Kill you?" I was so shocked that I blurted out the words. "But why?"

Rose turned away, unable to look at us. "Because he never really wanted me."

"Oh, Rose, what an awful thing to say," Belinda said.

"He must have loved you or he wouldn't have married you," I said gently because I could see how distressed she looked.

Her face was a picture of embarrassment. "He only married me because I was going to have a baby," she said. "One stupid night together and that happened. At least he did the right thing at the time. But I'm sure he never loved me. For me, it was a dream come true. I couldn't believe my luck. I mean, Tony Summers—the most eligible, gorgeous man I'd ever met and me as mistress of Trewoma."

"What happened?" Belinda asked. "About the baby?"

"I lost it," she said. "I had a miscarriage at three months. Tony was furious. I'm clearly not the sort of wife he wants. I have no social graces, I'm not good at the sort of things the upper crust do. So I think he's trying to get rid of me."

"What makes you think that?" Belinda asked.

"He's tried to trick me into things."

"What sort of things?" Belinda asked, giving me a worried, questioning look.

There was a rustling in the bushes above us. Rose glanced around nervously again, but it was just a bird. "We have a boat, you know," she said. "A small sailing boat. He keeps trying to persuade me to come out in it. He knows I'm a bad sailor. I could just picture what he had in mind. He'd get far enough out to sea and then he'd throw me over the side. He'd say, 'Poor Rose. She leaned over to throw up and a great wave came and she fell out. I tried to save her but the waves swept her away.'"

She put a hand up to her mouth. "It has to be an accident, you see. He's tried to get me to take up riding, knowing I'd fall off. And then there's the coffee."

"What coffee?" I asked.

"Remember last night I said it didn't taste bitter? It usually does, and I hate to admit I don't like it, so I pour it into one of the plants. Well, Tony usually stays on in the dining room to have brandy and a cigar while I go through to the drawing room for my coffee. Last night you were here so Tony came with us. And the coffee didn't taste bitter. Which made me wonder: does he usually put something in my coffee? Something that is slowly poisoning me?"

"But how could he do that if he stays in the dining room?" I asked.

"The coffee is left in thermos jugs on the table," she said. "He could have tampered with it before dinner. He sometimes goes for a call of nature. He'd have plenty of chances."

Belinda put a hand on Rose's shoulder. "Rose, I think you're imagining all this. Living alone in that big house, living the sort of life you are not used to, as well as the shock of losing the baby . . . well, maybe it's been playing on your nerves."

Rose shook her head. "No. I'm not imagining. I'm afraid, Belinda."

"You'll have another child soon, I'm sure, and then everything will be all right and Tony will be happy," Belinda said.

Rose shook her head. "The doctor says it's unlikely I'll have another. This one was in the tubes and something ruptured. That's another reason he wants to get rid of me."

"Oh, Rose," Belinda said gently. "Please don't get so upset."

Rose shrugged her off. "I don't know if he ever fancied me in the first place. I was just a friendly shoulder to cry on. And he's certainly lost interest now. I saw the way he looked at you yesterday."

"Men always look at me like that," Belinda said carelessly. "I'm just that sort of girl."

"You're the sort of girl he wishes he had married." Rose sounded as if she was close to tears. "Tony doesn't want me anymore and the most convenient way to get rid of me is to make sure I have an accident."

She started walking ahead of us, moving quickly between the giant leaves and the overhanging vines until a series of steps led us down to a little beach. We came out into a small cove with black water lapping a few yards from us. Cliffs rose on all sides, disappearing into the mist, and that little stream fanned out into rivulets through the sand to be swallowed up into the estuary. Somewhere above us we could hear seagulls mewing.

"So what do you plan to do about it?" Belinda asked.

"I don't know," Rose said. "That's the problem. I just don't know. Should I just admit defeat, tell him he can have a divorce and go quietly back to my old life, or should I wait around for the ax to fall?"

I didn't know what to say, but Belinda said, "Rose, I'm sure it's all in your head. Jonquil had a tragic accident and nothing you've said makes me think you are really in danger."

"The problem is that I have nobody to turn to here," Rose said. "My mum is far away in Bath. I never lived here, of course. I just came in during the holidays to stay with Mum at your granny's house. So I was a summer visitor like you. So there is nobody . . . that's why it seemed like such a miracle when I spotted you yesterday. Now I've got allies. Now I'll have proof."

No sooner had she finished the words than a pebble bounced down from unseen heights, landing with a thud on the beach beside us. It was followed by another, then another.

Rose grabbed at my arm. "You see," she whispered. "Someone has followed us. Someone is up there and any minute now a rock will fall on our heads."

"I'm sure it was just a bird landing on the cliff, dislodging some loose stones. You can hear them calling up there, can't you?"

"We must go back," Rose said. "We shouldn't stay down here any longer."

And she started toward the steps.

Belinda glanced at me again, then set off after Rose. I followed up in the rear, and found myself peering up into the mist above the cliffs. Like Belinda, I had thought that Rose was imagining things, but when the rocks started to rain onto us, I was not so sure.

Chapter 13

Are we really living in a house of horrors? When Tony came home for
lunch he seemed jovial and relaxed and I couldn't believe any of
the things Rose was suggesting. But down on that beach—for a
moment I wasn't so sure.

It wasn't until much later that I had a chance to be alone with Belinda.
Rose had stuck to us like glue all morning until Tony arrived with the
names of a couple of reputable local builders who would be willing to
come out to the cottage. Belinda suggested we could go and see them
after luncheon. The meal was excellent again: a leek and potato soup,
local John Dory—a kind of delicious flat fish—grilled and a steamed
sponge pudding with custard. When Belinda said we were off to see
the builders, Rose invited herself along. "I'd love to see the cottage for
myself," she said. "And I actually know one of the men Tony has mentioned. He did some work in our bathroom. So it would be useful to
have me along."

What could we say to that? We put on outdoor clothes and then drove out to the cottage. Rose pronounced it to be charming—or it could be charming if Belinda put in a proper bathroom and maybe a conservatory like the one they had at Trewoma. "But you wouldn't want to live out here, would you? It's so remote. Wouldn't you be scared to be on your own?"

"I've lived alone for years, Rose," Belinda said. "And I'd probably only come for short visits. I'd bring Georgie with me."

"I would be nice to have a friend nearby," Rose said and I heard the longing in her voice. I felt heartily sorry for her. I too had seen how Tony had looked at Belinda, how he had tried to flirt with her. I could, unfortunately, see why he might have tired of Rose and want to move on to pastures new. But as for trying to kill her? Well, that was hard to believe.

We left the cottage and went in search of Tony's builder. His office was in Wadebridge, which was the nearest town of any size.

"I'm sorry. Mr. Harris is with a customer at the moment," the receptionist said. "He shouldn't be long."

We had just taken a seat and had a cup of tea produced for us when two men came in, deep in conversation. The older man, with the weathered face of the outdoor life, clapped the younger one on the back. "Don't you worry about it then, Mr. Jago. We'll do a lovely job for you. Like one of those Paris boudoirs it will be." And he gave a hearty laugh that turned into a cough.

That's when I noticed that the younger man was Jago. He recognized us at the same time.

"Well, hello again," he said. "We seem to keep bumping into each other." His gaze lingered on Belinda. "Come about the cottage, have you? Old Harris here knows his stuff, but you can't have him for a while. I've got him working on a big project at Trengilly first."

"That's right, Mr. Jago," Mr. Harris said. "Now if you'd just like to step through so we can complete the paperwork, and I'll be with you ladies in a jiffy."

"Nice seeing you, Rose," Jago said. "How are you enjoying being lady of the manor, then?" He chuckled. "Do I have to touch my forelock when you approach these days?"

"None of your cheek, Jago," Rose replied, blushing scarlet. "Just because you've come up in the world yourself."

"I'm just a humble employee, not a landowner," Jago said. "Got to run. Bye, ladies."

"He's as cheeky as ever," Rose said as the inner door closed behind the men.

"What did you mean about coming up in the world?" Belinda said. "I told you I saw him on the grounds at Trengilly. He wasn't very friendly either. Is he the groundsman there now?"

"No, he works for that foreign man Tony was talking about. What's his name again? Panopolis? Something like that. Tony would know. I mentioned that he thinks this man is a bit dodgy, if you get my meaning. Not sure how he acquired his wealth or why he's bought an estate in the wilds of Cornwall. Anyway, Jago is his estate manager here but I understand that he also looks after his properties all over the place. Big vineyard in France, so I hear. Cattle ranch in Argentina. Oil tankers."

"Jago is his manager?" Belinda sounded horrified. "And I thought . . ."

"You thought he was a smuggler," I said, giving her a grin.

"Well, what was he doing at my cottage if he wasn't smuggling, then?" Belinda demanded.

At that moment the door opened and Jago came out. He nodded to us as he left the building. I wondered if he had overheard Belinda's last words because he had an amused look on his face.

"He and Tony don't exactly see eye to eye," Rose muttered as soon as Jago had closed the door behind him. "They had quite a run-in the other day."

"About what?" Belinda asked.

"Something to do with lobster rights, I believe. Anyway Tony told him in no uncertain terms he was getting above himself. It didn't go down very well."

She broke off as Mr. Harris came to join us. He promised to come out and take a look at the cottage as soon as he could find the time. "But I have to put in two more bathrooms at Trengilly first," he said. "The sort of guests that the foreign bloke brings down all like their own bathrooms, so it seems. And not just bathtubs either. They all want showers as well, if you can believe it. Not to mention them foreign bidet contraptions. And don't ask me what they are."

⁂

"You're rather quiet," I said to Belinda as we drove home. "Are you trying to decide whether it's worth going to a lot of trouble with your cottage?"

"No, I was thinking about Jago. I mean, he was a local boy. Surely he would have had very little schooling. How did he wind up in a position like that?"

"He got a scholarship to Oxford," Rose said. "I remember my mother telling me. I couldn't believe it because he was always—well, shy like me around you upper-class children. He hung around with us but I don't remember him ever saying much, do you?"

"I remember he was one who tried to save Colin," Belinda said. "He was a good swimmer, wasn't he?"

"He was. But it was hopeless. The currents are so strong when the tide is coming in. Colin was swept away and disappeared under the water."

We drove on in silent contemplation. I wondered how I'd handle it if I'd let a pal drown. They'd done all they could, at least Jago had done all he could. Presumably Tony too. But Jonquil had known that Colin couldn't swim. And now Jonquil was dead. I began to wish I had never accepted Belinda's invitation and had stayed safely but boringly at Eynsleigh.

Belinda was clearly having the same sort of thoughts. The moment we were together upstairs, sprucing ourselves up before tea, she tapped on my door. "What do you say we forget about the cottage for now and flee?" she said. "Darling, if I'd known what I was getting you into, I'd have left you alone." She closed the door behind her and came over to me. "Do you think that Rose is batty? I mean, I knew Tony pretty well and I simply can't believe that he'd go around murdering wives."

I nodded. "And yet it's clear she's scared, isn't it? And something must have prompted her to start wondering whether Jonquil's death was an accident. I don't know how you'd ever prove that it wasn't, unless there was an eyewitness."

"She said Tony got rid of all the staff, didn't she? Perhaps one of them saw something."

"Then you'd want to keep a close eye on them, not set them free to gossip. And he didn't get rid of Mrs. Mannering. If anyone was spying through a window, it would have been her."

"But she adored Jonquil," Belinda reminded me. "If she'd seen Tony giving her a push, she'd definitely have gone straight to the police."

I nodded, agreeing with this. "But I'm with you on fleeing as soon as we can. Since your builder can't do anything until he's renovated Trengilly, why don't you leave a key with him and ask him to get in touch when he's had a chance to inspect the place."

"Good idea," Belinda said. "We'll make our excuses and go in the morning."

"Do you think it's all right to leave Rose in the lurch like this? I mean, what if we go and then we find that she has had a horrible accident?"

"We can't stay on indefinitely, can we? She'll have to make up her mind what she wants to do with her life. And I still think the whole thing is in her head."

"I don't know about you, but I could do with a good cup of tea," I said. "This sort of weather has chilled me to the marrow. And those little cakes and scones yesterday were heavenly, weren't they?"

Belinda agreed that they were. As we entered the long gallery where tea was served we heard voices.

"Tony must be back," Belinda said. "Oh God. All right. Let's face the music, shall we?"

As we came closer we noticed that the hair appearing above the back of the armchair was dark, not fair. And parted in the middle.

Rose looked up from her teacup, with a strained smile on her face. "Ah, here they are now," she said. "A surprise for you, Belinda. Look who is here."

"Uncle Francis," Belinda exclaimed.

"He stopped by to give his compliments," Rose said. "He had just heard that I now lived here and he wanted to congratulate me on my marriage. Apparently he remembered me fondly from my childhood, and my mother's cooking. Wasn't that sweet."

"Very sweet," Belinda said in a voice that could have cut glass.

"And also delighted to find my one and only niece here too," Uncle Francis said. "I was hoping to give my regards to young Tony Summers as well. I remember him from those years. A fine young yachtsman, I remember. Does he still sail?"

"We have a small sailboat," Rose said, "but I don't think he has much time for sailing. He's very busy with the property and the farm."

"He should come and crew for me," Uncle Francis said. "I've a forty-footer. Handles a rough sea splendidly. So when do you expect that rogue of a husband to return home, Rose?"

"I've no idea. He comes home when he's hungry, usually. But why do you say he's a rogue?"

"He's raking in the money at the expense of poor creatures like me, that's why," Francis said. "Do you know he's doubled the mooring rents, and as for lobsters—he's created a monopoly. He owns all the best bits of coast around here. If you try to put down a pot, the blighter pinches it." He stopped, realizing perhaps that it might not be tactful to run down a woman's husband if he wanted her support. "He probably has no idea, of course. It's probably his estate manager or someone in his office who is in charge of moorings and licenses."

"Tony doesn't have a manager," Rose said. "He has a secretary and a man who oversees the farm, but that's about it. And I remember he mentioned those mooring fees. They hadn't been raised since before the Great War."

"That's as may be. But they've put chaps like me in a bind," he said. "Living on a pittance, you know. My mother—your dear mum's old employer—left everything to my niece here. Everything. Cuts off her son without a penny."

There was an awkward silence. "That's not quite fair, Uncle Francis," Belinda said. "When she sold Trengilly she settled half of it on you."

"Yes, in a trust, doled out to me like a child's pocket money," he said. "Not even enough for a decent Bordeau or a good steak."

Belinda was still standing, her hand on the back of the sofa. "Uncle Francis," she said, "I don't think it's right to come here and air your grievances in front of strangers. You are making Rose feel quite uncomfortable, and she was nice enough to offer you tea."

"It's all right for Rose," he said. "She's landed on her feet, hasn't she? And her mother too. I understand my mother gave her the money to start her own tea shop. If she'd done the same for her only son, I could have set myself up in some kind of business too."

Nobody spoke. Uncle Francis took a big bite of a chocolate éclair. "Such a treat," he said. "It's toast and dripping for a pauper like me." He stood suddenly. "Well, I can see that I've outstayed my welcome. I don't think I'll wait around to see if young Tony comes home. Probably not much point. I'll bid you all adieu. And thanks for the tea, Rose. Quite delicious. Quite up to your mother's standard. Did you bake the cakes yourself?"

"Of course not," Rose said. "We have a wonderful cook." She picked up a bell. "I'll have someone show you out."

"Don't worry. I can find my own way," Uncle Francis said. "I used to come up here a lot when I was a boy. I was friendly with Ferrers Trefusis—the one who was so tragically killed in that air crash. We used to run all over this place. Knew every nook and cranny. And the parties! What a great house for sardines, what?"

For a moment he had been smiling, then the smile faded. "I hope you'll bring it back to life, Rose. That's what we need around here. Gaiety, laughter! I also bid you farewell, niece. Enjoy your wealth while you can."

Then he stomped out, brushing against a statue of a Hindu god and making it teeter on its table.

Chapter 14

Belinda has suggested we go tomorrow morning. I couldn't agree more.
Having that little fracas with Uncle Francis was the last straw!
What an unpleasant relative. If Belinda had had to put up with
him and her stepmother, no wonder she wanted to get away from
family. I always felt that Fig was bad, but not that bad! Golly, if
I'm thinking fondly of Fig, I must be homesick.

"I must apologize for my uncle," Belinda said as soon as he had gone.
"Horrible man. I always thought so."

"I have to confess that I did too," Rose said. "I wasn't going to say
this but when I was visiting once he trapped me in the hallway outside
the kitchen and he groped me. He ran his hands over my front and
told me I was developing nicely. I was so shocked I never told anyone
but I made sure I stayed out of his way after that."

"I had similar experiences," Belinda agreed. "If he calls again I'd have the servants tell him you are not home. And warn Tony about him too."

Rose shifted uncomfortably. "The trouble is that he has been raising all the local fees and he's put a lot of backs up around here. Old men who have moored their boats in a particular spot all their lives now suddenly have to pay double. I did suggest it wasn't going down well, but Tony just said that they need to move with the times. You know what Cornwall is like. Nothing ever changes."

The embarrassment gradually melted away as a new plate of warm scones was brought in.

"Perhaps we shouldn't mention your uncle's visit to Tony," Rose said when his voice was heard in the foyer. "I don't like to upset him after he's been working all day."

That was strange to hear, I felt. At one second she was saying she feared he was going to kill her, but this sounded like a caring wife, concerned for her husband.

We went up to change for dinner. Belinda paused outside her door. "Uncle Francis really is the last straw, isn't he, darling," she muttered. "I can tell you, I nearly died of embarrassment. It was all I could do not to tip the teapot over his head."

I had to chuckle at this image. "I suppose he was using your being here to try and get more favorable terms from Tony."

"Of course he was. What a slimy snake he is. No wonder Granny didn't trust him. How dare he come here. First thing tomorrow we go."

As I entered my room I started in surprise. Mrs. Mannering was standing beside my bed.

"Ah, here you are, my lady," she said. "I came up to help you dress again. I have laid out the blue gown, or should I find you another choice for tonight if you don't want to wear the same thing twice?"

"Oh, Mrs. Mannering, this is very good of you," I said, "but I am quite happy to wear that beautiful dress again."

"It certainly suits you," she said. "It was made to compliment blond hair."

I had to stand there, feeling strangely embarrassed, while she eased my jumper over my head, helped me step out of my skirt and then put on the blue evening dress. I felt her cold fingers as she hooked at my bare back. There was something reptilian about them and I tried not to shudder or to push her away.

"If you'll take a seat at the dressing table I will take care of your hair, my lady," she said. She almost pushed me onto the stool, took the brush and started to brush my hair in long, even strokes. I saw my reflection in the looking glass, my tense uneasiness. My hair was short and easy to manage. A few strokes would have sufficed, but Mrs. Mannering went on brushing, stroke after stroke until I wanted to cry out.

"How I have missed this," she said. "I always brushed Miss Jonquil's lovely hair until it shone like spun gold. The current mistress of this house is not worthy of my ministrations. She would not appreciate them. It takes a true lady to allow a servant to do her job."

"She is trying hard, Mrs. Mannering," I said. "It must be very strange for her and she needs encouragement. You could help her fit in and learn this way of life."

"You have to be born to it, my lady. Breeding counts. That's what I've always known."

She slid a jeweled hair clip to hold back a curl. "Very nice. I will now go and make sure all is ready for your dinner."

I let out a sigh of relief as she closed the door behind her. I hurried down to join the others. Dinner was again outstanding. I hoped that I could find a cook like this one. Queenie's food was—well— satisfactory and filling. This was a gourmet treat. Oysters followed by a creamy cauliflower soup, then roast pheasant surrounded by tiny slivers of roast potato and creamed spinach, and finally floating islands followed by squares of grilled cheese. Each course was accompanied by plenty of wine. Feeling replete and content we went through for coffee. Again Tony joined us immediately and poured us a generous snifter of brandy each. "Come on, drink up," he said. I heard the belligerence in his voice and wondered if he'd knocked back a bit too much at dinner.

Belinda steered the conversation to White Sails, chatting about the possible renovations to the cottage and the reputation of the builder and what Jago was doing at Trengilly.

"That blighter," Tony said. "Don't tell me he's commandeered Harris for Trengilly. The money certainly flows freely there, doesn't it? And who knows how it's acquired?" He gave a knowing grin. "I think that Panopolis fellow has got fingers in a lot of suspicious pies. Shipping business? Argentina? I wouldn't be surprised if it isn't weapons. Probably selling them to the Nazis in Germany."

"Oh, surely not, Tony. You do jump to conclusions," Rose said. "I heard he was in banking."

"What would you know about banking?" Tony gave her a patronizing smile.

Belinda cleared her throat and mentioned that we were planning to go home in the morning.

"Since the builder will not be able to give his attention to White Sails for a while, I thought there is no point in waiting around here."

Rose reached out and touched Tony's hand. "Oh, but we love having you, don't we, Tony?"

"Absolutely," Tony said. "Livens up the place no end." He gave Belinda a quick glance.

"But Georgie needs to get home. She needs to be there when her husband returns from his trip," Belinda said. "She's newly married. Pining for him."

"Lucky chap," Tony said.

There was silence, then he said, "I know, why don't we play cards? There are four of us. Whist? Bridge?"

"I'm hopeless at cards as you very well know," Rose said.

"Well then, this is a good opportunity to improve your skills when you are among friends." Tony gave her a long look. "Come on, Rose. Don't be a wet blanket."

And so we played. As it turned out Rose wasn't nearly as poor a player as she described. Rather astute at times. She and I were partners and we won quite handily. Tony grudgingly handed over some money. "You see," he said. "You can do these things if you put your mind to it."

"Not really. It was all because of Georgie's skill that we won."

This wasn't true and we all knew it. I was again glad when the evening came to an end and we bid each other good night.

"I'm going to get some hot cocoa after all this excitement," Rose said. "Does anyone else want some?"

"Won't Cook have gone to bed?" Tony asked.

"I can make my own hot cocoa, Tony. I did fend for myself for several years," Rose said. "Are you sure I can't bring some for the rest of you?"

We declined. Rose headed off in one direction, toward the kitchens, while Belinda and I went upstairs together. There was no escaping the dreaded Mrs. Mannering, lurking to help me undress, but I did refuse her offer to brush my hair again. I thought of taking a bath, as there was a lovely large tub in the bathroom at the far end of the hall, but tiredness overcame me so I made do with a wash in the basin in my room. I had just been down the hall to the lavatory when I passed Belinda's room. Her door was slightly ajar and I heard voices. Belinda's voice, high and strained: "Tony, what are you doing? Are you mad? You have to leave immediately."

I knew I should not be listening in to other people's conversations but I wouldn't make myself move.

"Oh come on, Belinda. Don't be a spoilsport. I thought you and I had something special going once, didn't we?"

"I wasn't the one who was engaged to someone else and forgot to mention it," Belinda said.

"I know. It was stupid of me. I realized later it was you I really wanted. I allowed myself to be seduced by all that Jonquil offered. My own father had lost his fortune. I was in a boring, mindless job that I hated. And here was Jonquil, with Trewoma and properties around the world. An heiress. I knew it was a mistake the moment I married her."

"A mistake? I thought you were madly in love with her? You were grieving when she died."

"The truth, Belinda, is that she was a foul person. Completely self-centered. Didn't care a hoot about me. Invited her lovers down here. Can you believe that? Some chap moored his boat to our dock and Jonquil disappeared down there for the night. But she knew I couldn't divorce her. I couldn't give up all this."

"So it was rather convenient when she died?" Belinda asked.

I held my breath. She was treading on really dangerous ground.

"Convenient? It seemed like a miracle. I couldn't believe it. I was free."

"And yet you went and married Rose so quickly. You didn't come looking for me," Belinda said.

"I seem doomed to make mistakes," Tony said. "I bumped into Rose in London. I took her out for a meal. She seemed so pathetically grateful that I felt sorry for her. We both drank rather more than we should and we wound up in bed together. She was a virgin. A virgin at twenty-seven? Can you believe it?"

"And she wound up pregnant from that one night?"

Tony let out a large sigh. "Frankly I had forgotten all about her. It was just a spur-of-the-moment thing. It meant nothing. So you can imagine I got the shock of my life when she showed up on my doorstep a couple of months later and announced that she was pregnant. She was in a terrible state. She was going to lose her job when they found out. Her mother would never forgive her. She had nowhere to go."

"So you did the right thing," Belinda said.

"I did the right thing. I offered to marry her. She jumped at the chance. We were married right away in a registry office. And no sooner were we married than she had a miscarriage and lost the baby."

"Tony—" Belinda said. "Are you sure she was really pregnant?"

"Well, yes. I mean, I never questioned. But what does it matter? I was stuck with her. With Rose. Boring old Rose. You've seen how out of place she is here. And of course everyone knows she was the cook's daughter. She'll never be accepted into local society."

"She can learn if you are patient and help her, Tony," Belinda said. "Look how well she did at cards tonight. She always was timid. She needs patience and encouragement."

"The truth is that it's all boring as hell down here. No friends. No social life and only Rose to come back to at night," Tony said. "As for the sex—she just lies there, like a great beached whale under me. No passion. Nothing. Not like you. My God, we had a good time together, didn't we?"

"We did."

"So how about just once more, for old time's sake?"

"Tony, if you think I'm going to bed with you in your own house with your wife just down the hall, you can think again. I've made my own mistakes in life and I do not intend to make any more. Now please go before I raise my voice and Mrs. Mannering appears."

"Damn that woman," he said. "She may keep the house running but I can't stand the way she creeps around, spying on us. She'll have to go."

"And you'll have to go too, I'm afraid. You are keeping me from my beauty sleep and if Rose comes up with her hot cocoa she'll be mortally offended. She'll probably blame me for luring you into my room."

"You're a spoilsport, Belinda, and I'm still in love with you. How about I sell this place? We chuck it all up and go to Barbados?"

"Sorry, Tony. As tempting as it sounds, I'm kicking you out. Go on. Leave before you do something you regret."

"I think you're the one who is going to regret this."

"Probably, but not as much as if I let you stay."

I only had a moment to dive into my own room before I heard a slam and Tony came striding past my door.

Chapter 15

October 17
Trewoma

**Oh golly. I don't even know how to put down what has happened. I'm
still in shock.**

Good old Belinda, I thought as I heard the floorboards creak as Tony
walked down the hallway. She has learned her lesson and is now behaving like a sensible person. I climbed into bed and pulled the covers
over me because I was cold after wearing that blue silk dress. It was a
wild night. I could hear the wind moaning through the chimney and
it had begun to rain, peppering the window. I snuggled down, tucking
my cold feet into my nightgown and wishing someone had offered me
a hot-water bottle. One more night, I thought. One more night and I
can go home. And I wondered where Darcy was, what he was doing,
whether he was in any kind of danger and whether he was missing me.

    I was just drifting off to sleep when something awoke me. A cry. Had
the cry been in my dream? No, I was sure I had heard something. I

jumped out of bed and grabbed for my robe, fumbling to put it on in a hurry. I came out of my room and saw that Belinda's door was ajar.

"Belinda?" I called, hurrying toward her. "Are you all right?"

She didn't answer me. I pushed her door open and froze. Belinda was standing there, holding a large knife in her hand. The knife and Belinda's hand were covered in blood and her face was one of utter terror. Then I looked past her. The covers had all been tossed off her bed and were lying in a heap on her floor. Tony lay on the white undersheet, completely naked and with a large stab wound in his chest. A horrid red stain was spreading across that white sheet. His eyes were wide-open and staring in surprise and it was quite obvious that he was dead.

"I didn't . . ." Belinda stammered. Her eyes were also as big as saucers. "It wasn't me. I just found him. . . ." She started sobbing.

"It's all right," I said. "Calm down. And perhaps you'd better put down the knife. If he attacked you, it was self-defense."

"But he didn't. I didn't," she wailed.

"Then how exactly did he get into your bed?"

"I don't know." Her voice sounded close to breaking point. "Georgie, I swear. . . . He came into my room earlier tonight. He suggested he was getting tired of Rose and we could . . . get together again. But I told him no and he went off in a huff. I was a bit shaken up so I decided to have a lovely hot bath. When I came back everything was dark. I opened my door and I kicked something on the floor. I picked it up and it was all sticky and I turned on the light and it was this knife." She was still holding it, staring at it in disbelief. "And then I saw him, on my bed, lying there. Dead."

At that moment there were hurried footsteps. "What's going on? Is something the matter?" a voice called and Mrs. Mannering appeared at the open door, wearing a dark blue dressing gown and with her hair in curlers. She stood breathing heavily as if she had just come running. Her gaze went from Belinda's bloody hands to the bed. She opened her mouth as if to scream, then controlled herself, pointing at

Tony's corpse, her hand shaking. "Oh dear God. You've killed him," she stammered. "Poor Mr. Summers. You've killed him. How could you?"

"I didn't," Belinda whimpered. "It wasn't me. I found him here like this. I don't know who did it."

"Where is Rose?" I asked. I stepped out into the corridor but at that moment I saw her crossing the foyer down below.

"I can't believe how long it took me to make cocoa," Rose's voice floated up the stairwell toward us as she started to come up the stairs with a mug of cocoa in her hand. "I couldn't find the cocoa tin, then I found it in a tin marked Horlicks. Then I couldn't get the wretched stove to light for hours. And then the blasted milk boiled over and I had to clean that up—" She broke off, as Mrs. Mannering came out of Belinda's room. "Is something wrong? Has someone been taken ill? Is it Belinda?"

"Let us take that mug from you, Mrs. Summers." Mrs. Mannering stepped out to intercept Rose. "I'm afraid you're in for a nasty shock."

She took the mug and handed it to me.

"What is it? What are you saying?" Rose gave her a questioning glance, then looked toward Belinda's open door and started forward. Mrs. Mannering restrained her, then put her arm around Rose's shoulder. "I'm afraid you're going to have to be very brave. Your husband has been . . ."

Rose gave a little cry, wrenched herself free and pushed past her into the room. Then she let out a horrible scream. She turned on Belinda. "You killed Tony. How could you do such an awful thing? You're a monster. A vile monster. I'll never forgive you. I hope you hang."

"But I didn't do it." Belinda was choking back tears. "I swear I didn't. I came back from my bath and he was lying there."

"Then why is there blood on your hands?" Rose shrieked the words. "And you're still holding the knife, for God's sake."

"I didn't realize what it was," Belinda said. "I came into my room and it was dark and I kicked something so I bent to pick it up and it was this knife." She seemed to realize she was still holding it and put it down hastily onto a side table. "And it was all sticky with blood. I screamed and Georgie came."

I was able to observe now that it was not a knife as much as one of the curved oriental daggers that had been displayed in one of the rooms downstairs.

"Then if you didn't kill him, who did?" Rose demanded. "Call the police, Mrs. Mannering. If she really didn't kill him, then there is a murderer loose in this house."

"May I suggest that you all come out of this room," Mrs. Mannering said calmly. "It is a crime scene now. Nobody is to touch anything. I will call the police. And I will rouse the staff to search the house and grounds."

I put an arm around Belinda. "You'd better come and wash your hands in my bedroom," I said.

"She should leave her hands as evidence," Rose said angrily.

"We all know what we saw, Mrs. Summers," Mrs. Mannering replied calmly. "We all saw the blood on her hands and besides, her fingerprints will be on the knife."

"As well as the killer's," I added. "Don't worry, Belinda. It's going to be all right. They'll find out who is the real murderer."

"Come with me, Mrs. Summers," Mrs. Mannering said. "You've had a terrible shock. Let me put you to bed and get you a glass of brandy while we wait for the police to come." Then she turned to me. "I think you should stay with Miss Warburton-Stoke, my lady. She should not be left alone."

"Come on, Belinda. Come into my room." I put my arm around her. I could feel her whole body shaking. I led her through to my bedroom and ran the water in the washbasin until it was hot, then I held her hands under it, watching the sink spattering red as the blood washed away. All the time I was trying to calm my own racing thoughts. I wanted to believe her. I was pretty sure I did believe her, but there was still that nagging doubt at the back of my mind. Tony had come to her bedroom. He had propositioned her. I wasn't sure how long ago that was as I had drifted off to sleep, but it couldn't have been that long. If he had gone away in a huff, why had he come back again, taken off his clothes and gotten into her bed? And more to the point, where were his clothes? Had he run naked down the hall to her room, knowing she was in the bath, hoping to surprise her when she returned?

And the bigger question: if she didn't kill him, then who did? I dried her hands as if she were a little child. Then I sat her down in the armchair beside my fire.

"I'm going down to get you a glass of brandy too," I said. "You're in shock."

"I know I'm in shock," she said, "but don't leave me. The killer may come back for me."

"I'll be back in a jiffy," I said. "And the servants are all being woken up." I ran out and down the stairs. I didn't see anyone in the drawing room as I went to the sideboard and helped myself from the drinks table. Around the house I could hear voices as servants were roused. I heard hysterical crying and Mrs. Mannering's calm voice: "Pull yourself together, Elsie. No murderer will come after you, you can be sure of that."

As I went back up the stairs I spotted a footman creeping down the hallway carrying a candlestick. I made it up the stairs without running into anyone.

"What are we going to do, Georgie?" Belinda asked, taking the glass I offered her. "Nobody will believe I'm not guilty, will they? They saw the knife in my hands."

"There will be other fingerprints on the knife," I said. "They'll find who did it. Obviously Tony had some enemies. We heard that, didn't we? Raising all the fees?"

"Yes, but how could an enemy get into the house? And what's more, how did Tony get onto my bed, stark naked?"

"Maybe he crept back to your room and wanted to surprise you when you came out of the bath. He thought he might convince you to change your mind."

"But does anyone walk down a long hall naked?" she asked. "Wouldn't he at least put a robe on until he got here? He might have run into you or Mrs. Mannering, after all."

"Perhaps there is a robe somewhere among those bedclothes."

"Oh yes. That's possible. He could have stripped off the bedclothes in a fit of impatient passion. But I made it quite clear to him, Georgie. I really did."

"I know," I said. "I was coming back from the bathroom and I overheard some of it."

"But if anyone else overheard some of it?" Belinda said. "If anyone else spotted Tony going into my room. That creepy Mannering woman. I bet she spies on all of us. If she testifies that he crept into my room, I'm done for. She might even lie and say I invited him."

"Why would she do that? Did you detect any special dislike from Mrs. Mannering?"

"Not exactly. Not the way she dislikes Rose." She took a sip of the brandy, shuddered and said, "It's impossible, isn't it?"

"Of course it is. Everything's going to be all right." I put a hand on her shoulder.

Belinda covered it with her own hand. "I'm so glad you're here. I don't know what I would have done if I'd been alone. You do believe me, don't you?"

"Of course I do. We've known each other for years. I know very well when you are lying. And anyway, why would you want to kill Tony? You've had enough experience with men to stop his advances if you didn't want him."

"But why kill him in my room? Why put him on my bed? If anyone had a grudge against Tony, why not lurk around a dark corner, stab him in the back and then creep out again? For that matter, why take the risk that you'd be caught inside the house? Why not follow him to a distant corner of the property and then escape by sea?"

She stopped suddenly and put a hand to her mouth. "Uncle Francis!" she said. "That's who did it. How very clever. He came to the house this afternoon on the pretense of wanting to pay his respects to Rose and see his beloved niece again, and while he was here, he had a good opportunity to scout things out. And didn't he say he'd see himself out? I bet he never went at all. He found a disused room to hide out in until the proper time came to strike. He has killed two birds with one stone, don't you see? Not only Tony and his mooring leases but if I'm found guilty of murder and I hang, he'll get the money and the properties."

"Do you really think your uncle is capable of murder to get what he wants?"

"Oh, absolutely; he was a young soldier in the Great War, you know. He told me how they were trained to run a bayonet through somebody and fight in close combat. He boasted about sneaking up behind a German and slitting his throat."

"But that was war. Lots of men had to do things that were not really part of their nature because they were commanded to."

"I think it might be his nature to do anything to get what he wants," Belinda said. "My grandmother said he was a difficult child, prone to fits of temper and that he would lie smoothly to get out of trouble. Quite the opposite from my mother, who was the sweetest, gentlest person in the world." She gave a shuddering sigh. "My father probably won't do anything to help me. He might care but the wicked witch will tell him I'm not worth bothering with." I heard her voice tremble.

"Surely not, and anyway, it's all going to be sorted out very soon," I said. "Now drink that brandy and I'm going to tuck you up in my bed."

She gave me a watery smile. I smiled back, trying to seem more confident than I felt. Because in truth I did think that things looked very bleak for her and I had no idea how we would prove that she was not the murderer. Oh, Darcy, I thought, I wish you were here. You'd know what to do.

Chapter 16

October 17

Trewoma, where the most unbelievably horrible thing has happened. I hope the police can sort this out. Poor Belinda.

A loud hammering at the front door announced the arrival of the local police constable.

"So you're sure you've got a murder here, and not just a nasty accident?" I heard him saying in his broad Cornish accent as he came up the stairs. "Or is it possible that the young gentleman took his own life?"

"It was clearly not an accident." This was Mrs. Mannering's voice. "One does not run into a sharp dagger while lying on a bed. And also he could hardly have stabbed himself to death and then thrown the knife across the room. Besides, the young female guest was found still holding the knife, with blood on her hands."

I motioned for Belinda to stay where she was and crept out of the room to observe. Mrs. Mannering pushed Belinda's bedroom door open for the policeman, who was a stout older man with the round,

red face of a countryman and a fine head of white hair. He was holding his helmet tucked under one arm. I saw him take a deep breath
before he went inside, then I heard a gasp of breath. "Oh my Lordy,"
he said, quickly stepping back out into the corridor, his face ashen
white to match his hair. "Poor young blighter. I've never in all my
years seen something like this. There was Henry Blakely who fell into
the threshing machine that time and that was pretty grizzly. But I've
never seen an actual murder. In all my years on the force I've never
seen nobody murdered. Not lying on a bed like that, all naked. There
was that time that Tommy Hicks fell down the mine shaft but everybody knew he was up to no good and . . ."

"So what do you plan to do about it, Constable Hood?" Mrs.
Mannering asked curtly. "Aren't you going to start investigating?"

"Me? Investigate? That's not my job, my lovey. I'm a village constable. I see to drunks and lost dogs, not dead bodies. I'll have to call
the inspector from Wadebridge and he'll probably have to call the
inspector from Truro or maybe from Scotland Yard itself, seeing the
serious nature of the crime." He closed the door behind him. "Nobody
is to go in here until the inspector has seen it for himself," he said. "So
do we have any idea who might have committed this terrible crime?"
(He pronounced it *turrrrible*.) "I mean, is there likely to be a dangerous
lunatic running around the house at this moment?"

"I think that is highly unlikely," Mrs. Mannering said coldly. "The
servants are checking the premises and the grounds as we speak, but
I think you'll find that it's an open-and-shut case. A Miss Warburton-
Stoke who is staying here, a friend of the late Mr. Summers and his
wife, was found standing over the body holding the knife with blood
all over her hands. It is her bedroom, and her bed on which he is lying.
Quite naked too." And she gave him a very meaningful glance.

"Oh. Ah," the policeman said with understanding. "Case of fend-
ing off the young gentleman to preserve her honor, do you think? The
courts will go lightly with her if that's how it was. Always go soft on
young girls defending their honor."

"I couldn't tell you her motive," Mrs. Mannering said. "She had seemed a perfectly pleasant and stable young person until that moment."

"Where is she now?" He looked around and saw me, hovering just outside my bedroom door. "Is this the young woman in question?"

I stepped forward. "No, I'm her friend. I've put her to bed in my room since she was in a state of shock. She didn't kill him, Constable. She had been to have a bath. She came into her room and kicked something in the dark, picked it up and found it was the knife when she turned on the light. Then she saw Tony Summers lying on her bed, naked. She has absolutely no idea how he got there or who might have killed him."

"The two were well acquainted, were they?" the constable asked, giving me something akin to a wink. "Otherwise why would he be lying on her bed with no clothes on?"

"They were childhood playmates, when she used to come down here in the summers to stay with her grandmother Lady Knott," I said.

He brightened up at the mention of this. "Lady Knott, eh? She were a fine old bird, weren't she? I remember how she used to ride out in her little pony and trap. Well respected around here. So that's her grandmother. Well, that will sit well with the jury if she's tried down here, but if it's a case up to the Old Bailey, which it well might be, seeing as how it will be a capital offense, if you get my meaning. . . ." He paused, realizing he was rambling on. "So what has been going on since they were childhood friends, then?"

"Miss Warburton-Stoke had not seen Mr. Summers for some time and had no idea he was living here or that he was married to Mrs. Summers."

"In which case why are you staying here if she knew nothing about him or his wife?"

"We came down to Cornwall to look at a piece of property that Belinda inherited," I said. "We bumped into Rose Summers and she remembered Belinda from her childhood and invited us to stay."

"I see." He sucked air through his teeth. Then he ran his hand through his thick white hair. He was clearly at a loss what to do next.

"You were going to telephone the inspector?" I suggested.

"Right." He turned back to stare at Belinda's closed door and then at mine. "I'm not sure what to do about the young lady. By rights I should take her to the closest jail, I suppose. But the closest jail is in Truro at the county court and that's a good way in the dark and I don't have a proper vehicle to escort the young lady. I borrowed Alfie Fellows's motorbike, since the matter was urgent. She can hardly sit on the pillion, seeing as how it's raining out there."

"She'll be quite safe here," I assured him. "I'll make sure she doesn't run away."

"Right you are, then." He nodded with satisfaction. "I'll go and telephone the inspector. He'll be right shirty at being woken at this time of night, but needs must, as they say."

"This way, Constable," Mrs. Mannering said and led him down the stairs to the telephone in the foyer.

I lingered on the balcony. I heard him talking to the operator, then a long pause and then he said, "Sorry to trouble you, sir. . . . Yes, I do know what time it is. . . . Yes, I know it's the middle of the night and you were asleep . . . but it's rather urgent that you come here as soon as possible because I'm not sure what to do next. No, it's not a fight outside the pub, it's a young man lying naked and dead on a bed. At that big house called Trewoma. Stabbed through the heart, sir. A clear case of murder." There was another pause, then he added, "No, sir, it's not a prank, I promise you. It's a real honest-to-goodness murder. . . . The murderer? Yes, I do have an idea. I have her apprehended and under guard. Why, thank you, sir. I just do my best."

He looked quite satisfied as he hung the telephone receiver back on its cradle. "He'll be coming out as soon as he gets dressed," he said. "It shouldn't take him more than half an hour."

I went back to Belinda. She was sitting up in bed, hugging her knees to herself.

"The inspector is on his way," I said. "Why don't you try to get some sleep?"

"How can I possibly sleep, Georgie? I'm absolutely terrified. And the more I think about it, the more I am sure that Uncle Francis did it. Because if not he, then who could it be? It must be someone with a grudge against me as well as against Tony."

I thought about this. "Rose would be the most likely suspect," I said. "She told us today that she was scared Tony was planning to kill her. So why not kill him first? But I don't know what she could have against you, unless he was now interested in you and thought that you might also be returning that interest."

"She might have seen him going into my room earlier," Belinda said. "And come to the wrong conclusion."

"It would have been the right conclusion if you hadn't sent him packing," I said. "But the trouble with that theory is that she was down in the kitchen making cocoa," I pointed out. "We all saw her going that way, then when you cried out and we came running, she was still at the bottom of the stairs with the cup in her hand."

"The kitchen is at the back of the house, isn't it?" Belinda said. "A long way from these rooms. She couldn't have seen Tony going into my room, or the murderer, whoever it was, if she had been making cocoa."

"I think Mrs. Mannering might be capable of plotting a murder, don't you?" I said. "I mean, look at that face. But I suspect it would be the sneaky type—poisoning someone or arranging an accident. I can't see her stabbing with a dagger. Too messy and the sheets will need cleaning. You can see how she values cleanliness and tidiness." I glanced across at her and had to grin.

Belinda looked at me and started to laugh. "Oh, Georgie, it's not funny, is it?"

"Not at all. Absolutely terrifying. But if it really is your uncle Francis, then they'll find him soon enough."

"What if he's sailed off to the Continent or something? And how will we ever prove it's him?"

"He'll have left fingerprints on the dagger. Maybe in a room where he hid. He'll have touched door handles."

She grabbed at my hand. "Georgie, you're so good at all this. You've solved crimes before. You'll save me, won't you?"

"Of course I will," I said, again sounding more confident than I felt.

Chapter 17

Oh gosh, something absolutely awful has happened and everyone
thinks it's poor Belinda. I've promised I'll help her but I don't
know how. Who wanted to kill Tony? And harm Belinda too,
because the scene was clearly set up to make her appear guilty. I do
hope it is her uncle Francis because that would sew it all up so
neatly, and, besides, I don't think he's a very nice person. I hope
the inspector is not one of the bumbling sort.

I had crept into bed beside Belinda and we lay, side by side, staring at
the ceiling, neither of us either willing or able to sleep until we heard
a loud knocking at the front door. Then there were voices echoing up
from the foyer.

"Powerful beastly night, ain't it, sir?" came the constable's voice.
"Sorry to have called you out, but you'll see for yourself."

"This had better be good," the new, sharper male voice was saying.
"You know what people are like at these posh houses. They think it's

a tremendous joke to play pranks on poor stupid policemen like us. Are you sure they didn't stage a murder just for their own amusement? If I hear a background of chuckles, you're going to be in a lot of trouble, Hood."

"Oh no, sir, I can assure you nobody here was doing any chuckling," the constable's voice replied. "And I think I know a dead body when I see one."

"All right, lead on. Which room is it in?"

My curiosity got the better of me. I slipped out of bed and opened my door just enough to peek out. The newly arrived inspector was a much younger man but life had not been kind to him. Either that or he had spent the evening being rather too merry at the local pub. He had large bags under his eyes and he was scowling as if it was an effort to see. His sandy hair was already thinning on top. Not an encouraging sight.

"The next room on your right, sir," Constable Hood said and started to push the door open for him.

"Don't touch the door, man," the inspector barked. "There might be valuable fingerprints on it."

"I expect there will be if people have gone in and out over the last hundred years," the constable said with a chuckle. The inspector was not amused.

At that moment Mrs. Mannering came rushing down the hallway toward the two men. I stepped back hastily into my room as she went past.

"Inspector Purdy. How good of you to come at this time of night," she said. "I am Mrs. Mannering, the housekeeper. I'm afraid Mrs. Summers was so overwrought at the death of her husband that I gave her a sleeping powder. But I will be of assistance in any way I can."

"I don't need assistance, thank you, madam. But I hope you've made sure that any evidence has not been tampered with?"

"Oh yes. Indeed I did. Nobody has entered that room since the young woman was found holding the murder weapon."

"And where is she now?" the inspector asked.

"Her friend, Lady Georgiana Rannoch, sister of the duke, is looking after her in her own bedroom."

"Sister of the duke, eh?" The inspector gave a slightly nervous cough now. "And is the young lady suspect also a titled person?"

"Not titled but of good family. Her grandmother was Lady Knott—"

"Not what?" he asked impatiently.

"No, that was her name. Lady Knott. With a *K*. A true lady of the old school. Used to own a house very close to Trewoma. Now deceased unfortunately."

"I see." The inspector sucked through his teeth. "In my opinion just because you're highborn doesn't mean you're not capable of dirty deeds. I shall need to speak with both young ladies after I've viewed the scene of the murder."

"It's in here," Mrs. Mannering said. "Nothing has.been touched."

I watched as he stepped into the room. "Oh my God," I heard him exclaim. "And a young lady did this?"

"She was discovered clutching the knife, and her hands covered in blood," Mrs. Mannering said.

"Mentally unstable, obviously. A lot of them are. Too much inbreeding. They probably won't hang her but send her to one of those nice rest homes for batty aristocrats. And where is the murder weapon now?"

"The young lady was persuaded to put it down on the side table here."

I heard another grunt of surprise. "That's no ordinary knife. A nasty-looking weapon if ever I saw one. Where did she find a thing like that? I wonder."

"I regret to say that she found it in this house, Inspector. The former owner was a great traveler and collector. There are weapons from all over the world on the walls in the library and long gallery. It would have been all too easy to take one of them."

"I see. And the deceased was the current owner of this house?"

"Yes. Mr. Anthony Summers."

"I don't remember having heard the name. Wasn't it something different? A Cornish name?"

"It was the Trefusis family, Inspector. Unfortunately, Mr. Ferrers Trefusis and his wife died tragically in a plane crash. Mr. Summers came to the house when he married Miss Jonquil Trefusis, who had inherited the property from her parents. That would have been just over three years ago."

"So his wife is the heiress to this estate?"

"Not his current wife. His former wife."

"He's got through two wives in three years?" The inspector sounded incredulous.

"Unfortunately Miss Jonquil met with a tragic accident when they had been married for less than a year. She was standing on a cliff top when it crumbled under her and she plunged to her death."

"I remember reading something about that. I was stationed on the other side of Cornwall, at Launceston, at the time. Tragic thing to happen to a young girl."

"It was devastating. If anyone loved life, it was Miss Jonquil. I had looked after her since she was a baby," Mrs. Mannering said.

"And when she died he got his hands on all the property?"

"It wasn't like you make it sound, Inspector. I can assure you there was no indication of foul play. In fact Mr. Summers was over at the home farm when the accident happened. Anyway, they seemed quite happy together. They were a well-matched pair."

"But he didn't waste any time getting married again?"

"I'm afraid you are right. He rather rushed into it. Unfortunate circumstances, I think. It is not for me to gossip but I understood that the current Mrs. Summers was in the family way and Mr. Summers did the right thing by marrying her."

"And how was their marriage? Presumably not too happy if he was found naked in another woman's room."

"I don't think they were an ideal couple if you really want my opinion," Mrs. Mannering said. "She was not of his class. A lowborn young woman without any social graces. Quite unsuited to running a great house like Trewoma. I have tried to educate her but I can't say we have been making much progress."

There was a pause. I was dying to see what was happening. Was he taking a look around the room, examining those bedclothes? I started to sneak out of the room but then noticed Constable Hood standing guard in the doorway. Well, either standing guard or he didn't want to have to look at that body. I suspected the latter. I stepped back before he saw me.

Then the inspector spoke again. "As housekeeper you must have a pretty good idea about what goes on here," he said. "Was there hanky-panky going on between the master of the house and the young woman who killed him? Was he the sort who went up to London on business from time to time? Did he bring her here with hanky-panky in mind?"

"I doubt that, Inspector. He seemed genuinely surprised to see her. And I have to say frankly that I have not seen evidence of hanky-panky on his part since he came here."

"Nevertheless, he is lying naked in another woman's bed," I heard him say. I crept a little closer, trying to see through the crack in the door. Then I heard him gasp. "That's odd. His hair is wet. Had he just been out in the rain, do you think?"

"Oh no, sir. Mr. Summers always took his bath at night. I presume he'd just had his bath, which might also explain his nakedness. Should we perhaps cover him? It doesn't seem right to have him lying there, exposed to the elements, as it were."

"I'm afraid we should not move him or touch anything until I've made a thorough examination of the room. I can understand that it's a disturbing sight for a delicate and refined woman like yourself, Mrs. Mannering. May I suggest that you let the members of the household know that I shall want to interview each of them, starting with the young lady in question and her friend. I suppose that Mrs. Summers will be in no condition to talk to me, if you've administered a sleeping powder. I may have to wait until the morning for her. In any case, Scotland Yard will have to be called in. Given that we're dealing with highborn people and it's clearly a hanging offense, I feel that it's beyond my authority. Constable Hood?"

"Right here, sir."

"Round up the members of the household, both above- and belowstairs. I shall want to question them all. The members of staff can be interviewed in the kitchen. In fact you can take initial statements from each of them—"

"I hope you do not mind my interrupting, Inspector," Mrs. Mannering said, "but is it necessary to interview the staff? They had all gone to bed at that hour. I usually wait until Mr. and Mrs. Summers go up to bed and then I do one last tour of the house and lock the front door. I can assure you that there was no sign of any person other than Mr. and Mrs. Summers and their guests."

"That doesn't mean that they were necessarily asleep. Could have been lurking inside their room, ready to strike. Murderers are devious, you know, Mrs. Mannering."

"Hardly devious enough to attack the master of the household with a large dagger when he was in a guest's room, surely? That would take incredible bravado and be quite unnecessary. Besides, the staff are happy here and well treated. Local people. Simple people. Not the type who go around murdering their employers."

I heard the inspector give a sigh. "I suppose I must agree with you, Mrs. Mannering. When I was in training they told us to look for the obvious first. And the obvious in this case is that the young lady either invited Mr. Summers to her room with the intention of killing him or that he came to her room unwanted and unbidden and she grabbed a weapon to defend herself. Although how and why she had that particular dagger in her room, if it belonged on a wall downstairs, is another matter."

At that moment there was a tap on our door. "It's Constable Hood," said the voice. "Are you young ladies still awake? Inspector Purdy requests that you make yourselves respectable and come downstairs because he would like to question you."

"Very well, Constable," I called back through the door. I turned to Belinda. "Come on. We have to make ourselves respectable."

"All right for you," she said. "You've always been respectable. You were born respectable. I'm the one who has led a rather wicked life and for once, this time, I was behaving with absolute decorum and now I'm accused of murder."

"We'll make them see the truth, don't worry." I squeezed her hand.

"Do you think he expected us to dress again?" Belinda asked, "because all my clothes are in the room with the body."

"I'm sure dressing gowns are respectable enough," I said. "They don't reveal any more than an ankle. Although that might still be considered sinful down here in the wilds of Cornwall."

Belinda even managed a smile.

Chapter 18

In a way I'm hoping that the man from Scotland Yard will come
quickly, because this inspector seems to have jumped to
conclusions and isn't prepared to listen. But then again, not all
inspectors from Scotland Yard that I've dealt with have been
excessively bright. Oh dear. What on earth can I do to help? Poor
Belinda is in a terrible state.

Having not been directed to a particular room we went into the drawing room where the fire was still giving off warmth. We pulled up
armchairs close to the fire. Outside the windows the wind was now
howling and thunder rumbled somewhere in the distance. Belinda sat
hunched over, staring into the fire.

"Can I pour you another brandy?" I asked.

She shook her head. "I don't want the inspector to smell alcohol
on my breath. Then he'll say I was drunk and not in control of my
actions."

We waited.

"Do you think I should mention that Tony came to my room earlier? And that I rebuffed him?"

"Absolutely not," I whispered back. "That gives you a motive. You should stick to the story that he was a childhood friend and you haven't seen him since. That's what Rose believes."

"But what if that awful Mannering woman saw Tony going into my room and has told the inspector? And what if they decide to investigate further and somebody in London remembers seeing us together at Crockfords or at a restaurant? Won't that look even worse for me?"

"I think that's highly unlikely. Why would they ever investigate in London unless somebody told them that you and Tony knew each other? Nobody down here knows that."

"But maybe one of Tony's friends in London might know. Tony might have mentioned to them that he was seeing me."

"I doubt it, if he was engaged to Jonquil at the time. No, I'm pretty sure he kept your meetings secret, if he was wise."

"Oh God. I hope so," she said.

We lapsed back into silence.

"I wish he'd hurry up," Belinda said at last after an extra strong gust of wind buffeted the window. "I can't bear this waiting. What if they do take me to prison, Georgie? I didn't bring any suitable clothes for a prison cell."

"One doesn't, does one?" I replied, "and anyway, they'll make you wear a uniform with arrows on it, won't they?"

"Oh crikey. I bet it's a horrid stiff fabric that will irritate my skin and I do mark so easily."

We broke off this silly conversation as we heard the tread of heavy feet coming toward us. The inspector came in and stood staring at us.

"Good evening, or should I now say good morning," he said. "I am Inspector Purdy from the Wadebridge branch of the Cornish Constabulary. May I have your names?"

"I am Lady Georgiana," I said. "Formerly Rannoch but now married to Mr. O'Mara, and this is my friend Miss Belinda Warburton-Stoke."

His gaze fastened on Belinda. "Ah, so this is the young lady in question. Miss . . . what was it again?"

"Warburton-Stoke," she said.

"Warburton-Stoke," he said with something like a derisive snort.

"Well, we can't do anything about the names we were born with, Inspector," Belinda said. Like me, her voice became tight and so posh in moments of stress.

"No, I suppose you're right," he agreed. "My first name is Algernon. Can't say I like that too much." He pulled up a chair beside us. "Now I'd like to ask a few questions, if you don't mind?"

He seemed pleasant enough. I wondered if this was to trap us into saying something we didn't intend to.

Belinda nodded. "This has all been such a horrible shock," she said in a voice scarcely more than a whisper.

"So why don't you start off by telling me how you came to be here, at this house?"

Belinda was looking down at her hands, her fingers playing with the cord of her dressing gown. "I had just inherited some property nearby. I asked my good friend Georgiana to come with me to take a look at it. It turned out to be a little fishing cottage, not suitable for us to stay in. We were in the village of Rock when we met Rose Summers. She recognized me, but I don't think I would have recognized her. She was the daughter of my grandmother's former cook, you see. She'd stay with her aunt all through the school year and come down to visit her mother in the summer. I used to spend my summers with my grandmother, so we used to be part of a group of young people who played together."

"How very democratic of you," the inspector said. "Including the cook's daughter in your games." The sarcasm in his voice made me realize that he wasn't being nice at all. He wanted to catch her out.

Belinda glanced up at him and frowned. "We were children. We hadn't yet learned to be snobs."

He nodded. "Go on. So this girl recognized you."

"I couldn't believe it when she told me she was now mistress of Trewoma, and that she was married to Tony Summers. He was another boy who used to spend his summers here and we all played together. I had no idea he'd come back to this part of the world to live."

"So you hadn't seen any of these people since your childhood?"

Belinda shook her head. "My grandmother moved away when I was fourteen. I was sent to school in Switzerland and never came back here."

"School in Switzerland. How nice for you." He had the hint of a sneer on his lips.

"Only because my stepmother didn't want me at home, Inspector," Belinda said sharply.

"So you had this pleasant little conversation with Mrs. Summers?"

"And I said we were looking for a hotel while I made plans to update the cottage. And Rose insisted we come and stay with her at Trewoma. I wasn't very comfortable doing this, as they were practically strangers, but she said they didn't often have guests and really wanted us to come."

"She didn't check with her husband first?"

"No, she didn't."

There was a pause. Outside the rain still peppered the windows and one of them rattled in the wind.

"And what did Mr. Summers think when you turned up on his doorstep?"

"He was surprised to see me after all these years."

"Surprised and delighted?"

"I wouldn't say that, Inspector. Just surprised and pleased to have guests," Belinda said, her face flushing. "I imagine it's quite lonely living out here."

"And how long have you been here?"

"This is our second night here," Belinda said.

He turned to me suddenly. "And you, Mrs. O'Mara. Had you also known these people as a child?"

"No, Inspector. I grew up in Scotland."

"You don't sound Scottish to me."

I decided that attack was the best form of defense. "I think you'll find my relatives don't speak with a Scottish accent when they come up to Balmoral."

"Balmoral? The castle? The royal place?"

"Yes, I am the king's cousin."

"Blimey." I could see this had really thrown him. I felt absurdly pleased.

"I met Miss Warburton-Stoke when we were at school together in Switzerland," I continued. "This is actually my first visit to Cornwall."

He was looking at me warily now. "So should I be addressing you as 'your highness'?"

"No, Inspector, I am merely Lady Georgiana. I kept my title when I married Mr. O'Mara, who is also the son of a lord."

"I see." I watched his face twitch. "Not the best of circumstances to be introduced to our fine county, is it?"

"Unfortunately not. My poor friend is in an absolute state of shock."

"I understand you have the bedroom next to hers along that hallway. Is that correct?"

"It is."

"And you didn't hear anything strange? Raised voices? Hints of a struggle?"

I shook my head. "The last time I spoke to Belinda she said she was going to have a long hot bath. I undressed, got into bed and started to doze off."

"How convenient." The smirk was there again.

"We had had a long day in the fresh air. I usually fall asleep the moment my head hits the pillow."

"You say you're married?"

"Yes. I've been married three months."

"And your husband lets you go off jaunting without him?"

"My husband is currently out of the country. And if he weren't, I wouldn't need his permission to go on a trip with my friend."

"A most modern man."

"A wonderful man. I'm very lucky."

He realized he was losing his line of questioning. "So to come back to tonight. You fell asleep, having heard nothing."

"As I said, I was just dozing off when I thought I heard a cry or a scream. I wasn't sure whether I had dreamed it, so I put on my dressing gown and opened my door. There was a light in Belinda's room and she was standing there, holding that knife with a look of pure terror on her face. She told me she'd come back from her bath and kicked something in the darkness. When she picked it up, it was that knife. She turned on the light and found Tony Summers lying on her bed as you saw him. Naturally she screamed."

The inspector swiveled back to face Belinda. "So, Miss Warburton-Stoke, do you have any idea why Mr. Summers would be lying naked in your room?"

"No idea at all, Inspector." She paused, glanced at me, then added, "But I do have an idea who might have killed him and tried to frame me."

This made him open his eyes. "You do?"

"My uncle, Sir Francis Knott. He came to the house this afternoon. He wanted to see Tony Summers because he was angry that Tony had doubled the mooring fees and my uncle lives on his sailing boat and is frankly short of cash. I had met with my uncle earlier and he was also very angry that he had not been included in my grandmother's will. I was her sole heir. He tried to suggest that he had been cheated and that I divide the spoils with him, so to speak."

"She was his mother?"

"She was."

"And why was he excluded, do you think?"

"He had proved himself to be reckless with money. He had always been untrustworthy and a gambler."

"So you think that this uncle decided to take care of Mr. Summers and make it look as if you did it?"

"I'm afraid that is the only conclusion that makes sense, Inspector," she said. "With me out of the way, I presume he would inherit his mother's estate. He could easily have hidden out in an unused room until tonight. He would have seen the weapons displayed on the walls when he took tea with us. He was quite handy with weapons, having fought in the Great War. In fact he boasted about how he had killed Germans."

"Ah." The inspector was nodding now. "And where do we find this uncle of yours?"

"As I said, he lives on his sailing boat and moors it across the river in Padstow."

"Well, we shall naturally have to talk to him, if he and his boat have not fled from the area, that is. And if he really did commit this heinous deed, we'll find his fingerprints on the knife and around the house. I must say he took a heck of a risk in a house full of servants."

"It's a very large house, Inspector," Belinda said. "There is one wing that is not used at all these days."

"Why is that, do you know?"

"It's where Jonquil Trefusis used to have her rooms. Her nursery and her bedroom and also the bedroom where she and Mr. Summers used to sleep. Her death was such a horrible shock to everyone that those rooms are not touched any longer."

"There seems to be an awful lot of death associated with this house," the inspector said. "First the girl's parents die, then she has a tragic accident and then the new master of the house dies. What do you make of all that?"

"I couldn't tell you, Inspector," Belinda said. "As I said, I had not been back to this area since I was fourteen, and that was twelve years ago. Some people might tell you the house is cursed. I believe I did hear that once as a child."

"The curse of Trewoma, right?" He chuckled at this. But at that moment a great gust of wind struck the windows, flinging one of them wide open. The inspector jumped to his feet. "Bloody hell," he muttered. He went over to the window and wrestled it shut again.

"Is there anything else you'd like to ask us tonight, Inspector?" I said, "because I think Miss Warburton-Stoke needs to rest."

"I'm going to need fingerprints from everybody in the house but that can wait until morning. I can't think of anything else at the moment," he said. "Naturally you are not to leave this house. You are not to go into your room, miss. The constable will remain on duty."

"But all my clothes and things are in my room," Belinda said. "How am I going to dress in the morning?"

"You'll have to wait until the room has been dusted for fingerprints and photographs have been taken. I hope to have an inspector down from Scotland Yard by tomorrow evening. Then it will be up to him when he lets you have access to any of your belongings. In the meantime I expect your young royal friend can lend you some of hers."

Belinda shot me a glance that seemed to indicate she didn't think my clothing choices would be suitable for one so fashionable. She stood up and stalked ahead of me out of the room.

Chapter 19

This has been one of the worst nights of my life. I am so worried about
Belinda. I just pray that her uncle is found to be responsible and
that we leave this place and go home. I just wish that Darcy was
here right now. Or Granddad. Or both.

I don't think either of us slept a wink that night. I know I didn't. Every time I attempted to doze off, disturbing visions flashed across my
mind: bloody bodies, knives, Belinda locked up in the Tower of London, Belinda being hanged. I didn't say a word to her, just in case she
had managed to fall asleep, but in the morning the bags under her
eyes indicated that her night had been as awful as mine.

"I wonder when the inspector from Scotland Yard will get here," she
said as she got out of bed and went over to the window, pulling back the
curtains to let gray light filter into the room. It was another morning of
thick sea fog and the view was limited to ghostly shapes of the first trees.
"It's the waiting and not knowing that's so terrible, isn't it?"

"I know," I said. I sat up, swinging my legs over the side of the bed. "I just can't figure this out. Did Tony really come to your bedroom with no clothes on, hoping to persuade you to change your mind? Surely he risked his wife spotting him coming down the corridor. Or even one of the servants. That seems like a really reckless thing to do. Was he a reckless type of person?"

"He and Jonquil used to love to take risks when we were young," she said. "We built a raft that came apart in the current. We climbed cliffs and got stuck once. And of course that time we tried to cross the estuary on foot at low tide and poor Colin—" She broke off.

"I'm still trying to picture this," I said. I got up, went across to the door, opened it and peered up and down the corridor. There was no sign of life, except for the constable, now sitting on a chair at the bottom of the stairs and appearing to be asleep. I closed the door quietly again and came over to Belinda. "Was he lying on your bed so that you'd find him when you came back from your bath? And someone followed him into the room and stabbed him unexpectedly? That doesn't make sense unless he'd fallen asleep. Wouldn't he sit up when someone came into the room? And if it wasn't you, wouldn't he attempt to cover himself? There didn't appear to be any signs of a struggle, as far as I could see. And Tony was a strong and fit man. He'd have managed to fight off most people."

"Including my uncle? I wonder if he was taken completely by surprise," Belinda answered. "Do you think the local police have managed to chase up Uncle Francis? I do hope he hasn't sailed off to the Continent already."

"We can just hope they find his fingerprints in an incriminating place," I said, "because if it wasn't him, then it was someone else in this house."

"I know." She gave a shuddering sigh. "I keep wondering if it was really Rose. She was the only one with a good motive to get rid of Tony, wasn't she? If she really thought he was trying to kill her, then why not kill him first, as you said? And my arrival was perfect timing for her, wasn't it? She invites us here and then kills him in my room so that someone else is blamed for the murder. I always thought she was not too bright but she might be deeper than we know. This was a stroke of genius."

"I don't see how it could have been Rose," I said. "It's a long way from the kitchen. Unless she had only pretended to make cocoa and was spying on Tony all the time, waiting for the right moment to strike. She watches him go into your room, realizes this is her chance and catches him unawares. Then she dashes down again and makes her cocoa.

"The only thing against that was that she didn't seem at all out of breath when she appeared at the bottom of the stairs carrying that cocoa mug. You'd have thought rushing upstairs, stabbing someone and dashing down again, all the way to the kitchen and back, would leave her a little breathless. And she'd also have had to go and find the dagger in the first place. She wouldn't exactly carry a large dagger around with her, just in case she got a good opportunity to stab him."

Belinda had to smile at this. "I see your point. And she did sound genuinely shocked, didn't she? And angry. Perhaps she really loved him."

"The worrying part is that if it wasn't Rose, then who? The servants had gone to bed. Let's hope the police check into each of their backgrounds. There might be one of them whose family has been cheated out of mooring rights or lobster rights or something. But surely no servant would risk carrying out a murder in one of the bedrooms. They'd follow him around the property and kill him where nobody could see and probably wouldn't find the body for days."

Belinda nodded. "The only other person who was up and around was Mrs. Mannering."

"What possible motive could Mrs. Mannering have for killing Tony?" I asked. "Or for trying to pin it on you, for that matter? She hardly knows you and it's certainly not going to help her in any way. If Rose decides to sell up because she's had enough of big, gloomy houses, Mrs. M. will be out of a job."

"I suppose it could have been an intruder," Belinda said. "It must be easy enough to get into a house this size without being seen. Someone with a grudge against Tony—again we come back to Uncle Francis." She grabbed my hand. "Oh, Georgie, I do so hope it is him. Or should that be 'it is he'? My grammar was never the strongest."

"It's not very charitable to wish a murder on your uncle, however obnoxious he is," I said, wrestling with my own uncharitable feelings about Belinda's uncle. "Do you really want your uncle to hang?"

Belinda frowned. "But he's such a good candidate. And if he did do this, then he did it fully intending me to be the prime suspect. He wouldn't bat an eyelid if I was hanged and he got his hands on my lovely money." She let the curtain fall. "Oh, I do wish we'd never come here. I do wish I'd refused Rose's invitation. I really didn't want to accept."

"But it would have been rude not to," I said. "And it did seem like a godsend after a night at White Sails."

Belinda put on her dressing gown. "The only good thing I can think of is that I left my toilet bag in the bathroom last night. At least I'll have my face flannel and cosmetics. I don't know what I'd have done without those. But as for what I'm going to wear . . ."

"I didn't bring much with me," I said. "You're welcome to my spare skirt and jumper."

She opened my wardrobe and stood, eyeing them with obvious distaste. "Not wanting to be rude or anything, but they are not exactly me, are they?"

"I agree they are not the height of fashion," I said.

"Not the height of fashion? Georgie, you've had that old tartan skirt as long as I've known you. It's gone all saggy in the bottom."

"True," I agreed. "I didn't pack anything elegant because I thought we were driving to view a house and then coming home again. So I went for comfort over haute couture."

This forced her to laugh. I came over to stand beside her. "The jumper and skirt are pretty grim, aren't they? I've never had what you might call a large wardrobe and these are from my Castle Rannoch days. But in truth, I didn't actually think I'd need a change of clothes. I just threw them in at the last minute."

"But I can't be interrogated by a man from Scotland Yard in clothes like that," Belinda said. "He'll come up with all sorts of ulterior motives for murder."

"No, he would have expected you to kill off Rose and marry Tony for his money."

"That's true. But he'll never believe I'm a fashion designer." Then her face lit up. "I know. We could borrow something of Jonquil's. She and I are about the same size."

"Wouldn't Mrs. M. have a fit?" I asked, not wanting to confront that formidable woman.

"Jonquil's not exactly going to be needing them for the next twenty-four hours, is she?" Belinda said. She went across to my bedroom door, opened it and listened. We could hear voices coming from downstairs. A man's ponderous speech, then a woman's. It sounded as if Mrs. Mannering was speaking with the constable who had been on duty all night, probably offering him some breakfast. Belinda grabbed my hand. "Come on. Let's go and choose something while the coast is clear."

I hesitated. "Wouldn't it be simpler just to ask Mrs. Mannering?"

"If we ask anyone it would be Rose. She's the mistress of this house. Mrs. M. is only the housekeeper," Belinda said, tossing her head in the way that she did when she wasn't quite sure of her decisions. "I certainly don't want to go creeping to Mrs. M. for permission. Besides, I'm only borrowing something for a day. Not like I'm stealing it."

"Mrs. M. might report to the police that you've helped yourself to Jonquil's clothes."

"Well, I'm not staying up here in my nightclothes, waiting for Scotland Yard to call, nor am I going to be seen in your jumper and skirt. So if you'd like to find the dreaded woman and ask permission, then please hurry up about it. I am in serious need of a cup of tea and breakfast."

"Oh, very well," I said. "I suppose she did say that we could borrow Jonquil's dresses, didn't she?"

Feeling like naughty schoolgirls we crept across the balcony to the other wing. This corridor was dark and smelled musty, as if nobody had been there for a long while.

"Which room was it?" Belinda opened a door. I peeked inside. "No, that was the nursery," I said, glancing around. "Her bedroom was next door." I stood examining it. The curtains were drawn. They hadn't been on the occasion Rose had shown us the rooms. I guessed that Mrs. Mannering had been in and drawn the curtains herself. There was something about the nursery now that I found unsettling. As I was trying to analyze what it was Belinda shoved me out and closed the door as silently as possible, moving on to the next room. These curtains were also closed. Belinda went over and yanked them open. I looked out onto the sea of whiteness. The cliffs and the estuary beyond were hidden in fog. Belinda was already attacking the large cherrywood wardrobe.

"She really had some very nice things," Belinda said in a soft voice. "What a pity Rose isn't the right size."

"I don't think Mrs. Mannering would have let her wear them anyway, do you?" I whispered back. "Not the right class of person."

"Poor Rose," Belinda said. "I do feel sorry for her in a way."

"Unless she killed her husband and set you up to take the blame."

"Then probably not so much," Belinda agreed. "I say, look at this, darling. It's perfect, isn't it?" She took down a gray cashmere dress with a rolled collar. It hung long and straight, perfect for the woman with a boyish figure and the dark gray was somber enough to give the right effect to a visiting detective.

"Definitely," I said. "You'll look demure but presentable."

"I shall need shoes and stockings," she said, taking out a pair of black court shoes. "Oh, my size. That's good."

"And you'll need underclothes," I said as she handed the shoes to me.

She rummaged in drawers and carried an armful back to my bedroom. "If anyone complains, I shall point out that I am being kept from my own clothes and, unlike Tony, I do not enjoy appearing naked in front of other people."

I was glad to see she was a little more combative this morning. I thought that was the right touch for dealing with bombastic policemen. We crept back to my bedroom and I helped her put on the dress. She looked stunning, as she so often did. I completed my own morning toilette and then we went down to breakfast together. The dining room was deserted but there were several tureens keeping warm on the sideboard and we helped ourselves to smoked haddock, poached eggs, bacon and toast. We had just sat down to eat when Mrs. Mannering came in. She gave no indication of having had a troubled night's sleep. Her face was still smooth and unwrinkled and her graying curls were exactly in place.

"Oh, my dear young ladies, I am sorry I was not here to take care of your needs. I was feeding the constable in the kitchen. He was loathe to leave his position at the bottom of the stairs, bless his heart, but I pointed out that you were hardly likely to make an escape when I had your cape with the motorcar keys in it, hanging in the hall cupboard." She gave a satisfied little smile. "Is everything to your satisfaction? Is the tea hot enough? I could have a fresh pot made."

Then I saw that she had taken in what Belinda was wearing. "Miss Jonquil had a dress just like that," she said. "I believe it came from Harrods."

"I believe it did," Belinda answered. I stared down at my smoked haddock.

When she had left the room I glanced at Belinda. "You're not going to tell her the truth?"

"It will be interesting to see if she dashes straight up to examine Jonquil's wardrobe, won't it?"

"Belinda, you really are naughty sometimes," I said.

"I just felt I ought to do something," she said. "After all, someone in this house has put me in a frightfully awful position. I've been questioned by a rude policeman. An even worse one is on his way. I had to strike a blow for independence."

And she went to get herself another cup of tea.

WE FINISHED BREAKFAST and still there was no sign of Rose. I presumed the sleeping powder she had been given had truly knocked her out and I wondered whether it had been administered deliberately so that she could not be interviewed by the local inspector. We went down the hall to the morning room to read the newspapers that had been delivered. I thought it didn't say much for their security that a newspaper boy had been allowed up to the house on his bicycle.

I saw that Belinda couldn't settle down. She flicked through pages, then got up and walked around, peering out of windows, then perching on the edge of the sofa before wandering again.

"Nobody from London could possibly get here yet," I said to her. "It's at least a six-hour train ride and then he'd have to be driven from the nearest station."

"I know. I just want it to be over. I do hope Uncle Francis hasn't done a bunk. I wonder if anyone spotted his yacht moored near here yesterday. Do you think that Inspector Purdy will be back or will he wait for the man from Scotland Yard?"

"Belinda, I have no idea. Now will you sit down and try to relax."

"Easy for you to say. It's not your neck, is it?"

"Let's hope it isn't yours either," I said. I went back to the *Times* crossword. "What's a seven-letter word for obstinate?" I asked, looking up. But Belinda was no longer in the room.

"Belinda?" I called. I got up and went to the door. No sign of her. Of course, she could have paid a visit to the lavatory. I waited, but she didn't return and I began to feel a little uneasy. The constable had now

resumed his place at the bottom of the stairs. A chair had been provided for him, and he looked as if he had just woken up from a little
snooze.

"Has the other young lady come up the stairs?" I asked him.

He was glancing around, looking a little guilty. "No, missy. No
one's come past this way."

I turned back in the other direction. Down the dark hallway,
through the long gallery and at last I found myself in the library. The
curtains were drawn and the room lay in gloom but I could make out
a figure that stood there. Belinda was standing on the other side of one
of the glass-topped tables and in one hand she held an impressive
dagger.

Chapter 20

OCTOBER 18
TREWOMA, CORNWALL

I can't wait for this day to be over. I wonder if the inspector from
   Scotland Yard will get here by nightfall. Golly, I hope so. The
   waiting is nerve-racking. There is something about this house
   that is definitely unsettling. And now I'm having worrying
   thoughts about Belinda. . . .

"What on earth are you doing?" I demanded, my voice louder than I
intended.

She looked up, startled, and dropped the dagger. It landed on the
glass table with a clatter. "Georgie, I didn't hear you coming in. You
frightened me."

"You frightened me too, standing there with that menacing object
in your hand. What were you doing with it?"

"I just wanted to see how easy it would be to help oneself to one
of the weapons without being seen. No problem, if you hadn't followed me. And then I noticed that this dagger actually had precious

stones down the side of the scabbard—is that what this is called?" She held it out to me. "So that made me start to wonder if the dagger that killed Tony came in a similar case, and if so, where is it."

"Good point," I said, "but you really are a chump, you know. You've now put your fingerprints all over a second weapon."

"Oh gosh. So I have. That wasn't very bright of me, was it?"

I handed her my handkerchief. "For heaven's sake wipe it clean as quickly as possible, then put the darned thing back."

Belinda did as I told her and together we placed it back on its hook on the wall.

"Now wipe the wall," I said. "Your left hand touched it when you stretched up to hang the dagger."

We scrubbed at the wall, then Belinda said, "So where was the other dagger hanging? Perhaps the person who stabbed Tony also touched the wall when they took it down."

We searched the room but couldn't find where the dagger had hung. Then we looked through the long gallery and drawing room and again there seemed to be no empty hook.

"So where could the murder weapon have been displayed?" Belinda asked. "If it wasn't easily visible, how could anyone say that I found the dagger and stabbed Tony with it?"

"That will be a good point in your favor," I said. "Now please come back to the morning room and don't do anything else that could incriminate you."

"You're right," Belinda said and allowed herself to be steered back to her armchair beside the fire.

Shortly afterward a young constable arrived and took our fingerprints. He seemed rather taken with Belinda, as were most men, and blushed when she smiled at him. If only the inspector was as influenced, she'd be all right. But my experience was that most inspectors were older men with no susceptibilities to pretty faces or long sexy legs. The morning dragged on and there was no sign of Rose. I began to wonder about that too. What if Rose was lying dead in her bed, if the killer had finished her off at the same time as Tony? I was tempted to go and ask Mrs. Mannering to check on her, but I didn't feel like wandering around this house looking for the housekeeper. But I did find myself glancing across at Belinda. Seeing her standing there with the dagger in her hand and a strange look on her face had definitely shocked me and made me wonder. I thought I knew Belinda pretty well. We had slept side by side in the dorm room at school. We had had adventures together. But she had always been a free spirit, an opportunist, so different from me in so many ways. She had certainly had more than her share of men. But since she had had a baby and had to give it away she had become less sure of herself, more cautious, vowing to stay away from men. Was it possible that something inside her had snapped and when Tony came into her room, perhaps tried to force himself on her, she had taken revenge for the times she had been betrayed? I didn't want to think that. I told myself that it was just the brooding atmosphere in this house that was making these strange thoughts pop into my head.

Mrs. Mannering came in at eleven with a tray of morning coffee and a plate of gingerbread. "Mrs. Summers has awoken but with a bad headache. She asks me to excuse her but she will take her meals in her room today. She has, of course, had the most terrible shock. As have we all. But we must be brave, put a good face on it and soldier on."

She gave a curt little bow and left us.

Luncheon was an uneasy affair with Belinda and me sitting across from each other at the large dining table. It was a simple meal, as befitted the solemnity of the occasion: a thick soup, a piece of poached fish and a milk pudding. Almost nursery food but frankly I didn't feel like eating anything. I wondered whether I might be able to take a look at Belinda's room and see if I noticed anything before the inspector from London arrived, but every time I went out into the hallway the constable was sitting there, stoic in his duty. Until I was heading for the lavatory after lunch, that was. The chair in the hall was empty but I could hear voices coming from up above. Cautiously I made my way up the stairs. If questioned, I would be retrieving a handkerchief from my bedroom.

Belinda's door was open and through the crack I could see several figures moving around inside.

"Take a picture of that, Simms," said a voice I recognized as Inspector Purdy's. "And careful with that fingerprint powder. The bloke from Scotland Yard will want good clear prints."

"This pillow is all wet, sir," came another voice. "What do you put that down to? Outside in the rain last night maybe? Or could the rain have blown in through the window?"

"The housekeeper reckons the bloke washed his hair in the bath last night," the inspector said. "His hair was wet when we first saw him. Still a bit damp, isn't it?"

"Washed his hair in the bath? Who does that right before they go to bed? My mum would say you'd catch your death of cold."

"These upper-class types are different from you and me," came the inspector's voice. "They take baths every night, some of them. And bloody great bathtubs too, not a tin bath in front of the kitchen fire like you're used to, sonny."

"Rather them than me," the other voice said. "You wouldn't catch me having a bath every night. It don't seem natural."

"What about the murder weapon, sir?"

"Have you taken the fingerprints off it?"

"Yes, sir. Shall I put it aside for the inspector from London?"

"Make sure you don't handle it, boy. We don't want your fingerprints on it, do we?"

"Righty-o, sir. And should we leave the window open? The rain's still coming in."

"Yes, leave everything exactly as we found it." There was a pause. "Right. I think that's all we can do at this moment. Let's go and have a cup of tea in the kitchen, then."

I retreated to the top of the stairs so that it appeared I was just coming up as they emerged from Belinda's room. The inspector raised a questioning eyebrow at me. "Did you want something, my lady?"

"I'm just retrieving my handkerchief from my bedroom, Inspector."

"Your room is next door?"

"Yes, it is."

"Do you mind if we take a look around?"

"By all means, Inspector," I said. "Miss Warburton-Stoke had to share my room last night so you'll find her fingerprints in there, but apart from that there is nothing of interest, I can assure you."

"No matter. Just a routine check. And I'd like to test how easy it is to hear through the walls."

I waited while they rummaged around in my room, then he sent a younger sergeant to speak, then shout in Belinda's room. I was delighted to observe that they could hear nothing until the loudest shout.

"The walls are pretty darned thick here, aren't they, sir?" the young sergeant said, returning.

"They seem to be," the inspector admitted. He turned back to me. "We won't trouble you any longer, my lady. We're off for a cup of tea."

I took a handkerchief from the top drawer, made as if I was straightening items they had moved during their search and as soon as they were safely far away, I slipped into Belinda's room. The first thing that greeted me was a blast of cold air. The window was wide-open. That was interesting as I didn't think Belinda was usually the hearty type who slept with her window open in bad weather—unlike my own experience growing up at Castle Rannoch where windows were open in blizzards. Tony's body had now been covered with a white sheet. I could just make out the shape. I went over to the bed and lifted the sheet a little, shuddering at the sight of his body, so white and cold. His eyes had now been shut but his hair, apparently washed during his bath, had gone into attractive blond curls.

Such a waste, I found myself thinking. Tony Summers, who clearly loved life, lying there dead. And who could possibly benefit? Rose had lost a husband and would have no one to run the estate. She might well sell up and then Mrs. Mannering and the staff would be out of a job. Belinda's uncle Francis did seem like the best bet. With Tony dead perhaps mooring rates would go back to their old level. I tiptoed over to the window and looked down. There was a sturdy creeper growing up the wall. Had someone dared to climb in or out during last night's storm? That indicated a very foolhardy and reckless person.

I glanced out. There was a flower bed immediately below the window, then an area of gravel with lawns leading to a kitchen garden on one side and the more wooded part of the estate. Somewhere among those woods was the strange little dell that led down to the beach. I thought how easy it would be for someone to move around hidden on this estate, apart from the last part of crossing the lawn. But on a blustery night who would have looked out of a window?

It was still raining and I stepped back from the window before I got too wet. There was a puddle on the parquet floor. Mrs. Mannering wouldn't be too pleased about that! I moved quickly over to the bed and went through the bedclothes on the floor. A top sheet, two blankets and an eiderdown. No dressing gown. If Tony had come to the room wearing his robe, then it wasn't anywhere to be seen. I tried to picture him sprinting down the hall with wet hair, stark naked. It seemed unlikely, to say the least.

An idea was beginning to form in my head. I checked the floor and walls around the bed. There was no trace of blood that I could see on the light rug, apart from where the knife had fallen and Belinda had picked it up. That was strange. Surely Tony couldn't have been stabbed while he was lying down? If he had been on the bed, waiting for Belinda, and someone else had come into the room, wouldn't he have jumped up, wrestled the intruder for the knife? It was just possible that he had fallen asleep. He had, after all, consumed quite a large amount of alcohol, as had we all. But if he had been awake, how had the intruder managed to stab him without getting any blood spatters anywhere in the room? I had seen stabbings before (yes, I know, I have led a rather strange life in recent years) and they were quite messy.

This led me to wonder: had he actually been killed somewhere else and brought here, arranged on Belinda's bed to incriminate her? What if he had been stabbed in the bathroom? In the actual bathtub? I crept out of the room, checking the surroundings before I went along the corridor in the direction of where I suspected Tony's bathroom would be. As I went I examined the floor for any spots of blood. I found none. When I reached the end of the hall I opened doors and found to my annoyance that there was no other bathroom accessible from the corridor apart from the one that Belinda and I used. That must mean that Tony's bathroom was entered from their bedroom at the far end of the hallway. And Rose was still in bed. How annoying. I tried to think of an excuse to go in—wanting to see how she was? But I realized she probably wouldn't want to see me, given her outburst of accusation directed at Belinda the night before. I'd have to wait until she got up. And it was quite possible that the bathroom had already been cleaned.

I thought of that open window in Belinda's bedroom. Uncle Francis was rather portly. Could he have climbed in or out? In the middle of a storm? It did stretch the imagination. The only person I could think of who had proven himself to be opportunistic was the enigmatic Jago. He had already entered someone's home by way of a cave in the rocks. He was working for a man whose dealings were described as underhanded, and he and Tony had had some sort of run-in recently. Had Tony discovered that Jago was helping to smuggle something, maybe weapons, and Jago had to silence him? I could picture Jago stabbing someone, but why would he deliberately incriminate Belinda? He seemed rather attracted to her.

The other explanation that I didn't want to delve into was that Tony was lying on Belinda's bed, relaxed and waiting for her to get into bed beside him. And instead she picked up a dagger she had brought from downstairs and stabbed him. But why would she ever do that? Because he had deceived her and married Jonquil? Because she was now angry with all men and the way they treated her? Golly, I hoped that wasn't true.

Chapter 21

This is the most puzzling murder I have ever seen. I'm praying the
inspector from Scotland Yard finds the truth quickly and we can
go home. And I'm really hoping that the truth does not involve
Belinda!

Defeated, I went back downstairs. When I had a chance I'd question
the servants. Someone must have cleaned that bathroom this morning. I'd have to find out which maid was responsible. Unfortunately
as in any well-run household one hardly ever saw servants. Mrs. Mannering brought in the tray of coffee herself. A footman helped to serve
the meals but fires were magically stoked, curtains drawn and floors
swept when we were not around.

By midafternoon the fog had lifted. "Do you feel like getting some
fresh air?" I asked Belinda.

"I don't know if I'm allowed to leave the house," she said. "I'm the
prime suspect, aren't I?"

"Don't be silly. Nobody could prevent you from going for a walk in the grounds. And besides, I think the inspector and his team have already left. I don't hear voices, do you?"

Belinda got up. "It might be a good idea. I'll go mad if I have to sit here any longer."

We reached the foyer and were about to open the coat cupboard under the stairs when Mrs. Mannering appeared in that unnerving way she had. "You young ladies are not thinking of going out, I hope?"

"Just for a walk in the grounds," I said. "Miss Belinda is upset and needs fresh air."

She frowned. "Well, I suppose a walk in the grounds can do no harm, but the inspector was quite insistent that nobody was to leave the property."

"Don't worry. I'm not about to run away," Belinda said. We retrieved our outdoor things and went out into afternoon sunshine.

"Not that way," Belinda said as I headed for the right. "That leads to the cliffs. I don't want to be reminded where Jonquil died." She turned to me. "Georgie, do you think there is a curse associated with this house?"

"I certainly don't think that some malevolent spirit pushed Jonquil or stabbed Tony," I said. "Frankly I don't know what to think. Rose tells us that she suspects Tony pushed Jonquil and now wants to kill her. I don't know where she got that idea from, but now Tony is dead, not Rose."

"What do you think she wanted to achieve by telling us what she suspected about Tony? Do you think she really believed he wanted to kill her? Did she want witnesses to say she feared for her own life in case she was accused of his death?"

I shrugged. "I thought she was just being overdramatic at the time. Living cut off from the world she knew in a house like Trewoma can certainly play tricks on the mind. She is suddenly mistress of a big house, with a housekeeper who clearly disapproves of her. She's lost a baby recently. She is lonely without any friends or family. Personally I tend to believe that Jonquil's death was a tragic accident and that Tony inviting Rose to sail or ride horses was just trying to get her to embrace her new lifestyle."

"So you don't think she killed him?" Belinda asked.

I shook my head. "I don't see how she could have. Besides, you saw her face when she realized he had been killed. She was shocked and then angry, and I don't believe she was acting."

We had reached the entrance to the little dell and the path that ran down to the beach.

"Shall we go down here again?" Belinda said. "It was quite interesting, wasn't it? And we didn't have a proper chance to examine the plants once Rose started pouring out her secrets to us."

"All right," I said, with a slight hesitation. I was remembering those huge leaves, like giant food trays, looming over us in such a strangely menacing way. But I followed as she started down the narrow path. The little stream had increased in size from last night's rain and now rushed and tumbled over rocks, overflowing its banks in places. The air smelled damp and heavy, like going through a tropical greenhouse. It felt hard to breathe.

Suddenly I thought I heard a movement behind us, maybe the crack of a twig or the swish of a branch. I touched Belinda's arm. "Someone is following us," I whispered.

Belinda turned and stared. We both waited, holding our breaths. I didn't want to say that I thought it was stupid to come down here in the first place when there was a killer on the loose. I looked around for a weapon—a rock from the streambed? A dead branch?

Then there was a flapping and a pigeon flew out of a bush. Belinda looked at me and we exchanged a relieved smile.

All the same I was glad when we saw the glint of water ahead of us and came down the steps to the little beach. Except there wasn't much beach to be seen. The tide was now coming in and the water lapped at the cliffs on either side, leaving just a few feet of shingle between us and the steps. We could see the green slopes of the opposite shore, but the cliffs of the little bay cut off the view up or down the estuary. It felt horribly hemmed in and wasn't a pleasant place to linger.

A fishing boat passed, returning with a catch and followed by seagulls. Then another boat came into view, sailing out from somewhere near us and heading across to the far side of the estuary. It was a small yacht, towing a rowing boat behind it. There was one man at the tiller.

"Isn't that Jago?" Belinda asked.

"It looks like him," I agreed.

He had his back to us and was soon lost to view.

"Up to no good again," Belinda said.

"You don't know that."

"That's what Tony thought, wasn't it?" Belinda said. "He thought this foreign man got his money through illegal means and Jago was his willing henchman." She broke off. "Oh gosh, Georgie. What if Tony found out what was going on and Jago silenced him? It would be so easy to moor the boat, come ashore in the rowing boat . . ."

"Hold on a minute." I held up a hand to stop her. "That really is leaping to conclusions. How on earth would Jago know where to find Tony? Or where to find the dagger? And why stab him in your bedroom? He's clearly interested in you. . . ."

"Oh, I wouldn't say that." She turned red. "He's a natural flirt."

"Anyway, if Jago wanted to kill him it wouldn't be in that dramatic fashion. It would be a knife in the back where nobody could see and then his body taken out to sea and dumped."

Belinda nodded. "Yes, that does make sense. I'm so desperate to find someone who might have a good reason to want Tony dead. Oh, I do hope they've nabbed Uncle Francis. I am tempted to just jump in my little sports car and drive back to London as fast as possible."

"Don't do that, please," I said. "It wouldn't look good if you ran away at this moment."

"No, you're right." She nodded. She turned to go up the steps, then she shrank back and grabbed my arm.

"You were right. Someone is watching us."

"Where?"

"I saw a movement behind those bushes."

I had had enough of suspicion and drama. Had Mrs. Mannering sent one of the servants to keep an eye on us? Or perhaps one of the policemen?

"Come out and show yourself," I said in my loudest voice. Instead of echoing, it fell flat in the heavy air of the dell. "If you don't come out, I'll go and report you to the policeman who is up at the house."

There was blundering among the bushes and the old man who had given me directions appeared, looking flustered.

"I weren't doing no harm," he said. "Don't you go setting the police on me, missy."

"I'm sorry," I said, gently now, because he looked really agitated. "I just thought that someone was spying on us."

"Them policemen who came to the house," he said. "They weren't looking for me, were they? I didn't mean no harm."

"No, they weren't looking for you," Belinda said. "Why, what have you done?"

"I didn't mean no harm by it, did I? It was there. No one wanted it." He looked warily around. "She said she'd have the police on me and they'd lock me up," he said, sounding close to tears. "But I never said nothing, I promise. I told her I wouldn't and I didn't. Even though I saw what I saw. . . . But when those policemen came today, I thought . . ."

"There's been a death at the house," Belinda said. "Nothing to do with you."

"A death? Accidental, you mean? Not another . . ."

"Another murder?" I asked.

He shot me a look of pure panic. "I didn't say nothing." And he turned and blundered back into the bushes, leaving us alone.

"That was strange," Belinda said. "I wonder what he knows. He was really frightened, wasn't he? I wonder why someone threatened to call the police on him in the first place."

"Do you think he saw Tony push Jonquil?" Belinda asked. "He said he saw what he saw. He's skulking around the grounds all the time."

"But he said 'her,' not 'him,' didn't he?"

"You know how it is in Cornwall," Belinda said. "They get their pronouns muddled up all the time. And inanimate objects are given a sex too."

"All the same . . ." My brain was examining various possibilities. It was more likely that he had seen Jonquil with one of her lovers. Didn't someone mention something about docking a boat and Jonquil going down to join him for the night? Seeing them would have shocked an old countryman like him. And Jonquil might have threatened him if he told Tony.

We returned to the house to find that tea had been laid out in the gallery. There was no sign of the policemen nor of Rose. The fresh air had given both of us the appetite we had lacked all day and I noticed that Belinda set upon the watercress sandwiches and slices of plum cake as readily as I did. The time was approaching when one would normally go up to change for dinner.

"What do you think we should do?" I asked Belinda. "I am certainly not going to wear Jonquil's evening dress tonight. If Rose is not coming down, why don't we ask Mrs. Mannering if we can just have a simple supper instead of a formal meal?"

"Oh yes. Good idea," Belinda said. She walked toward the bell-pull, and was reaching up when a voice from the doorway said, "May I assist you young ladies with something?"

And Mrs. Mannering stood there, impassive as ever.

She came into the room. "Mrs. Summers has requested a tray in her room tonight. That being so, might I suggest that you do not change for dinner, but that I serve a simple supper—some soup, cold meats, pickles and a pudding?"

"Thank you. What a good idea," Belinda said.

Mrs. Mannering gave her customary little bow and retreated. The moment she had gone Belinda turned to me. "Do you think she was outside the door listening, or does she just read our minds? She really is the most unnerving woman I have ever come across. I bet she really is a witch."

"Shh, if she hears you she might turn you into a frog," I whispered.

"I wouldn't be at all surprised," Belinda retorted. "In fact nothing that happened in this house would ever surprise me again."

Chapter 22

OCTOBER 18, LATE EVENING
TREWOMA, CORNWALL

**Still waiting for the inspector from Scotland Yard. It feels like waiting
for doom to fall.**

I was just thinking that I was feeling a little peckish when there was a
loud knocking on the front door. Belinda reached out and grabbed my
hand. "Don't leave me, Georgie," she whispered.

"Of course not." I gave her what I hoped was a reassuring smile.

We heard voices, but after a long pause there was still no sign of a
visiting inspector. I motioned to Belinda to stay put and I went down
the hall, around the corner and to the foyer. Mrs. Mannering was
standing at the top of the stairs and I could hear male voices coming
from farther down the corridor, presumably from Belinda's bedroom.
The inspector was viewing the crime scene for himself.

I went back to Belinda. "I think you and I should request some
dinner first, don't you? We need to fortify ourselves before the inter-
rogation."

"How can you think of food at a time like this?" Belinda asked. "I don't think I could swallow a morsel."

I felt that I could swallow quite a few morsels. "A little soup, perhaps. You should eat something."

I rang the bell—something that had felt strange and uncomfortable to me all my life—and Mrs. Mannering appeared almost immediately. "My lady?" she asked.

"I presume that the inspector has arrived," I said. "We heard voices. May I suggest that we have something to eat while we can, in case the inspector wants to talk to us at length later?"

"Certainly, my lady. I'll have James bring your supper immediately. Would you perhaps prefer to eat in here, by the fire? I can bring you trays."

"That would be very nice, thank you," I said.

She gave me a smile—the first attempt at a smile I had seen from her, and a little nod of a bow before she went out. Almost immediately a footman and maid appeared, each carrying trays. On the tray was a bowl of thick vegetable soup, a plate of ham, pork pie, a wedge of cheese, a small dish of pickled cabbage and several slices of bread. Mrs. Mannering followed, carrying a bottle of white wine and two glasses. She poured us a glass each without waiting to ask and placed them on the low table in front of the sofa. Then she left.

Belinda toyed with the soup while I'm afraid I tucked in with gusto. "It's very good," I said. "And the pork pie is delicious. And this pickled cabbage."

"I just can't swallow," she replied. "I'm so scared, Georgie."

"I'm sure it will be all right." I reached across to pat her hand. "Do try at least a few sips of soup. You need to keep your strength up."

She brought a spoon to her mouth. After two or three attempts she put down the bowl.

"At least have the wine and cheese," I said.

"If I drink the wine, they'll think I have an alcohol problem and that I was intoxicated last night."

"Of course they won't. And you drank exactly the same amount as the rest of us. I'll tell them that."

"Except for Tony," Belinda said. "He drank more, didn't he? He had several brandies after dinner."

"He did," I agreed.

I toyed with this thought as I ate in silence. Tony was definitely tipsy by the end of the evening. Had that fact made it easier for someone to kill him? Had he, in fact, passed out on Belinda's bed? Not that this would make it any better for Belinda—just explain how easily she could have stabbed him to death. I suddenly experienced what she was feeling, that I could not swallow another morsel. One of the maids appeared with another tray, this one with dishes of blancmange and stewed apple. Both of us managed those quite nicely. We had moved on to coffee when Mrs. Mannering appeared again.

"The inspector would now like to speak to both of you young ladies. He suggested speaking to you in the library but I pointed out that the fire is not normally lit in the library during the evening and it might feel rather cold for all of you. So he said he will come in here instead."

"What is he like, Mrs. Mannering?" Belinda asked. "Is he terrifying?"

"He seemed a most mild-mannered man, Miss Warburton-Stoke. Quiet in his speech. Thoughtful. Observant. No, I do not think you will find him a bullying type of policeman. His name is Detective Inspector Watt, by the way."

"What?" Belinda asked.

"Yes."

Mrs. Mannering gave a little nod and left us.

"What did she say his name was?" Belinda turned to me. I was grinning.

"Yes," I said. Then I had to chuckle. "That's his name. Inspector Watt." I suppose it was the tension but I couldn't stop giggling. "And do you know what? If your grandmother had married him, she would have been a Watt-Knott."

Even Belinda managed a smile at this. "It's not funny, Georgie," she said, fighting to look serious. "How can you laugh when the situation is so dire?"

"I thought we both needed cheering up," I said. "And it's good to see you smile."

"Watt-Knott. You're awful, you know that?" We were both still giggling like schoolgirls when the door opened and the inspector came in. "I'm glad to see you ladies are in good humor," he said. "I am Detective Inspector Watt." (I pressed my lips together so that I didn't allow a chuckle to escape.) "Which one of you is Miss Warburton-Stoke?"

"I am," Belinda said.

"And your name, miss?" He turned to me. He was a thin man probably in his forties, wearing a brown suit that matched his sandy mustache and thinning sandy hair. The sort of man one might never notice in a crowd, but I observed his eyes, as they fastened on me, were narrow and shrewd.

"I am Mrs. O'Mara," I said, omitting that I was still to be addressed as "lady."

"A friend of Mrs. Summers?"

"No, I'd never met either Mr. or Mrs. Summers before Wednesday. I am a friend of Miss Warburton-Stoke. We came down here to look at a property she had just inherited."

"I see. I shall want you to give my man your full name and address, if you don't mind. But I have some questions for this other young lady, in whose room I understand that the body was found."

"That is correct," Belinda said stiffly.

"Now, in your own words, if you don't mind, perhaps you'd like to tell me how this unfortunate scene came about." He pulled up a spindle-backed chair and sat directly opposite Belinda.

"There is almost nothing I can tell you," Belinda said. "I went to have a bath, about ten thirty or thereabouts. I came back to my room and didn't bother to turn on the light as I was already dressed for bed.

My foot kicked something. I couldn't think what I could have left on the floor. I bent to pick it up. It was sticky. I turned on the light and saw that it was a knife, covered in blood. Then I looked up and saw Tony Summers, lying on my bed as you have just found him. I believe I might have screamed."

"You are telling me that the gentleman was already dead when you came into your room?"

"That's exactly right."

"I heard her scream, Inspector," I said. "I was just dozing off in the room next door, but her scream woke me. I came running and saw her standing there, holding the knife and looking petrified."

"So, Miss"—he consulted his notes to remind himself—"Warburton-Stoke. I'd like you to think carefully before you answer this. Do you have any idea at all why Mr. Summers would be lying on your bed, naked?"

"Absolutely no idea at all, Inspector. I certainly did not invite him into my room."

"How well did you know the man?"

"Hardly at all," Belinda said. "I used to spend my summers with my grandmother in this part of the world. Tony Summers and his wife were also children who spent their summers here. We all used to play together. I was completely surprised when I bumped into Rose Summers coming out of the post office and she recognized me and I found out that she and Tony were married and now living at Trewoma."

"So that was the first you'd seen of them since childhood?"

Belinda hesitated. Then she said "I had bumped into Tony once at a club in London several years ago. But certainly not kept up the acquaintanceship with either of them."

I nodded. Good answer, Belinda. She had told the truth, or at least part of it.

"So what are you doing staying at this house, then, if these people were relative strangers now?"

"In the course of our conversation outside the post office I mentioned that we were in search of a hotel room as the little cottage I had inherited was not in a fit state to stay in. Rose immediately suggested we come to stay at Trewoma. I was hesitant to accept, because I really didn't know them anymore, but she kept insisting, didn't she, Georgie?"

"She did. She wouldn't take no for an answer and went on about how seldom they had guests and essentially how lonely it was. It would have been rude not to accept."

DI Watt nodded slowly. "So it was Mrs. Summers and not Mr. who invited you?"

"Yes, it was," Belinda replied.

"And what did Mr. Summers think about it?"

"He seemed rather pleased to have guests and was proud of the way he had built up the home farm. He showed us his herd of Jersey cows."

"He didn't, at any time, show . . . uh . . . special interest in you, Miss Warburton-Stoke?"

Again Belinda paused. Then she said, "Since his wife was present at all times I find that a strange question. We went around the farm together with Rose Summers. We ate dinner together. We played cards together and then I went to have my bath. Lady Georgie can verify this."

"Lady who?" He looked confused.

"My friend, Lady Georgiana."

He spun back toward me. "I thought you said you were Mrs. O'Mara?"

"I am, Inspector. I recently married the Honorable Darcy O'Mara, but I still retain my title as daughter of a duke."

"I see." This clearly had thrown him. He glared at me as if concealing this all-important fact was a criminal offense.

Then he sighed, turned back to face Belinda and said, "So you want me to believe that you go to stay with a man you haven't seen since childhood, he shows no interest in you at all and yet he winds up naked on your bed with a large knife wound in his chest?"

Belinda eyed him coldly. "As strange as that sounds it's the truth, Detective Inspector."

He leaned toward her confidentially and lowered his voice. "You know you wouldn't be the first young woman who has defended her honor. A man comes to your room, perhaps having drunk too much, late at night, you fight him off, grab the first weapon that comes to hand. . . ."

"How many men do you think walk the whole length of a hallway stark naked, Inspector?" Belinda demanded. "And where do you think I might have had a large dagger lying around handily?" Her face was now bright red. "And if he had come into my room in such circumstances I would have screamed for help, not stabbed him. And Lady Georgiana would have heard me and come to my aid."

He swiveled back to face me. "So let me ask you, Lady Georgiana, now Mrs. O'Mara. Did this man maybe show any interest in you? I understand that wife swapping is an accepted sport in some circles."

It was my turn to eye him coldly. "It might be among some of my class, but I assure you that I intend to stay absolutely faithful to my husband. Furthermore Tony Summers treated me only with the politeness that one gives to a guest. And he'd hardly have invited me into my friend's room for a little hanky-panky while she was in the bath, would he?"

"I wouldn't know. The ways of your class are quite unfathomable to me. And I would have expected you to close ranks," he said with a sniff. "So let me ask you this: if neither of you killed him, then who did?"

"We have no idea, Detective Inspector," Belinda said. "The only person I can think of who might have both motive and means would be my uncle, Sir Francis Knott. I did mention this fact to Inspector Purdy."

"Ah yes, the wicked uncle." Inspector Watt managed a smile. "And your reason for this was?"

"My uncle is in difficult financial straits, Inspector. He was furious with Tony Summers because he had raised the mooring fees and my uncle lives on a boat. Also he is angry with me because I inherited my grandmother's estate, not him. So why not kill two birds with one stone? He came to the house yesterday afternoon, on the pretext of wanting to see Tony, but left without seeing him. Actually saying he would see himself out. So it would not be hard to hide and wait in a place like this." She paused, then added, "Whoever did this deed wished to pin it on me, didn't they? Or else why not lurk somewhere in the estate and stab Tony as he went about his work? Why not hide the body in a remote part of the estate? Why not fling him into the river?"

"So you believe your uncle capable of killing, do you?"

"Absolutely. He always used to boast about how he killed Germans during the Great War. I think he was quite handy with a knife."

The inspector remained silent for a while, examining Belinda. Then he said slowly, "The only thing against that is that there was one set of fingerprints on the knife, Miss Warburton-Stoke. And those fingerprints were yours."

There was a long silence after this. Outside the wind had picked up and a branch was tapping against a window somewhere. The logs shifted in the fireplace. The tension became unbearable. I felt that I had to say something.

"Of course her fingerprints were on the knife," I said. "She told you that she kicked it and then picked it up. She was holding it when I found her."

"Holding it when you found her. Right." He gave a little smirk of satisfaction. "Might the scream you heard not have been hers at all, but the poor man breathing his last as she plunged the dagger into him?"

"That is so silly," Belinda said. "Do you think that I had a large ceremonial dagger handy in my room? Lying by my bed for self-defense just in case anyone wandered in?"

"There must have been other fingerprints on the knife," I interjected.

"No others. Just this lady's."

I frowned. "No other fingerprints on a dagger that is at least a hundred years old? Isn't that a little suspicious?"

"Not necessarily," the inspector said. "The housekeeper tells me that the servants were instructed to dust and polish all the artifacts every week."

"But surely one of them would have left a stray fingerprint as they hung it back on the wall?" I suggested.

"Unless they were instructed to hold the artifact with a cloth. I am sure some of these old things are priceless and have to be handled with care."

"There is another explanation that you don't seem to want to address," I said. "That the person who stabbed Tony Summers wiped the weapon clean of his or her own fingerprints, made sure there was plenty of blood on it and left it on the floor for Belinda to pick up."

"That would be a possibility," he said, giving me a long stare with those shrewd little eyes. "So that would indicate someone who wanted to incriminate Miss Warburton-Stoke."

"Exactly," I said. "That is exactly what she suggested earlier."

His gaze moved back to Belinda.

"As I explained before, my uncle, Sir Francis Knott, is seething that I was left my grandmother's estate. If I were to die I expect it would come to him."

There was another long pause. The log on the fire shifted again, sending up sparks.

"The local police have checked on your uncle. Unfortunately for you he has a perfect alibi," he said. "It has been verified that his boat was at its mooring across the river in Padstow all yesterday evening and that he was playing dominoes in the pub with a group of men until closing time."

"Oh. I see." Belinda looked crestfallen. "How annoying."

"You wanted your uncle to be arrested for a crime?"

"No, but I wanted you to find someone else who had a good motive so you didn't think it was me."

"Which brings me to my next question: can you think of anyone else who might dislike you enough to pin a crime on you?"

My mind skipped unbidden to that time in the dell and what Rose had told us about Tony. If I said something, it gave Rose a good motive for murder. I decided to remain silent at this moment.

"I really can't," Belinda said. "As I told you before, I have had no real contact with the occupants of this house since I was fourteen and in those days we all got along well, having great adventures messing about on the river."

"And it appears that you are the only guests in the house. The only outsiders in the immediate environment. We will naturally be checking on the backgrounds of all the servants," the inspector said. "And any other suspicious people seen in the neighborhood, although this hardly looks like a crime committed by a member of the lower classes. The person would be taking a huge risk to steal the dagger from the wall in the first place and then be seen in the corridor of a guest's bedroom."

"One small point," I said, making him swivel back to me rapidly. "Miss Warburton-Stoke's window was open when I saw the room. She told me she had closed the window because it was raining hard that night."

"So you are suggesting . . ."

"That someone could have come in from the outside, and climbed up to her window."

"An outsider, you mean?"

I nodded.

"And how would this outsider know which room was her bedroom? And more to the point, that he'd arrive at the right moment to find Mr. Summers naked in that room?" He gave a satisfied little smile as if he'd just scored a point in a courtroom. "To me the whole crux of the matter comes down to this: Mr. Summers was killed on this lady's bed. He was naked."

"Was his robe found among the bedclothes?" I asked.

"Not that I've been told," he said, glancing down at the notebook he held in his hands and then jotting down a couple of words.

"And you don't find that odd?" I went on. "How many people walk down a long hallway with no clothes on after a bath?"

He gave another small smirk. "From what I hear about you aristocrats, there are all kinds of funny goings-on. And it was his own house, after all. I've been known to come out of my bathroom with just a towel around me."

"Yes, but not walk the length of a very long hallway when he knows there are female guests in residence. It would be horribly cold, for one thing. And certainly shocking for me if I'd opened the door and bumped into him."

"Perhaps he had something else around him—a towel, a sheet?" DI Watt said.

"Was a towel found among the bedclothes?"

"Not that I know of." Another glance down at the notebook.

"Detective Inspector," I began, a little hesitantly this time, "is it at all possible that he was killed elsewhere and his body brought and dumped on Belinda's bed?"

He was frowning now—well, scowling, actually. "In my experience I'd say no. People do not go on bleeding for long after they die. There's no heart to pump the blood around, you see. And there is a good-sized bloodstain on the sheet where he is lying. Also surely someone in the house would have reported seeing blood spatters in another room or along the hall."

I had to agree this was a good argument.

"You seem to have a morbid fascination with this case," he said. "Do you read a lot of detective novels? See yourself as one of those clever lady detectives who are so far removed from real life that it's laughable?"

"No, actually I've been involved in a few real murders, Detective Inspector," I said.

"You have? And how is that, pray? Trying to solve them when you read about them in the newspaper?"

"No, I just happened to be on the spot when someone was killed on more than one occasion. Once I had to solve a murder that they wanted to pin on my brother. Fortunately I was able to do so."

"Really? Good for you." He leaned closer to me and for a moment I thought he was going to pat my hand. "You can rest assured that my forensics team will give the place a good going over, little lady," he said. "And we're the professionals, so don't you worry your little head with the case."

This was now war, I decided. Nobody calls me "little lady."

Chapter 23

This is absolutely horrid. It's like my nightmare, only worse. I wish I
    knew what to do.

Detective Inspector Watt looked up as someone came into the room.
It was Mrs. Mannering, come to tell him that Mrs. Summers had had
a little supper and now felt strong enough to answer his questions.
We were told to confirm all of our details with the sergeant who
had apparently come with him from London. He took down our ad-
dresses.

"And where might your husband be, Mrs. O'Mara?" he asked.

"Off on business somewhere," I said.

"And how would we contact him?"

"I don't think you would, at the moment. He's abroad."

"What line of work is he in?"

"He works for the government, Sergeant," I replied although I was
never quite sure this was true. This seemed to satisfy him.

Rose did not put in an appearance that evening and eventually we were told that we would not be wanted again and could go to bed. I poured us both a large brandy. I felt we needed it to help us sleep.

Mrs. Mannering offered Belinda another room to sleep in, but Belinda said she'd rather stay with me. She did not want to be alone. I could understand how she felt. If someone had tried to pin a murder on her, then she might not be safe alone. But I couldn't fathom who that person could be. Apart from servants there were only Rose and Mrs. Mannering in the house. And neither had any reason to dislike Belinda. Perhaps Rose's husband had been a little flirty with her, but that wouldn't drive someone to kill. And we'd already decided the kitchen was just too far away for Rose to have done the deed.

I got undressed and crawled into bed beside Belinda.

"I'm glad you are here, Georgie," she whispered. "You're clever at these things, aren't you? You've solved murders before. You'll find out who did it, won't you?"

"I'll do my very best," I said, "but at the moment I'm stumped. I've been thinking that Rose could have chosen you as her alibi if she wanted to kill Tony, but how would she have known that he came to your room and was on your bed, naked, if she was down in the kitchen? He'd hardly have told his wife that he was off to have his way with Belinda while she was making cocoa."

"Oh, shut up, Georgie." She gave a half laugh. "What could he have been thinking?"

"His hair was wet," I said. "Apparently he washed his hair when he had a bath at night. So maybe this has something to do with bathrooms. Did you see him at all when you went to have your bath?"

"No. I didn't see anybody," Belinda said.

"Oh, that's a pity. I thought he might have just come out of his bath, spotted you going in to your bathroom and, in a fit of passion, decided to sprint down the hallway and lie in wait for you."

"Except that he would have taken his bath in his own bathroom, not the one in the hallway."

"Ah yes. Of course." I sighed.

"And he would have grabbed his bathrobe. That corridor is freezing cold with a wicked draft coming down it."

I nodded. "True."

"It's hopeless, isn't it?" she whispered.

"No, it's not. There is a logical explanation and we'll find it. Perhaps it has to do with his former life in London. His financial dealings. His father was in banking and lost all his money, you say. Perhaps Tony had borrowed heavily and hadn't paid back the debt and whoever he owed it to sent a henchman to finish him off." Then I shook my head. "No, that doesn't make sense, does it? They'd want him alive to pay back the money."

"And I don't think he was the sort to be involved in shady deals. He always struck me as absolutely straight."

"Apart from not telling you he was engaged when you had your little fling."

"Apart from that," she agreed, "but remember how scathing he was about the foreign gentleman at Trengilly and his shady dealings. And Jago being mixed up in them? I say, Georgie—I wonder if they are smuggling arms or something and Tony found out about it when he checked on the moorings he now owns and someone had to silence him?"

"As we decided the only thing against that is how would an outsider have known where to find a ceremonial dagger or where to find Tony, for that matter?"

"Good point." She hesitated. "And you still don't think Jago might have climbed in through my window, do you?"

"How would he have known that Tony was going to visit you?"

"You're right. He wouldn't." She sighed.

"Besides, he fancies you. I can tell that. He wouldn't want to harm you."

"Do you think so?" She sounded almost hopeful.

"Let's try and get some sleep, shall we?" I said. "Perhaps things will look brighter tomorrow. Perhaps the police will have turned up some useful evidence that will clear your name."

"I do hope so," she said.

I tried to sleep but again was plagued by strange dreams. Again I was running down dark corridors looking for something. I didn't know what it was but when I found it everything would be all right. And then the hallways turned into a prison and Belinda was in one of the cells. I could hear her calling for me. Help me, Georgie. You are the only one who can help me. And when I found the cell, I looked in it, but it wasn't Belinda behind those bars, it was Darcy. I awoke, clammy with sweat. Was this some sort of awful warning? Was Darcy in danger somewhere? Beside me Belinda was blissfully asleep. I lay listening to the night noises, the cry of a screech owl, the sigh of the wind until eventually I managed to fall back to sleep.

⁂

THE NEXT MORNING I awoke with a crick in my neck, having slept on the outside edge of a sagging mattress. I sat up, delighted to find that the fire had been banked up while we were sleeping and that the room was pleasantly warm. Hooray for servants, I thought, remembering again my first days alone in London when I had learned how to light my own fires. Outside the window the first rays of sun were shining on the water of the estuary. I spotted movement in the grounds and saw two policemens' helmets among the trees. I wondered what sort of clues they were looking for or if they'd actually found a good lead. This made me a trifle more optimistic. The police were here. They were actively working on the case. As the inspector had said, I didn't need to trouble my little head with it. Except that I probably wouldn't take his advice!

I heard a sigh coming from the bed. I looked around. Belinda opened her eyes, looking rested and beautiful as ever. I don't know how she did it. No wonder men found her irresistible if she woke up looking like that every morning!

"Oh goody. There's a fire," she said. "Do you think they'll be bringing tea? I'm starving, actually. I wonder when breakfast will be ready."

"You certainly bounce back from adversity quickly," I said.

"I had a good night's sleep. It works wonders on the constitution and I do feel more hopeful today." She sat up, stretched like a cat, then got up, putting on her dressing gown.

I went down the hall to bathe. The bathtub was a huge clawfooted affair and I only filled it a few inches, thinking that it would have taken hours to fill it properly. As I sat in the warm water I found myself wondering about Tony Summers again. He had just bathed. His hair was wet. Was it possible that someone had killed him in the bathtub and then brought him to Belinda's room? But Detective Inspector Watt had said that, based on the bloodstain, he did not think Tony was already dead when he was lain on the bed. And there was the added complication of how he could have been moved from a bathroom inside his own bedroom all the way to Belinda's room. That would be a mighty feat indeed.

Belinda was dressed when I returned to my room. We went downstairs, not encountering anybody, and found breakfast laid and ready. Belinda helped herself to generous amounts, but today I was the one who could only face a small portion of scrambled egg and toast. We were halfway through when we heard the tap of footsteps and Rose came in. She looked pale and lifeless and gave us the slightest nod as she went to pour coffee.

"How are you feeling?" I asked as she sat down.

"Numb," she said. Then she added, "Look, I'm sorry, but I simply can't speak to you. I should never have invited you here. I want you out of this house now."

"I'm afraid we can't leave. The police said so," I replied. "Not until the investigation is complete."

"How can it not be complete?" Rose snapped. "My husband is dead and you killed him."

"Rose," Belinda said, "I didn't kill Tony, I swear."

"You must have." Rose's voice sounded high and hysterical. "He was lying on your bed. And don't think I didn't know what was going on."

"Nothing was going on," Belinda said.

"Oh no? I wasn't born yesterday, you know. I saw him looking at you. And you looked back at him. It's that look between people who have slept together." She took a big breath. "You came here deliberately, didn't you? You hoped to renew your relationship with Tony. You arranged to bump into me and got yourself invited to our house."

"Rose, think about it," I said. "If Belinda was still attracted to Tony, why on earth would she want to kill him?"

"Because he rejected her, of course. He told her he was married to me now and he wasn't interested."

"And why was he on her bed naked if he wasn't interested?" I asked.

She flushed angrily. "How do I know? All I know is that he was killed in your bedroom, Belinda. What was he doing there?"

"I have no idea," Belinda said.

I wondered again whether Rose had possibly happened upon Tony going into Belinda's room earlier when she was supposed to be making cocoa. But she couldn't have. I'd been in the corridor and no one else was around.

"If it wasn't you, then who could it be?" Rose said, her face now bright red with anger.

"I wish I knew," Belinda replied.

"It could have been an outsider," I said. "Belinda's window was open when she had closed it earlier. Perhaps someone climbed in and killed Tony."

"Who happened to be lying naked on another woman's bed?" Rose spat out the words. "Oh, come on, Georgiana. Face facts. Look, I don't know your friend the way you do, but perhaps she's one of those women who lure men to their beds and then get a kick out of killing them. All I know is that my husband is dead and I don't know what will happen to me or to Trewoma."

"It wasn't long ago that you told us you were afraid he was going to kill you," I said quietly. "How do we know you didn't decide to kill him first?"

"Well, that's stupid, isn't it?" Rose said. "I was at the other end of the house, downstairs in the kitchen, trying to get the blasted stove to light. If you want to check, ask the kitchen maid about the mess I left when the milk boiled over. I made a half-hearted attempt to clean it up, but then I thought why bother? I'm mistress of this house, aren't I?" And she gave a bitter little laugh. "Mistress of this house." She stopped talking as Mrs. Mannering came in.

"Oh, Mrs. Summers. There you are. The inspector would like a word with you when you've had breakfast."

Rose sighed. "I don't feel like eating anything. I'll take a cup of coffee and go through to him now."

"You must eat," Mrs. Mannering said. "You need to keep your strength up at a time like this." She went over to Rose and put a hand on her arm. "We'll get through this somehow. I'm here. I'll take care of you now."

"Thank you, Mrs. Mannering," Rose said.

What remarkable transformations happen after a death, I thought. Rose had talked of her husband wanting to kill her and now was playing the grieving and vengeful wife and Mrs. Mannering had clearly shown her disgust for having to take orders from a lower-class girl and now was mothering her.

Rose and Mrs. Mannering went off. We went into the morning room to read the newspapers. As yet there was no news of Tony's murder. At least that was one small blessing. I supposed news took a long time to travel up from Cornwall.

The morning passed and we saw no one.

"How long is this going to go on?" Belinda said. "When do you think we'll be free to leave?"

"I've no idea," I said. I didn't like to say that it probably wouldn't be until they had found a more likely suspect than Belinda.

Then just as the grandfather clock was chiming twelve the door opened and Detective Inspector Watt came in, followed by Detective Inspector Purdy. He cleared his throat before addressing us.

"Belinda Warburton-Stoke, I am arresting you for the murder of Anthony James Summers," he said. "You have the right to remain silent but anything you say may be used against you in a court of law."

Chapter 24

What am I going to do? Poor Belinda. I have to help her but I can't do it alone.

Belinda and I rose to our feet at the same time. "No!" she exclaimed. "No. That's not true. I didn't kill him."

I put out my hand to hold on to her, as much to stop her from bolting as for support.

I felt that I had to do something. "Detective Inspector, what makes you so sure that Miss Warburton-Stoke killed him? Are you jumping to conclusions only because you found her prints on the knife or because you can't come up with anyone better?"

He gazed at me long and hard, the hint of a frown on his brow before answering. "Actually new evidence has come to light," he said. "Rather compelling evidence, as it happens." He turned to Belinda. "I'm afraid you weren't quite honest with us, young woman. Pretending that you hadn't had any contact with Mr. Summers since childhood.

According to his wife you and he acted like old friends. He knew about your mews cottage in London. You were seen flirting together."

"I was there all the time, Inspector," I said before Belinda could answer. "If there was any harmless flirting it was from Tony, not Belinda. And it was in front of the rest of us, including his wife."

"I did tell you that I bumped into Tony several years ago at a club in London," Belinda said. "One does. But I hadn't seen him since, I swear. I didn't even know he was living here. Why won't you believe me?"

I thought I detected the hint of one of those smirks.

"Then why had he written 'Belinda!' with an exclamation point after it in his diary on the day you arrived? Oh, and we went through the papers in his study. Your name and address are in his address book. I don't know what exactly you'd been to him in the past but I'd say you came down here trying to win him back, and when he told you he wasn't interested, you stabbed him."

"That is simply not true," Belinda said.

"When I was in detective training we were told to go with the obvious before we looked beyond," the inspector said, turning to Detective Inspector Purdy for confirmation. "And everything points to you, young lady. You had the means, you had the motive and your prints are on the weapon that you were holding. If you will please come with us . . ."

"Where are you taking me?" Belinda's voice rose as Inspector Purdy took a firm grip on her arm.

"To be held for your own safety."

"Where is she being taken?" I stepped between them. "To London?"

"To the country courthouse in Truro for the time being," Inspector Watt said. "We can't risk flight at this point."

"Inspector Watt, I'll vouch for her. I'll keep her under constant supervision if she stays here. Surely it's not necessary to incarcerate her?"

"I see no reason that she should be treated in any way differently from any other person who has committed a capital offense," Inspector Watt said. "So I'm afraid the young lady comes with us to be held until I get word from headquarters on what's to be done with her next."

Belinda turned back to me. "Georgie, do something, please. Don't let them take me away."

"Are you ready, miss? Do you have an overcoat?"

"My cape is in the cupboard in the foyer, I believe," she said. She turned back to me. "Oh my God, I can't believe this is happening."

"Can't I please come with her?" I asked. "She's very upset." I turned to the local inspector this time.

"I'm sorry, my lady," Inspector Purdy said, shaking his head. "This woman is now under arrest. There's nothing you can do."

"Isn't she allowed to make telephone calls?" I demanded. "Her lawyer should be notified."

"Oh yes, please let me call my solicitor. Although I don't know what good he'll be." Belinda sounded desperate. "He's good at wills and things but I don't know if he's ever had to deal with a crime and a court case."

"He'll know which barrister to contact, don't worry," I said.

"And my father," Belinda said. "Can't I call my father?"

"You'll be allowed one telephone call as soon as you are in custody," DI Watt said, showing no compassion at all.

"I'll telephone your father, Belinda. You talk to your solicitor," I said.

"His number is Broxham two five one. Can you remember that? Oh, and I need my things. My handbag and my cape." Belinda said. "I can't go without my things. And what about my nightclothes and toilet bag? Will I be staying there overnight?"

"It's not a luxury hotel, miss," Inspector Purdy said, glancing across at the senior man from Scotland Yard. "What do you think, Inspector? Can I send someone up for her possessions?"

"This young lady can go and get them," Inspector Watt said. "She'll know what a lady might need."

"Thank you," Belinda said.

I needed no urging. I ran up the stairs and into Belinda's bedroom. Tony's body had been removed in the meantime and the bed had been stripped. It was hard to believe what we had seen. I looked briefly on the floor around the bed but saw nothing. Think! I was commanding myself. What could I do to help her? I went into my room and shoved her nightdress, dressing gown, hairbrush and sponge bag into her suitcase. Then in her own room I added her underclothes, then lipstick and powder. She'd want to look her best, wouldn't she? I thought about changes of clothes but that might have been going too far. When I retrieved her handbag I opened it, quickly tearing off the solicitor's address from the envelope of Belinda's letter about the cottage, just in case I had to telephone him at some stage.

Then I ran down the stairs again.

"Here," I said, offering the train case and bag to Belinda. DI Purdy intervened, stepping in to go through each item before he nodded and handed them to Belinda. "Nothing untoward there," he said. "Right. We're ready then, are we?"

"My cape," Belinda said, not taking her eyes from me. "I need my cape." As I retrieved it from the cupboard I felt a weight in the pocket, reached in and touched her car keys. Would they impound Brutus? If so, how would I be able to get around? In a split second I took the keys and shoved them into my pocket before I draped the garment around her shoulders, fastening the clasp for her as if she was a little child. She gave me a pathetically grateful smile.

"Don't worry," I whispered, giving her a kiss on the cheek. "It will be all right. You'll soon be back with us."

I followed them to the front door. As DI Purdy escorted her down the flight of steps the other inspector came back to me. "It has just been brought to my attention exactly who you are, my lady," he said leaning close to me so that we couldn't be overheard. "Your connection to our king and queen. If I may make a suggestion, would you please go home as quickly as possible. The news of this crime will be in the papers before we know it and we don't want any embarrassing publicity for the royal family, do we? If you go home now, I believe we can keep your name out of the papers."

"Absolutely not, Inspector," I said angrily. "Do you really think I would desert my friend in her hour of need? I'm going to do everything within my power to prove her innocence."

He gave me a sad smile. "You are a loyal friend, I can see that. But I'm afraid you might have to face facts. Miss Warburton-Stoke might not have been quite upfront with you in this matter. She knew this man. She might well have been his mistress. And I'm afraid she will turn out to be guilty."

I followed him out of the front door and stood on the threshold as they bundled her into the back of a police motorcar. She gave me a last frightened glance as they drove away. I felt sick. I'd let them take my best friend. I hadn't been able to stop them. And I realized the frightening truth that it was all up to me, yet I had no idea where to begin.

MY HEART WAS pounding. I tried to stay calm and think logically. Should I get into Brutus and drive after them to see where Belinda was being taken? I dismissed this as being a waste of time when time was of the essence. They presumably wouldn't let me keep her company so what good was being in Truro when the murder had happened here? Think, Georgie. Step number one would be to do as Belinda had asked, to call her father. I was going to ask for permission to use the telephone when I came to a decision. I would not make the telephone call from the house where I could be overheard, but from the telephone box in the nearest village.

I needed to escape for a while anyway for my own sanity and to formulate my plans. I went to find Rose. She was sitting in the morning room with an untouched cup of tea in front of her.

"I shouldn't impose on you any longer," I said. "I'll pack my things and go to find a hotel in Truro where I can be close to Belinda."

"That's not necessary. You don't have to leave. I have no quarrel with you, Lady Georgiana."

"But I'd feel most awkward staying on in this house of mourning. You certainly don't want to entertain a stranger."

To my surprise she grabbed my hand. "Don't go. Please."

I hesitated. I would certainly be of more use to Belinda if I stayed on in this house. I could snoop around for clues, talk to the servants and see if they had noticed anything that might be helpful. I could find the old man again and get to the bottom of who had threatened him with the police and what he might have seen. But I was certainly uneasy about staying on here. Someone had killed in a most violent manner and while I couldn't think that anyone had a grudge against me, I might find myself in danger if I tried to delve into the manner more deeply. But it had to be done.

"I'll stay on for the moment, if you really want me here," I said. "But you don't have to be polite, Rose."

"I don't want to be alone," she said.

"All right," I said. "But you should know that I believe wholeheartedly that Belinda is innocent. So I think it wiser that I leave as soon as possible."

"At least stay for tonight," she said. "Until my mother can come and be with me. I telephoned her and she's on her way."

"Very well," I agreed. "But at this moment I need to be alone, if you don't mind. I need fresh air."

She nodded. "I have to tell Mrs. Mannering to make up a room for my mother." She went across to the wall and tugged on the bell-pull. "And we will need to plan a funeral, won't we? When do you think the police will release Tony's body to us? They said something about an autopsy, but that's ridiculous, isn't it? We all know how he died. He was stabbed to death. I told the police that I didn't want his body cut up any more but they said it was standard procedure. Horrible." She shook her head.

"You rang, Mrs. Summers?" Mrs. Mannering appeared. "Oh, you've let your tea get cold. Should I bring you another cup?"

"No, thank you," Rose said. "I'm finding it hard to swallow anything. But I've just spoken with my mother and she will be arriving by this evening so I wondered if you could . . ."

"I have already instructed Elsie to make up the blue room for her. It is suitably close to your room."

"Thank you. You're an absolute brick, Mrs. M.," Rose said.

The older woman gave a little nod of appreciation. "I do my job, Mrs. Summers."

Chapter 25

I feel as if I am fumbling blindly in the dark. There must be some logic
    to this. It is as if I'm living my nightmare over and over.

I retrieved my overcoat from the cupboard, took the key to Brutus
from my pocket and came out into the fresh air. A stiff breeze was
blowing and clouds raced across the sky. It would be a grand day for
a ride or better still a hunt. Or a walk through the estate at Eynsleigh
with my grandfather. Anywhere, other than here. I really wished I
hadn't agreed to come. If only Zou Zou had been in London or
Granddad hadn't been busy I would not have been home when Belinda came calling. Then I rebuked myself for being selfish. It would
have been so much worse for her if I hadn't been with her. She needed
me here.

I found Brutus where we had left him beside the stables and ten-
tatively climbed in. Even more hesitantly I put the key into the igni-
tion, and, with my foot on the clutch, turned it. The motor sprang to

life with a roar like an impatient tiger. I slid the gear into first (which it did with no grating and grinding at all) and gradually let the clutch out. The motorcar sprang forward eagerly and we headed down the drive. I had driven cars before, including Sir Hubert's Daimler, which was now mine to use, but never anything with such raw power as Brutus. I could feel him straining like a powerful horse, willing me to give him his head and let him gallop. I kept us in a sedate second gear as we negotiated the turns of the driveway and then turned into the road. Here I moved to a daring third gear, but the nature of Cornish lanes is such that one can never drive fast. Once I dropped from the headland, the lane ran between high banks, with tree branches reaching out from them, so winding that I could never see around the next corner. I slowed to a crawl, holding my breath as I came around each bend. Then I noticed a motorcar had come up behind me. Very close behind me. In the rearview mirror I saw a big black shape. I tried to go a little faster. I was sweating. Then I told myself, "He'll just have to wait."

I came to a place of the first houses, where the lane opened up a bit. Suddenly the other car swept past me. I noticed the Rolls-Royce emblem on the front. "Show-off! Road hog!" I shouted after it. I knew he couldn't hear me but it made me feel better.

I continued on into the village of Rock and pulled up outside the little post office where I had spotted a telephone box. And there was the Rolls-Royce, parked next to me. I wondered whether I dared to give the driver a piece of my mind when he came out of the post office, holding a bundle of mail. It was none other than Jago. He recognized me and gave me a friendly nod.

"Oh, it's you," I said, reformulating what I was about to say. "Nice motorcar."

He gave a cheeky grin. "Not mine. My boss's." Before I could say anything more he said, "Sorry if I gave you a scare back there, but my boss has just arrived with a big party and they want lobsters tonight. So I'd been out to my pots, but no luck again, I'm afraid."

"There aren't any lobsters around at the moment?"

He scowled. "There should be plenty, just not in my pots. I have my suspicions that someone is helping himself. I've tried to catch him at it but no luck so far. That's what I was doing when I surprised you and Belinda at the cottage. I'd spent most of the night out at sea, watching my lobster pots. Between us, my money is on that bugger Tony Summers, or someone who works for him. That's the sort of thing he would do. He's not a local man. He doesn't know our traditions. Not really popular around here."

"Oh," I said.

He saw my face. "What's wrong? And where's Belinda?"

"You haven't heard. Tony Summers is dead."

"Dead?" He looked astonished. "Heart attack or accident?"

"Murdered. And Belinda has been arrested for his murder."

"Belinda? How could Belinda have killed Tony Summers? And why?"

"She didn't, I'm sure, but he was found in her bedroom, lying naked on her bed. . . ."

"Was he?" Jago gave another cheeky grin.

"It wasn't like that at all," I said huffily. "She was off having a bath and she has no idea how he got there. Anyway, by the time she found him he had been stabbed with a large knife."

"Crikey," he said. "And what's happening now?"

"They've taken her off to the county courthouse in Truro," I said, and to my mortification I heard my voice quiver. "I don't know what's going to happen. She wants me to telephone her father."

"I'm really sorry. That's awful." He put a hand on my shoulder. "Is there anything I can do?"

"Not unless you can find the real murderer for me."

"I wish I could give you more time but my boss arrived out of the blue yesterday, so I've been racing around, getting household help, arranging for food to be delivered. He's a bugger with a terrible temper if everything doesn't go exactly as he likes it."

"Do you like working for him?" I asked.

He made a face. "He pays well. It's good experience. And I've been able to see parts of the world I'd never have seen otherwise." He let his hand fall. "Sorry. I have to get going. Look, come and find me if you need help. Once I've got them settled I should have a moment to breathe."

"How do I find you? I don't think that your boss wants me to trespass onto the grounds."

"There are people coming and going with deliveries right now. And my cottage is off to the left, next to the kitchen garden. But what about Belinda? Can we go and see her?"

"I'm going to try, but it sounds as if she's in jail. Do they let people in jail have visitors?"

"I'm sure they do in Cornwall," he said. "It's not like the Old Bailey here." This time the smile was reassuring.

"The problem is that if it wasn't Belinda who killed Tony, then who could it have been?"

"Who else was in the house?" he asked.

"Just Tony's wife, Rose, and the servants."

"And did she have a reason to want him dead?" Jago asked.

"She seems grief-stricken," I said, not wanting to divulge that conversation about believing Tony was trying to kill her. "And anyway she has a pretty good alibi. She was in a distant part of the house. The one interesting detail was that someone opened Belinda's window, so I'm wondering if an intruder got in."

"Someone from Tony's shady past, you mean?"

"Did he have one?"

Jago shrugged. "I've no idea. I do know he's not popular around here. He's raised rents, raised mooring fees, and of course Jonquil was never liked. She ran over a local child once, so there has been bad blood for some time with Trewoma."

"That's a thought," I said. "The servants. Is it possible that someone who now works at the house was related to the little boy that Jonquil killed years ago?"

"I'm not sure who works there now," he said. "Elsie Trelawney, doesn't she?"

"There's an Elsie. And James is the footman. But I don't know the name of the cook or other maids. They are all new, I gather. I understand that Tony—or was it Rose?—got rid of the old servants. One of them could have been bitter about being given the sack."

"I heard something about that," he said. "Poor old Gladys who'd worked there for years. And Will and Margie Stokes."

"Was one of them related to the boy?"

He frowned. "I think Gladys was his auntie or second cousin or something. Everybody's related to everyone else around here." Then he grinned. "They were all pretty ancient. I can't see Gladys climbing a drainpipe into someone's room. Or any of them, for that matter."

"Mrs. Mannering is still there, of course."

"Ah yes. The housekeeper. She's not local, I don't think. And she's been there donkey's years. Started off as a nursemaid for Jonquil."

The wheels were now turning in my head. A servant who was related to the dead boy—but then it was Jonquil who ran him over, years ago, not Tony. But Mrs. Mannering . . . she had obviously worshipped Jonquil. If she suspected, as Rose did, that Tony had pushed Jonquil off the cliff, might she have been waiting for the perfect moment to take revenge? But why Belinda? Belinda had nothing to do with Jonquil or the house. And Mrs. Mannering didn't like Rose much. Why not implicate her? I sighed again. Nothing made any sense. But at least I had a slim lead to go on. Someone in the neighborhood who hated Tony or hated Trewoma for some reason and had a relative working at the house now. A relative who could take the dagger and signal for the right moment to climb into the room. It was far-fetched but better than nothing.

"I'd better get going, then." Jago interrupted my train of thought.

"I'll keep my eyes and ears open, just in case. And when this lot leave again, I'll try to see Belinda. I don't like the thought of her shut up like that."

He opened the door of the Rolls-Royce, climbed in and set off at a great pace, tires spewing up loose gravel. I decided to do a little sleuthing right away. I went into the post office.

"Oh, it's you, miss," the postmistress said, eyeing me with interest. "Staying at Trewoma, so we've heard. What's it all about with the police, then? Constable Hood called out in the night and Dan Struthers says he saw a big police car going past—driving real fast, he was, and he turned into Trewoma, so we're reckoning something's wrong."

"You're going to find out soon enough," I said. "I expect it will be in the newspapers. Tony Summers has been killed."

"Well, I never!" She put a hand to her ample bosom. "I can't say he was the most popular of men around here—seeing as how he was trying to modernize everything and make folks pay up for mooring their boats and all—but who would have wanted to kill him? Poor Mrs. Summers. Just when she thought she'd landed nicely in clover, she's a widow with a big house to run."

"I was just wondering about the servants," I said.

"The servants?" She was frowning.

"Are they all from these parts? I wondered if any of them might have a grudge or perhaps have a family member with a grudge against Mr. Summers."

"Well, lovey," she said, "I dare say that Elsie Trelawney's old dad is not happy with the mooring fees, but that don't make someone decide to kill, does it? No, if you make up your mind to kill somebody it needs to be a pretty important reason. Something that means life or death to you personally and I can't think of anyone around here who could have so much hatred for Mr. Summers that they had to kill him." She paused. "Unless, of course, he was having his way with one of the maids. He was a good-looking chap, wasn't he? And I've heard how these lords of the manor behave—forcing themselves on young girls who would lose their jobs if they fought back. How did you say he was killed?"

"I didn't. He was stabbed."

"Well, there you are then." She gave me a knowing nod. "Stabbed in self-defense. That's what I'd be looking for."

"Thank you," I said. "Now, could you possibly change a half crown for some pennies? I have to make a couple of telephone calls and I don't want to run out."

"Of course I can, my lovey," she said and obliged. I came out and went to the telephone box. I put in what I hoped would be enough pennies. "Broxham two five one," I said when the operator came on the line. "Just a minute. I'll connect you to trunk calls," she said. I waited, then a voice said "Broxham two five one. Major Warburton-Stoke's residence." I pushed the button and heard the pennies drop before I said, "This is Lady Georgiana O'Mara. May I please speak to Major Warburton-Stoke?"

"I'm sorry, my lady," the smooth male voice said. "This is Hextable, the butler. But the master and mistress are off at their lodge in Scotland. They've gone shooting with friends."

"Oh dear," I said. "Do you happen to have the telephone number where I can reach them?"

"I'm afraid you can't reach them. There is no telephone at the lodge. It is purportedly very remote."

"When do you expect them home?"

"Not before next week at the earliest. The master said if the shooting was good they might stay on for a while."

"This is awful," I said. "Miss Belinda is in trouble. She has been wrongly accused of a crime and she begged me to telephone her father. Is there no way we can contact them?"

"We could send a telegram, I suppose. The post office would have to deliver it, wouldn't they?"

"Yes, that's a good idea," I said. "Could you send it?"

"It would be more suitable coming from you, my lady," he said in that expressionless and even voice that so many butlers have.

"Very well." I tried to stay calm. "What is the address?"

"Let me double-check for you." There was a pause, then he said, "It is Glenbrae Lodge, Perthshire."

I didn't think that sounded like the sort of address that could easily be found on a map and I doubted that a telegram would reach it within days, but I replied, "Thank you. I will send the telegram immediately."

"I do hope it's nothing serious concerning Miss Belinda. She always was a high-spirited young girl, wasn't she?"

"It's very serious, I'm afraid," I said. "She has been accused of murder."

Then I hung up. There was nothing more to say.

I went back into the post office and composed a telegram. "Belinda in trouble. Accused of murder. Truro, Cornwall." I was going to add "Return home immediately" but I decided those words were obvious and would cost more. So I handed the telegram to the postmistress and watched her face as she read the words. "Miss Belinda?" she asked. "Well, I never did."

"And neither did she," I replied, my nerves now close to snapping point. "She's innocent and we have to find a way to prove it."

Having done what I could with Belinda's family I made a second telephone call to my own house. Mrs. Holbrook answered and I explained that I was staying at a house called Trewoma in Cornwall and that I was in a spot of bother. If Mr. Darcy telephoned or returned home would she ask him to come immediately? I gave her the address, directions and telephone number.

"Of course I will, my lady. Is there anything I can do? Has someone been taken ill?"

"No, it's worse than that, Mrs. Holbrook," I said. "There has been a murder and the police think that Miss Belinda is guilty."

"How terrible for you. Why don't you come home right away and let us take care of you?" she said.

"I can't leave Belinda. She needs my help," I said.

"Of course. But don't you worry. The moment Mr. O'Mara telephones, I'll send him straight to you."

I felt a little better as I put down the telephone. Just hearing a friendly voice was somehow reassuring. Darcy would telephone, I thought, and come racing to my side. Unless . . . unless he was currently on a steamer heading for Argentina or in the wilds of Siberia. Or in danger somewhere himself, my mind added, unbidden. One never knew.

"Drat the man," I said, fighting back tears that threatened to come.

Chapter 26

OCTOBER 19

HEADING BACK TO TREWOMA BUT NOT SURE THAT I WANT TO
STAY . . .

I seem to be getting nowhere. There is nobody I can turn to for help
and yet Belinda is counting on me. Should I even go back to
Trewoma? What if I am in danger now?

I drove back slowly, trying to think calmly and rationally. I had been
involved in strange crimes before. I had managed to find clues, trace
suspects, figure things out. And now it seemed it was all up to me. I
suspected the police were sure they had found the right person in
Belinda and were not going to look any further. Think, Georgie, I
commanded myself. The most promising direction seemed to be the
servants. Someone in that house had a grudge against Tony. Perhaps he
had tried to force himself on one of the maids. Perhaps her brother or
father had come to take revenge. Or a relative had lost his fishing rights
and with them the family income. I would go back to Trewoma and
try to talk to them. Somewhere, someone knew something critical.

The moment I said that a figure flashed into my mind. Old Harry appearing behind us on the beach in an agitated state and mumbling something about what he saw and how he never said anything. I should try to find him and get out of him what he knew. Now with a clear plan of action ahead I drove up to Trewoma and parked Brutus well away from the house. I didn't want the police to find out it was Belinda's motor and to seize it as evidence. I glanced up at the windows, wanting to see if anyone was watching me, but saw nobody. So I started to wander the grounds, looking for the old man. After a frustrating half hour I decided he was the sort who knew how to make himself invisible when he wanted. I came out from the woods, onto the open lawns leading to the cliff tops. This was where Jonquil fell, I thought, and found myself drawn to take a look. I knew her death and Tony's could not be connected but I had also learned that when things seem to be coincidental, there is often a hidden connection. I stood at the cliff edge and looked down. It was not an enormously high cliff, but there were vicious-looking rocks below. At high tide they would have been covered but at this moment they lay exposed with tide pools in the crevasses. If Jonquil had fallen from this spot, death was almost certain.

I don't know how I sensed someone coming up behind me. I'm sure footsteps would have made no sound on the springy turf, but I turned around.

"This is where she fell," said a voice right behind me.

I jumped and almost lost my footing when a hand reached out to grab me. Rose was standing there. "Steady on," she said. "We don't want a second accident, do we?"

"Golly, you startled me," I said. "I didn't hear you coming."

"That's because of the noise of the waves," she said. "I spotted you crossing the lawn and I guessed where you must be going. I thought I'd better keep an eye on you, just in case."

She moved away from the cliff-edge and I followed. "You don't suspect . . ." I began hesitantly. "I remember you said that you thought that Tony must have pushed her."

"That's what I believed," she said. "But since he's been killed, I've been thinking and wondering. Perhaps it wasn't him at all."

"Then who?"

"That's what I've been asking myself. Who wanted them both out of the way? And of course the next question is am I next?"

I stared at her. Had she now come to believe that Belinda was not guilty after all? And did she have a suspicion about who the real murderer might be?

"Why should anyone want to kill you?"

She shrugged. "I don't know. I can't think that I've upset anyone. But living in a place like this sort of plays on the mind. I don't think I want to go on living here alone. I'll sell it and buy a nice house in town somewhere. Maybe in Bath, next to my mum. Maybe in London. Maybe in Paris. It hasn't quite sunk in yet that I'm a rich widow."

I glanced at her and she gave a nervous little grin.

"My mum will be arriving any moment," she said. "I should get back to the house to make sure Mrs. M. has made up a nice room for her. Of course she will have. Silly me. She does everything perfectly, doesn't she?"

Then she walked off ahead of me across the lawn, leaving me standing and wondering. The disturbing thought that had been nagging at the back of my mind was how she knew the exact spot where Jonquil fell to her death. Did someone tell her? Show her? Because when it happened she had been living in London. Unless . . . unless she had it all planned. She read that Tony had married Jonquil. Her two idols now living in the perfect house. What if she had come down here, taken her chances and pushed Jonquil over the cliff? Then arranged, after a suitable time, to meet Tony in London, to get him drunk, lure him into bed with her and claim she was pregnant. Then she'd say she'd had a miscarriage and at the right moment, get rid of Tony.

It was preposterous. Almost beyond belief. But I had seen when we played cards that she was much shrewder than she claimed. Belinda had mentioned that she had been a sneaky child. As she said, she was now a rich widow. The only thing against this was Tony lying naked on Belinda's bed. The inspector did not believe he had been killed elsewhere. Had Rose been spying on him, seen him going naked to Belinda's room and stabbed him? Had she only pretended to go to the kitchen? But the mug of cocoa I was given to hold had still been hot. And the kitchen was at the other end of the house. And the other ridiculous question: what man walks naked down a long corridor, knowing that female guests as well as servants might encounter him?

Instead of going straight to the house I continued to walk through the grounds. I came around to the kitchen garden, with the last of the apples on the apple trees and neat rows of cabbages planted out in the beds. Like everything else in the house it appeared to be well-run and I wondered if Mrs. Mannering's rule applied out here as well. Or was it Tony who supervised? A gardener was at work—a young, fit-looking lad, who was shoveling leaves onto a bonfire. He broke off when he saw me coming and tipped his cap.

"Morning, miss," he said.

"Plenty of leaves at this time of year to keep you busy, aren't there?" I said, giving him a smile.

"There certainly are, miss. No sooner have I swept them up, then more of the buggers come falling."

I nodded to him and he went off with a wheelbarrow to get the next load of leaves. Because everything was damp, the fire was not blazing but smoking. I stood savoring the sweet smoke that I always find so evocative. I was about to walk on when I saw something poking out from among the leaves. Something white and soft. I grabbed a stick and attempted to drag it out. It was smoking, or rather steaming, but I could see that it was the corner of what looked like nubbly fabric—a towel, maybe, or even a toweling robe. It was soaking wet and too heavy to lift, with the great mound of leaves and branches on top of it. I wasn't sure what to do next and then noticed the young gardener was coming back. I hurriedly covered it with leaves again.

"How often do you light this fire?" I asked.

"It weren't much use trying to light it after the last rain," he said. "So I haven't touched it for a few days now." He emptied the wheelbarrow. "See, even now it don't want to burn, do it? I reckon I might have to resort to tipping some petrol onto it to get a nice blaze."

A nice blaze, I thought. Consuming all evidence. Had he noticed there were things other than leaves in the pile? Or was it possible . . .

"What's your name?" I asked.

"Trevor, ma'am," he said.

"Have you worked here long?"

"Two years now."

"Your family lives nearby, I suppose?"

He nodded. "They do, miss. My dad's a fisherman but the catch hasn't been too good these days. So it's up to me and Elsie to help support our mum and the little ones."

"Elsie? She's a maid here?"

He nodded again. "That's right. Mr. Summers took us both on a couple of years ago. He got rid of the old staff and said he wanted to modernize the place with new young people. Had lots of grand ideas, he had, more's the pity." He threw on another shovelful of leaves. "That Mannering woman is a bit of a pain, if you'll pardon my saying so, but otherwise we're treated well here. And the pay's good."

I couldn't think of anything else to say. All I knew was that what I'd seen now seemed to confirm that Tony Summers had been wearing a robe, or had a towel wrapped around him, and that someone must have thrown it out of the window where it was later retrieved and hidden in the bonfire. But why? Was it because Tony had not really been stabbed on that bed but killed elsewhere and brought to Belinda's room? But the inspector had said he was sure Tony had not been killed elsewhere. So why throw the robe out of the window and hide it on a bonfire if it didn't have telltale bloodstains on it?

I was deep in thought when I came back into the house to hear voices coming from the hallway upstairs.

"No, I'm sure it will be lovely," said a woman's voice I couldn't recognize.

"Are you sure, Mummy? We have much nicer rooms. I don't know why Mrs. Mannering chose that room for you."

"I thought your mother would like to be close to you, Mrs. Summers. I had suggested the blue room but on consideration I thought she would feel more at home in a smaller room, since she is not used to houses of this size."

"Please don't get upset, Rose. I shall be quite happy here. Honestly. I'll just unpack, shall I?"

There was an awkward silence.

"I have laid tea in the salon," Mrs. Mannering said in her calm, cold voice. "Please take your mother downstairs, Mrs. Summers. I will have Elsie unpack your mother's things."

Rose came to the head of the stairs, followed by a round and pleasant-looking woman. I noticed that Rose had changed into a smart black dress which actually made her look quite stylish and slim. She saw me in the foyer. "Oh, Georgie. My mother has arrived. Isn't that nice? Mum, this is Lady Georgiana I told you about."

"Pleased to meet you, your ladyship," Rose's mother said, coming down the stairs to greet me. "I'm sorry we meet at such a sad time. My poor Rosie. She was so happy, married to that lovely man and now he's struck down in his prime. And I was so shocked to learn that it was Miss Belinda who did this awful thing. Miss Belinda of all people. Such a kind and friendly little girl when I looked after her. I used to let her help me with the baking and she loved it. I'm only glad old Lady Knott is not around to see this. It would be the death of her. Ever so proud of her family and her granddaughter, old Lady Knott was—" She broke off, flushing with embarrassment.

"I'm so sorry, Mrs. Barnes," I said. "But I really don't believe that Miss Belinda killed him, however bad it looks now. We will get to the bottom of it and find out who is responsible, I promise."

"Come on, Mum. Let's have some tea, shall we?" Rose stepped

between us and shepherded her mother away and down the hall. I waited until they had disappeared and then I sprinted up the stairs. The door was open to a room close to the end of the upstairs corridor. I peeked inside and saw the young maid, Elsie. I went in, closing the door behind me. The maid dropped the jumper she had just folded and regarded me warily. "Can I help you, my lady?" she asked.

"Do you enjoy working here, Elsie?" I asked.

She looked confused. "I don't know if anyone enjoys scrubbing and cleaning, but it's a good job and I'm paid fairly."

"And treated well?"

She glanced up, then said, "Well, Mrs. Mannering can be a bit of an old cow sometimes but apart from that I've no complaints."

"Mr. and Mrs. Summers both treat you well?"

"She's really nice. Grateful for everything. But Mr. Summers . . ." She paused.

"Wasn't so nice?" I suggested.

"Oh, he was friendly enough but a bit of a slob, if you get my meaning. I mean, left his clothes all over the place and his bathroom . . . well, it was always a mess."

"Elsie, are you Mrs. Summers's lady's maid?" I asked.

"I'm the upstairs maid, your ladyship. I take care of Mrs. Summers but she don't really want to be fussed over like some of the ladies. I also do the upstairs cleaning."

"When Mr. Summers was killed, were you already in bed?" I asked. "Or did you wait up to undress Mrs. Summers."

"No, my lady. She said she didn't need no help and I could go to bed."

"So you didn't find out that Mr. Summers had died until the police came and the servants were woken up again?"

"That's right." She nodded.

"Did the police check Mr. Summers's bedroom and bathroom, do you know?"

She looked puzzled now. "I couldn't really tell you. They told us to wait in the servants' hall until we were questioned."

"And were you allowed to clean the rooms the next morning?"

"Well, I wasn't allowed in the bedroom because Mrs. Summers took to her bed for the day. I was going to clean the bathrooms but Mrs. Mannering told me to leave them and not disturb Mrs. Summers. Mr. Summers's bathroom was a mess but Mrs. Mannering said she'd take care of it."

"You saw his bathroom? What kind of mess was it?"

"Oh, you know. The usual. Wet towels all over the place and water on the floor."

"It was always like that?"

"Well, this looked a little worse than usual. More wet towels on the floor. He got through ever so many towels. I couldn't understand it personally. At home we all took a bath once a week in front of the fire and used the same towel." She gave an embarrassed grin.

I was trying to find a way to ask whether she had noticed any blood on the floor but I couldn't come up with a way to phrase it before she said, "Why are you asking me all these questions?"

"I'm sorry," I said. "Mr. Summers was murdered and the police are saying my friend did it. I am sure she didn't. So I am just trying to get straight in my own mind how he could possibly have been killed and whether any of you servants noticed anything."

"But he was stabbed in the lady's room." Elsie looked perplexed. "That's what we heard."

"While she was in her bath," I pointed out. "She came back and found him lying there." I hesitated. "Do you know, was Mr. Summers in the habit of walking around with no clothes on?"

She really looked shocked now. "Oh no, miss. I've never seen nothing like that. Nor heard about it from the rest of the staff. He was always quite a proper sort of gentleman. In fact he apologized to me once when I was cleaning in the bath and he came in in his underclothes."

She clearly wanted to get back to her task but I couldn't resist asking, "Is everyone else happy to be working here, do you think?"

She shrugged. "Everyone has a little gripe every now and then, you know. Same as it is in any big house, I'd imagine. But we're all glad to have the work. There's not much to do around here, apart from fishing or working on the farm."

"So you can't think of anyone who might be happy Mr. Summers is dead?"

She shook her head. "Quite the opposite. We're all worried about our positions now. What might happen to us if Mrs. Summers decides to up and leave." She looked up suddenly as the door opened and Mrs. Mannering came in.

"Elsie?" she asked. "My lady? Is something wrong? Can I help you?"

"I just came to ask Elsie if she'd help me pack up Miss Warburton-Stoke's possessions and also mine. Now that Mrs. Summers's mother is here, I feel that my presence is a little awkward."

Mrs. Mannering nodded. "I quite understand, my lady. But I'm sure Mrs. Summers intends you to stay the night and leave in the morning. You would not have time to drive to your home before dark and I fear another bout of rain is approaching."

"Very well," I said. "But I will leave first thing in the morning, and I'll be taking Miss Warburton-Stoke's things with me. I presume the police have gone over everything with a fine-tooth comb?"

"I expect they have, my lady." She ushered me out of the bedroom. "Mrs. Summers would be delighted if you join them for tea first." And she stood sentry at the bedroom door until I had walked down the stairs.

Chapter 27

Maybe I'm getting somewhere at last.

It was an awkward teatime to say the least. I realized that I had missed luncheon and was quite hungry but it didn't seem fitting to be tucking in when the house was in mourning. So I nibbled dutifully at a cucumber sandwich, answered politely when spoken to and waited for the moment when I could excuse myself again. I was also conscious that the other occupants of the room were wearing black, whereas I had brought no black garments with me. One doesn't expect a death in every household one stays in, does one? My bright green jersey seemed almost garish and out of place. Perhaps I could just slip away after tea. But then where should I go? To Truro so that I could be close to Belinda, if they would let me see her? But what good could I be there, apart from being a comforting presence?

The question was what good was I here? I didn't seem to be getting anywhere, other than finding what appeared to be Tony's towel or bathrobe on the bonfire. I was beginning to wonder more and more about Rose. She was the one with the motive and I couldn't stop thinking about the way she had appeared behind me on the cliff top. If I hadn't sensed her coming and looked around, would she have given me a push? And there had been a tiny gleam in her eye when she had proclaimed herself a rich widow. Except for that wretched cocoa in the kitchen which would have made a well-executed murder almost impossible. I waited until tea was over and Rose suggested we take a turn about the grounds before the weather turned wet again. I replied that I thought she'd rather be alone with her mother and off they went. The moment they were well away from the house I made my way toward the kitchen. I had a good excuse. The gingerbread had been delicious and I would love to give the recipe to my cook.

A long narrow hallway led to the back of the house. I went through the door that divided the lives of those belowstairs from those above and found myself in an even darker, narrower hallway. Great houses are never built with convenience and comfort of servants in mind! From the far end came the clink of pots and pans. I walked toward it, then just outside the entrance to the kitchen I stopped. Ahead of me was a large, well-lit kitchen but through the gloom to my right I noticed a stone staircase cut into the wall. Of course, all the best houses had servants' staircases so that the masters were never offended by the sight of people actually working for them. Instead of going into the kitchen I crept up the stairs. The steps were steep and uneven and I thought of a servant trying to carry coal scuttles or hot water up to their masters this way.

I was a little out of breath when I came to a door on the floor above and opened it. I was standing at the far end of my bedroom corridor, right next to Rose and Tony's bedroom. I glanced around, then tiptoed into the room, carefully closing the door behind me. It was a lovely big room with a four-poster, a pretty dressing table in the window, and Rose's dress flung carelessly over the stool. An enormous oak wardrobe took up a lot of one wall. It was in many ways a woman's room. I spied a door beside the wardrobe and found myself in a large bathroom. On the other side of that was yet another door that led to a gentleman's dressing room and beyond that what must have been Tony's bathroom. Yes, there were his shaving things on the shelf and an enormous claw-foot tub. I stood, staring down at it, picturing Tony in that bath. If someone had come in unexpectedly, he would have been taken off guard. Someone with a knife, or in this case, a dagger. It was not the sort of tub from which one could have made a speedy exit.

The only thing against that scenario was that there would have been blood in the water. Someone would have had to have enough time to clean up the bathroom, and there would have been blood on the towels too. Besides, how could anyone have carried him through the whole bedroom suite, down the length of the hallway and laid him on Belinda's bed? Rose might have had time to run up those back stairs from the kitchen and kill him, but would she have had time to carry him the length of the hallway without being heard? I was in my room, after all, and it would have taken superhuman strength. Wouldn't I have heard a body being dragged? Maybe not on the carpeted hallway. But wouldn't she have let out a grunt of exertion that I might have heard through my door? Unless this was some sort of conspiracy and the killer had a helper—one who got away through that open window. I wondered who might have been Rose's ally.

I shook my head in frustration. How was I ever going to prove that Belinda didn't do this? I realized then that I was trapped in a bathroom in a potentially dangerous house. I looked around and there was a white-painted door, blending in nicely to the white-paneled wall. I opened it and found myself back on the corridor, right next to the room Mrs. Mannering had given to Rose's mother. How convenient. Not so far to drag a body after all, but still a goodish way. I went back to Belinda's room and started to pack up her clothes. Then I opened the wardrobe and saw Jonquil's evening dress hanging there. I'd have to put that back, plus the one that had been lent to me. I certainly had no wish to keep it now, after what had happened. I finished packing Belinda's things, retrieved both the dresses and crossed the balcony to the forbidden hallway without Mrs. Mannering appearing in that uncanny way behind me.

This side of the house felt so much colder. Was it just that no fires were lit here, that the wind came directly off the Atlantic, or was it something else? I found myself glancing back down the shadowy hallway. Then I opened the door and stepped into the bright light of . . . drat. I'd made the same mistake again. This was the nursery. The bedroom was next door. I stood examining it with pleasure. The rocking horse so like the one that still resided in the nursery at Castle Rannoch. All those wonderful dolls. Again I found myself picturing a nursery like this at Eynsleigh, a sweet little person, with Darcy's dark curly hair, asleep in that cot. If only. . . . Then I frowned. Something was different. The dolls were now sitting on the doll bed in the corner and the soft toys in the crib. Surely they had all been together . . . in the red cart. The red cart was no longer here.

I was breathing rather fast. It had been a sturdy replica of a farm cart, big enough to transport a child. In fact there among the photographs on the mantelpiece was a snapshot of an adorable, curly-haired Jonquil riding in the wagon with a small friend, being towed by an older boy. It had rubber wheels. Was it possible it was big enough to transport a dead man along a hallway? His legs would have dragged along the floor, of course, but I thought it could have been done. Why else would it now be missing?

I slipped out of the nursery without being seen, returned Jonquil's two evening dresses to her wardrobe and went back to my own room, where I packed my own suitcase. Should I try to find what had happened to the wagon? But if I did, what would it prove, unless there were bloodstains on it? It must have been disposed of, possibly out of that window, or one of the staff would have reported seeing it in an unlikely place. Why had it not been returned to the nursery? Either because there were bloodstains or because Tony had been so heavy he had damaged it. Either way it would be something to present to the police, a small piece of evidence that Tony had not come naked into Belinda's room of his own free will.

I felt a glimmer of hope. Should I leave quietly now and spend the night in Truro? Maybe be allowed to see Belinda? Or should I search the grounds to see if I could find any evidence of that wagon—perhaps being burned at this moment on the bonfire? I realized I ought to do that. And my excuse would be that I had decided to join Rose and her mother after all. Out I went into the blustery afternoon. The wind had now picked up, driving a great bank of dark cloud from the ocean. Already I felt the first spots of rain. I reached the kitchen garden and saw no sign of Trevor, the young gardener. The bonfire was still smoking and was piled higher than my head with dead leaves. I took a stick and dug into it but could not feel any large object. With so many acres of wild grounds it would be easy to hide the wagon elsewhere. I started to wander through the more heavily wooded section until the rain arrived with a vengeance and I was quite soaked by the time I made it back to the house.

"My dear lady Georgiana. I rather fear that an expedition was quite unwise given the inclement weather," Mrs. Mannering greeted me as I took off my sodden overcoat. "I hope you have not caught a chill. I will have Elsie run you a bath right away."

An image of that large bathtub flashed into my mind. "That won't be necessary," I said. "I grew up in Scotland. I really am quite hardy and I feel that I should perhaps take this opportunity to leave Mrs. Summers and her mother in peace. I really am not comfortable being an intruder at this awful time."

"I do understand," she said, "but may I suggest again that you leave in the morning. The conditions tonight will not be suitable for driving. Some of the lanes around here flood very easily."

I tried to study her face. Did she perhaps want me in the house? Did she suspect Rose? Given the way she seemed to know exactly what was going on all the time, did she want me to get at the truth?

"I have nothing suitable to wear for dinner," I said. "I brought no black dress with me."

"Please do not concern yourself," she said. "We will not be dining formally tonight. Only a simple meal."

I hesitated. The thought of a meal with Rose and her mother was not appealing, but I had told my housekeeper I was staying at Trewoma. If Darcy came looking for me, he'd expect to find me here. Also Belinda's father might show up. Then I decided that I could always telephone my house again when I'd found a hotel or boarding house. I just wanted to be away from this place. "You have been very kind," I said, "but now that Mrs. Summers's mother is here, I feel I should go to Truro to be close to Miss Warburton-Stoke. Please thank Mrs. Summers and explain to her that this situation has made me feel most uncomfortable."

She nodded. "Of course. If you feel you must leave. And I hope for your sake that your friend is not found to be guilty in this matter."

I wanted to ask her about the wagon, about the mess in Tony's bathroom, but I felt those were questions better coming from the police. So I collected the bags and had James carry them to Brutus for me. The rain had proved to be just a squall and had now settled down to a drizzle. The light was fading and I began to regret my impulsive decision. I was not looking forward to driving all the way to Truro in the dark along the precarious Cornish lanes. I turned on the headlights and windscreen wipers and gripped the wheel as I negotiated the narrow lane. I just prayed that I didn't meet any large vehicles coming the other way. I wasn't sure I knew how to reverse!

Before I reached the village of Rock with its post office and shop I came upon several vehicles parked beside the road. One of them was an ambulance and I recognized another as a police motorcar. As I slowed to a crawl, trying to negotiate past them, a group of men came up from the seashore, two of them carrying a stretcher on which a form was covered in a blanket. And following this procession was Jago. Of course my curiosity was now overwhelming. I drove to a spot where I could pull off the road and walked back to where the action was taking place, noticing as I did so that we were beside Trengilly, right at the spot where Belinda and I had accessed the grounds from climbing over the rocks at the seashore. The men were now loading the body—for body it must have been, into the back of the ambulance. Jago was deep in conversation with a policeman.

I went up to them. They broke off as they saw me approaching. "Has something happened?" I asked. "I noticed the ambulance."

"Just a sad accident, miss," the police constable said. He was one I hadn't encountered before, a friendly looking lad not much younger than me. "Local chap. Simple sort of fellow. Not quite right in the head, you know."

"Old Harry, you mean?" I asked, glancing at Jago for confirmation. "What happened to him?"

"Drowned," the policeman said. "He must have got caught by the tide. He often hung about on the seashore, didn't he?"

"Where did you find him?" I asked.

"He'd washed up on the rocks where you and Belinda were the other day," Jago said. "I was just telling the constable, some of our visitors were taking an evening stroll and spotted something at the water's edge. They came to find me."

"What was he doing on the rocks here? I wonder," the policeman said. "Nothing for the old man around here. Do you think he was trying to get onto the Trengilly estate?"

"I doubt it," Jago said. "I'd made it very clear to him once before that I'd hand him to the police for trespassing if he came here, and he was mortally afraid of the police, you know." He looked out up the estuary. "The tide's coming in. I reckon he must have fallen in somewhere closer to the headlands."

I followed his gaze. The land ahead of us curved in a sweeping bay and on the far side of that bay would be Trewoma. I pictured that narrow beach where we had met him once before. And the high cliffs where rocks had rained down . . .

"Did he have any injuries?" I asked.

"He was battered around a bit by the rocks," Jago said. "That's to be expected, I suppose, poor old fellow."

"Did he have any family?" The ambulance doors were now shut and the two ambulance drivers were climbing into the cab.

Jago shook his head. "Nobody. He just sort of slept rough. People used to let him use a shed or cow barn, you know. He'd do odd jobs. There was no malice in him."

"Well, thank you, sir," the constable said. "If I could just get the names of your guests who discovered him."

"Certainly," Jago said. "Here they come now."

And a group of people was coming up a narrow path from the shore. The woman at the front was wearing a fur coat. The men wore overcoats with collars turned up, hats shielding their faces in the fading light.

"How long is this going to take?" the woman demanded in accented English. "The rain is picking up and I'm getting horribly wet. You had better go and get the automobile for us, Jago. I do not want to have to walk back to the house."

"I only need your names, madam," the constable said.

"Helga von Dinslaken," the woman said as she approached us. "Can you spell that, do you think? I doubt it." And she laughed.

"And these are Baron von Stresen, Señor Arguello, Mr. and Mrs. Greenslade and Mr. O'Connor. I'll write them down for you and drop them off at the police station tomorrow, all right?" Jago said. "I don't want to keep our guests out in the rain. I'd better go and get the motorcar."

"That's fine with me, sir," the policeman said. "Sorry to have disturbed you. Thank you for your help. We'll be getting along, then."

"I'd better be going too," I said to Jago.

"Are you going back to Trewoma?"

"I was heading into Truro but I think I'll stay at White Sails tonight. It's quite upsetting about the old man." I started to walk away, feeling awkward as Jago's guests were joining him. I crossed the lane, heading back to my motorcar.

"Quite a little adventure." An American woman was allowing one of the men to help her over the stile.

"For God's sake, get the motorcar before we are soaked," the German woman said huffily. "Why didn't any of you men think of bringing an umbrella?"

"It's not too bad, Helga. We can walk back along the road. Come on," one of the men said. There was something about his voice that made me look back.

Then I almost stepped into the water-filled ditch beside the road. It was Darcy.

Chapter 28

I think I might be going mad. I know what I saw.

He had his hat low over his face and his collar turned up, but the man looked just like my husband.

"You are such a brutal slave driver, Mr. O'Connor," the German woman said and took his arm.

The man she had called Mr. O'Connor said, "I enjoy it, Frau von Dinslaken." He did not appear to have noticed me. I hesitated. I stood and watched them. He walked at a brisk pace, propelling the German in her fur coat, never once looking in my direction. Jago had run on ahead. The rest of the group followed, hurrying toward the main gate of Trengilly.

I reached Brutus, fumbled with the door lock and half fell into the driver's seat. My heart and my thoughts were racing. I sat, gripping the steering wheel, staring out ahead of me. Was I going mad? Was all this worry and staying at Trewoma affecting my brain? Surely I recognized my own husband but there had not been one flicker of recognition in his eyes that I could see. Had I made a mistake? After all, the light was poor and his hat was shading his features, and his voice did sound a lot more Irish than the way Darcy usually spoke. I had to tell myself that I was wishing him to be here, fooling myself.

I started the motor and drove to the village shop. The proprietress was just closing up and wasn't too happy about serving me, so I had to make some quick decisions—which wasn't easy in my current state of mind. I came away with a tin of soup, six eggs and a treacle tart. Not exactly a balanced meal but it would have to keep me until the next morning. There was no sign of life as I passed Trengilly this time. The gates were shut and no vehicles were parked nearby. I kept on driving, past the last of the houses, past the gates of Trewoma and up to the headland.

"Round Little Rumps," I muttered to myself as I slowed to a crawl, letting the headlamps cut a beam of light into the utter blackness ahead of me. We had laughed at that, not a care in the world only three days ago. It seemed like another age.

Now the rain was coming down hard and I was conscious of the fearful drop on my side of the road. What on earth had made me think it was a good idea to spend the night at White Sails? I knew the answer to that one. Because old Harry's body had washed up on the rocks and because someone who looked a lot like Darcy was staying nearby. Both of those things had to be examined in daylight.

I almost drove past the little gate leading down to White Sails. I cursed myself for not having a torch and left the headlamps on as I took the steps one by one and then located the front door. I opened it with Belinda's keys. Once inside I found matches and managed to light the lamp before I braved the steps again and brought down my luggage, carefully locking the front door behind me. Now I was safely inside I got the fire going and cooked myself boiled eggs and soup over the hob. It felt very lonely and remote, sitting by that fire with the hissing light of the oil lamp, but I told myself that Belinda would be feeling so much worse, spending the night in a prison cell. When would the telegram reach her father? I wondered. When would her solicitor come? Would they be able to arrange bail for her?

And if they couldn't? Would she be shipped to London to face trial at the Old Bailey? In my mind I went over the events of the day. Rose appearing behind me on the cliff top and, most disturbing of all, the old man's body washing up on the rocks at Trengilly. He had been frightened of "her." She had threatened to have him locked up but he had never said anything about what he saw. Had he seen Rose pushing Jonquil over the cliff? And now paid for it with his life . . .

Outside a great gust of wind buffeted the cottage. I should be making plans. Tomorrow I would visit Belinda, but did I have anything hopeful to tell her? Just my suspicions. And the fact that she did not kill old Harry. But then the police would say that nobody did. He was always wandering around on the seashore. Perhaps he fell and hit his head on a slippery rock and a wave took him. There would be no way to prove that his death wasn't accidental. I sighed, carried my dishes over to the sink and decided that I was not going to bother to heat water before the morning. Then I undressed for bed, wishing fervently that there was a hot-water bottle in the place. I curled into a little ball and lay listening to the wind and the waves.

I suppose I must have eventually drifted off to sleep when something woke me. Was it the creak of a floorboard? The lamp must have run out of oil and I was in complete darkness. I held my breath, remembering those steps coming up from the cave that would admit any intruder who knew about them. I thought I could hear breathing over the noise of the waves. I held my own breath, but nothing seemed to be moving. Then I felt the bedclothes cautiously lifted as someone was trying to slip into bed beside me. I sat up. "Jago, is that you again?" I demanded.

"So Jago has been visiting you frequently in bed, has he? I must speak to him about that," said my husband's voice as Darcy slid into the sheets beside me.

"Darcy!" I exclaimed. Then I did the sort of thing one does on such occasions. I flung my arms around him and burst into tears. "It was you. I knew it was you," I said. "Why didn't you let me know you'd seen me? I thought I was going mad."

He was stroking my hair, kissing my cheek. "Don't cry. It's all all right. And thank you for not recognizing me. It would not only have compromised what I'm doing but put me in danger."

"You said you were going on a boat train," I said, still allowing the occasional sob to escape. "I thought you'd be in South America or somewhere."

"I did take the boat train, to Paris," he said, "to meet up with certain gentlemen."

"They called you Mr. O'Connor."

"I'm an Irish gunrunner, working with the Republican Army," he said. "And some of these gentlemen are making a good living by trafficking in arms."

"You are dealing with smugglers?"

"It appears that way."

"So Jago was smuggling guns! Belinda was right," I exclaimed.

Darcy gave a little chuckle. "Jago? This is strictly entre nous but Jago is one of us."

"As in . . . ?"

"Yes. And not another word about it. He's in deeper than I am. And, by the way, what was that about his getting into bed with you again?"

"The first night we were here he didn't know the cottage was occupied and he tried to climb into bed with us in the middle of the night. We were all equally scared."

"I see. I suppose I'll have to take your word for it—the part about being scared, I mean." He paused. I felt the warmth of his arm around me, his sweet breath on my cheek. "I had no idea you were in Cornwall. I had as big a shock as you did. Look, I only heard a little of what's been happening. Belinda arrested for murder of a local man? What on earth is this about?"

"Oh, Darcy, it's been so awful," I said, and told him the whole thing. The words came out in such a rush that I'm sure he had trouble making sense of them.

"Hold your horses a minute," he said. "So you didn't go down to Cornwall with the intention of staying with these people?"

"No. We came down to see this cottage. Belinda has just inherited it. We had no idea it would be this remote or so primitive. How did you get in, by the way? I locked the front door."

"I came up from the cave. Jago told me how to. I borrowed a speedboat to get here. Quite nasty clambering over those rocks in the dark, let me tell you. So you came to this place, and . . ."

"It obviously wasn't suitable for us at the moment and we went into the nearest village and bumped into Rose Summers. She recognized Belinda. They chatted and she insisted we come to stay."

"Insisted?"

"Yes. Belinda wasn't at all keen. Rose had been the cook's daughter and was apparently not all that nice as a child. But Rose wouldn't take no for an answer and we had nowhere else to stay in the neighborhood so we went to Trewoma. That's the name of the house. They all have funny names down here."

"So Belinda hadn't seen Rose since childhood? What about the man who was murdered?"

"Ah, well, that was slightly different," I said and told him the truth about the affair.

"Crikey. That's bad. That gives her a perfect motive, doesn't it?"

"She managed to get away with not telling the police the whole story about that—only that she met him in London, but I think they guessed. Her name and address were in his book, for one thing, and if they ask his London friends, perhaps one of them would have known about her. But it only lasted a couple of weeks and it was several years ago. She did the right thing. She stopped seeing him when she found out he was engaged."

"So she stopped seeing him because he was about to marry Rose?"

"No, he was about to marry Jonquil," I said.

"Jonquil? Who is she? Where does she come into this?"

After a lot more explaining and a lot more questions Darcy said, "So you think that Jonquil's death is somehow linked to Tony's?"

"I think it has to be, don't you? She was wonderfully athletic, apparently. Why would she fall off a cliff?"

"And who could be behind two such different murders? One is stealthy and sneaky and one is brazen and violent."

"That's true," I agreed. "Maybe I'm wrong and Jonquil's death was an accident, but then there's old Harry—"

"Who is he?"

"The old man whose body you found today. He wasn't quite right in the head but he was clearly afraid of someone—a female, he called her 'she,' and he promised he'd never said anything about what he had seen. So Belinda and I thought he might have seen someone pushing Jonquil."

"And that person decided he was a bit too much of a risk?"

"Exactly. After the second murder the person is either becoming desperate or no longer has any qualms about killing. It would have been easy to finish him off. He's often wandering on the seashore and it wouldn't be hard to drop a rock or two on him and let the tide carry him away. We had a trickle of stones come down on us once when we stood on the beach. Rose thought that someone was up there, spying on us. We thought at the time that it was only maybe seabirds, but now I wonder . . ."

"So they arrested Belinda today. Why did you come here?"

"I couldn't very well go on staying at Trewoma, could I? It felt so awkward as the friend of the accused. Besides, Rose's mother arrived and I was no longer needed to provide company."

"So you didn't move out because you didn't feel safe?"

"It did cross my mind that I could be in danger," I confessed, "but then why me? I had no connection to anybody there."

"It's bloody cold in here." Darcy shifted position so that we were both under the covers. "Why didn't you go to a decent hotel?"

"I was going to stay close to Belinda in Truro," I said, "but after old Harry was killed and then after I thought I'd seen you I wanted to stay nearby."

There was a silence, then Darcy said, "Georgie, are you sure Belinda didn't do it?"

"Absolutely," I retorted. "She was taking a bath when he was killed. Actually he did come to her room earlier and try to suggest that they get back together, for old time's sake, but she told him to get lost. So how or why he ended up naked on her bed is a complete mystery."

"Unless someone saw him going into her room earlier and decided that it would be perfect to implicate her in his murder."

"Yes," I said.

"You must suspect somebody. Who else was in the house?"

"Only Rose and the servants," I said. "Belinda's window had been opened, so we wondered whether anyone had come in from the outside. But then how would they have managed to get a naked Tony into her room?" I paused. "I've been thinking, Darcy, and it has to be Rose. She likes to say that she's not very bright, but I think she's quite clever really. What if she has managed to pull off this whole thing?" And I went through my train of thought, from pushing Jonquil, claiming she was frightened of Tony, insisting that Belinda come to stay so she'd have a perfect setup for murder, to my own encounter with her on the cliffs and old Harry.

Darcy grunted. "It does make sense, if she had reason to believe he wanted to divorce her. But how would you ever prove any of this?"

"I don't know," I said. "I think she could just have managed it physically if she ran up the servant's staircase, but I was a bit out of breath when I went up those stairs. If she'd had to kill her husband in his bath, lift him into a wagon she had previously hidden nearby, drag him the length of a hall and arrange him on a bed, then go back the same way and appear with a mug of cocoa in her hands she would at least be breathing heavily. And she wasn't. She sounded quite relaxed when she came up the main staircase toward us."

"Interesting," Darcy said. "Do you think she might have enlisted someone's help? She was a cook's daughter, after all. Might she have been chummy with one of the servants? Actually brought them in for this very purpose?"

"It's a good point," I said. "The housekeeper has been with the family for ages—she used to be Jonquil's nursemaid, I gather, and she doesn't approve of Rose—getting above her station, you know. I tried to talk to one of the maids. She's a young local girl. Her brother works in the garden. The footman is another young local lad. I haven't met anyone else. There could be another gardener or chauffeur or someone. I do know that the staff were replaced not too long ago. The old faithful retainers were all let go."

"There you are, then. That gives us a good lead to follow. I'll try and get in touch with a chap I know at Scotland Yard."

"There is already an inspector from the Yard here," I said. "His name is Watt."

"Watt?"

"Precisely. Belinda and I laughed about it." I sighed. "Oh dear. Poor Belinda. We must do something quickly, Darcy."

"I'll do what I can, but obviously I don't have much time at the moment. I'm a guest at a house party with some pretty interesting people. And if I don't want to wind up floating in the river like old Harry, I have to tread rather carefully."

I touched his cheek. "Oh, Darcy. Please be careful."

"I'm always careful," he said. "Don't worry about me. You have enough on your plate."

"But if these people are smuggling guns . . . Do you think you should go back before you are missed?"

"Before daylight, yes," he said. "But before I brave the murky ocean I'm not going to waste the chance of being in bed with my wife."

And after that we didn't talk for quite a while.

Chapter 29

Things are finally happening! It's so wonderful to know that Darcy is close by.

When I awoke in the morning Darcy had gone. I found myself still smiling as I got out of bed. He was nearby. That was all that mattered. Until I was rekindling the fire and remembered that he was probably in a lot of danger. Why oh why did he have to take such stupid assignments? Why couldn't he settle down and be a farmer like Binky? I knew the answer. Because he enjoyed what he did. He loved the thrill.

We had arranged to meet at the village shop in Rock at noon. He would do what he could to help, but obviously he had to be extra cautious at the moment. "If necessary and I can't get away, you can give a note to Jago," he said. "He's a good man. Quite trustworthy."

I made tea and ate an egg plus the last of the treacle tart for breakfast, then set off for Truro. I encountered no vehicles on the road before I reached the village of Rock. As I passed the gate to Trengilly I slowed and glanced inside but there was no sign of movement that I could see. I felt a pang of apprehension that Darcy was in there with a group of potentially dangerous people. I had seen how easy it is to have a body wash up on the shore here. I had to tell myself that he knew what he was doing. This was old hat to him.

After that, I followed the signposts, leading me through villages with more unbelievable saints' names until I came to the city of Truro, nestled between hills with the three spires of its cathedral rising above the narrow streets. I was startled to hear the sound of church bells and realized that it must be Sunday. I had lost all track of time, shut away at Trewoma. The day was confirmed by smartly dressed people walking toward the cathedral.

I found a policeman directing traffic, and he showed me the way to the Crown Court, a little out of the center of the town. I asked to see Belinda, half expecting to be turned down, but a nice policeman led me to a room with a table and chairs in it. I sat and waited and after a little while Belinda was escorted in to sit opposite me. She looked hollow eyed and so scared and I wanted to get up and hug her, but the burly attendant stood right behind her.

"How are you holding up?" I asked.

"It's awful. I had to pee into a bucket," she said. "And I got a bowl of disgusting porridge for breakfast and there is no mirror for me to put on my makeup. I'm sure I look a fright."

Only Belinda would worry about her makeup in such circumstances.

"Did you manage to talk to Daddy?" she asked.

"He's away. At your hunting lodge in Scotland, I understand," I said. "I sent a telegram but I've no idea how long it will take to reach him."

"Oh damn and blast. That stupid hunting lodge. It's miles from anywhere."

"What about the solicitor? Did you telephone him?"

"I did and he's coming down today. I hope he can arrange bail.

But how can he do anything? They'll tell him the facts and he'll think I'm guilty too." She reached out to touch my hand but a cough from the attendant made her sit up straight again. "What are we going to do, Georgie?"

"Well, I have one piece of news. I'm not sure if it's good or not, but you remember the dotty old man? His body washed up yesterday. They said he was bashed about a bit on the rocks but I wonder if any of his wounds might have been the result of a blow to the head."

"Crikey. So you're saying that somebody killed him? Why would that help me?" she asked.

"Well, if the person who killed Tony also killed him, you had the perfect alibi."

"Not if we don't know when he was killed. It's probably hard to tell whether bodies that have been in salt water have been there twelve hours or three days. So who do you think might have killed him? You must have had time to think this through by now, Georgie."

I leaned closer to her, although I was sure the policeman could hear everything we were saying. "I'm wondering if Rose planned the whole thing. She was so insistent in inviting you, wasn't she? And going on about how she was scared of Tony? What if this was all one large and glorious scheme to get what she wanted? What if she had come down before and pushed Jonquil off the cliff and the old man had seen her? Remember how scared he was of 'her'?"

Belinda nodded. "I've been trying to think of ways that might tie Jonquil and Tony and me together. Was I only brought in as an alibi? And do you really think Rose could have managed to rush upstairs, kill Tony and get back down again?"

"It's just possible," I said. "There is a convenient back staircase. If she came up, spotted him coming down the hall to your room with just a bathrobe on, perhaps she might have stabbed him. . . ."

"And just happened to have a handy dagger with her?" Belinda said.

"You know what else," I said. "The wagon is missing from the nursery. The one with all the toys in it. It was quite big and sturdy for a child's plaything, wasn't it? I think it might have been used to transport Tony down the hall from the bathroom. I think it's possible he was killed in the bath."

"But someone would have had to clean up the blood," Belinda said. "You can't stab somebody in the bath and not have a lot of blood around."

I nodded agreement. "Mrs. Mannering cleaned up that bathroom," I said, "but that was the next morning. If it was Rose who killed him, she would have had plenty of opportunity to dispose of bloody towels before the police checked bathrooms. There was what looked like a wet towel on the bonfire. I didn't have a chance to see if there was any blood on it."

"We're never going to be able to prove anything, are we?" Belinda said in a small voice. "We can throw ideas around all we like, but there is absolutely no proof. If Rose killed him, then it's only natural that her fingerprints would be everywhere in the house. And apparently nobody has come forward to say they saw anything." There was a silence. The clock on the wall ticked loudly. "I was awake all last night, lying on that hard bed. Trying to make sense of things. And you know what kept going through my mind? The only thing that links the three of us was Colin."

"Colin? The boy who drowned all those years ago?"

She nodded. "We were all partly responsible for his death."

"But it was an accident. You didn't know he couldn't swim. And you were just a child, following older children. Nobody could have thought you were responsible."

"I suppose not," she said. "Although, according to Tony, Jonquil did say later that she knew he couldn't swim."

"And how many years have gone by? Twelve? If someone in his family wanted revenge, why wait this long?"

"Because we weren't in the same place before?" Belinda said. She sighed. "I know, it's a stupid thought and I don't know why I came up with it. But at this moment I'm willing to grasp at straws."

"What was his last name?" I asked. "The least we can do is see if any member of his family has been in the area."

"I can't even remember that." Belinda stared out past me. "An interesting name. Different. Huckleberry? Something like that." She waved a finger excitedly. "Hucklebee, that was it. Colin Hucklebee. I remember Jonquil making some sort of chant about it and Colin going red. They liked to tease him."

"And you?"

"I was sort of a background player. I suppose I went along with it. Jago was the only one who stood up for Colin."

"Jago? He's—" I started to say something, then remembered I was sworn to silence.

"He's what?"

"Remember you thought he was up to no good?" I said. "That night he came to the cottage he was out checking his lobster pots because someone had been helping themselves."

"That's what he says," Belinda said. "I suppose I had better give him the benefit of the doubt."

"He was very concerned when he heard about you, you know."

"Was he?" She tried to sound unimpressed by this but I knew her well enough to see the spark in her eyes.

"So back to business. Colin Hucklebee. Where did he live, do you remember that?"

"The Midlands somewhere. He had a Midlands accent. We teased him about that. Birmingham?" Then she waved her hand. "Look, just forget it. It's clutching at straws, as I said. It's all hopeless."

I didn't know what else to say. I could see all too easily that the police might question Tony's friends in London who might remember about Tony boasting about spending the night with Belinda. How could I promise to help her when I had no way of proving that Rose wanted her husband dead? We could hunt for the wagon, I thought. There might be a useful fingerprint on it, or even the fact that it had been hurled into a ravine or hidden beneath the bushes might make the police believe that Belinda wasn't responsible. But then Belinda could equally have killed Tony elsewhere and transported his body. It seemed hopeless.

"I'm not sure what to do," I said. "Should I find a hotel in Truro so that I can be near you, or should I keep on staying at White Sails so that I can be around in case anything useful happens or your father turns up?"

"You're staying at White Sails?"

"Well, I could hardly stay on at Trewoma, could I? Rose and her mother glaring at me suspiciously and a murderer among them too. At least this way I'm close by."

"Very brave of you, old thing," Belinda said. "Especially now we know that anyone can creep in from the cave below."

"That is a concern," I said, thinking of Darcy's arms around me last night. "But there is nowhere else nearby, is there?"

"I suppose not. But how will I get in touch with you if I am suddenly taken up to London?"

"You can telephone Trengilly. Jago knows where I am."

"And he's really concerned about me?"

"He is," I said.

"I'm sorry, miss, but you've had your allotted time," the policeman said. "You have to leave now."

I hardly thought this was the right time to tell him that I was "my lady" or at the very least "Mrs." and not "miss." It didn't seem worth worrying about in the grand scheme of things.

"Am I allowed to hug my friend?" I asked.

The policeman's expression softened. "Not really. Well, go on, then. I'll turn the other way."

I was just giving Belinda a hug when heavy footsteps approached and the door was opened. Inspector Watt came in, followed by the sergeant.

"Lady Georgiana," he said. "You're still here. I do wish you'd take my advice and go home."

"I'm not leaving until my friend has been proven innocent," I said.

"As to that . . ." He paused, frowning at Belinda. "Interesting development."

I thought he was going to say what Belinda feared—that the police had contacted Tony's London friends and someone remembered his affair with Belinda. But instead he said, "They've just concluded the autopsy on the dead man, and it seems that someone tried to drown him. Remember he had wet hair? Well, he also had water in his lungs. Not enough to have killed him, according to the police surgeon, but maybe to have rendered him unconscious."

"Well, that lets Miss Warburton-Stoke off the hook, doesn't it?" I said.

"How do you figure that, Lady Georgiana? The lady has confessed herself that she was taking a bath. So I'm thinking, knowing what these aristocrats get up to, what if they were in the bathtub together . . . what if things got . . . rather playful and she saw her chance to hold his head under the water?"

"But you still believe that he was stabbed on the bed and not transported from the bathroom already dead?" I asked.

"From the amount of blood on the bed I'd say he was alive and stabbed there," he said.

"Presumably you'd be able to check the bathroom for microscopic amounts of blood that had not been wiped away to confirm this?"

"We could do so, certainly, but I've seen stab wounds before. And if he'd been stabbed in the bathroom we'd also find blood in the corridor. My men did check that out."

"So what you are saying," I began carefully, making sure I presented this perfectly, "is that my friend, having half killed Mr. Summers while in the bathtub with him, decided not to finish him off there and make it look like an accident but dragged him the length of the hall and stabbed him in dramatic fashion on her bed, thus implicating herself and nobody else?" I paused. "Really, Inspector!" I laughed. "Any defense lawyer would make mincemeat of that."

His face had gone rather red. "Put like that you do have a point. I suppose the whole thing comes down to how easy it would have been to get him down that corridor. It's a long way from the nearest bathroom."

"It certainly is," I said. "But I think I might be able to help you." And I told him what I had observed about the wagon, also about the wet towel on the bonfire. "I think someone might have thrown them out of the window to be retrieved later," I said.

"Since you have been doing a bit of deducing and snooping," he said, "who do you think might be responsible if it is not your friend?"

"If you are suggesting that Tony Summers almost died, probably passed out, in the bathtub, then we have to look at who would want to implicate Belinda," I said. "If he'd been found floating in his bath, dead, it could have been perceived as an accident and certainly hard to prove it was murder, so the killer would have got away with it easily. Why risk taking him the length of the hall and stabbing him on Belinda's bed if not to involve her in the crime? Until now we have thought that somebody specifically wanted to kill Tony Summers, but what if that person equally wanted to kill Belinda Warburton-Stoke?"

"And who might come to mind, in your opinion?"

"The only person who had means and motive is his wife, Rose," I said, and I told him about the strange confession that Tony wanted to kill her, my own encounter on the cliff top and the gleam in her eye when she said she was now a rich widow.

DI Watt nodded. "Certainly she'd have had the best chance of catching him unawares in his bath, but why would she dislike Miss Warburton-Stoke? You said yourself that she hadn't seen you since childhood, didn't you?"

"I can't think, Detective Inspector," Belinda said. "Unless I was the privileged one and she was the servant's child and that had always rankled."

"Or she might be off her head, sir," the sergeant suggested. It was the first time he had spoken and he blushed scarlet when we all looked at him. "Perhaps she enjoys killing people. Some do, don't they?"

"Not many, in my experience," the inspector replied. "In the cases I've followed there has been a compelling reason for murder—fear or greed or vengeance. Not many people kill for the sport."

"In any case, Inspector," I said, "I take it this means that my friend is no longer your prime suspect and is free to go?"

He scratched his nose, considering this. "I suppose I have to say that she would no longer be our prime suspect, Lady Georgiana, given the facts that have been discussed this morning. However, this case is far from solved. I am willing to release her from custody at this moment but I don't want her leaving the vicinity for the time being. Is that clear?"

"Oh yes, Inspector," Belinda said. "And anything we can do to help?"

"I think it might be better if you don't go near Trewoma while we are conducting our inquiries," he said hastily. "Let's hope that the lady breaks down and confesses or someone at that house knows something, because frankly this whole thing still is a long way from making sense to me."

Chapter 30

OCTOBER 20

IN AND AROUND TRURO

I am so happy. Belinda is free. Now all we need to do is to have Rose
confess and we can go home. If there are no further complications,
that is.

"So what do we do now?" Belinda asked as we stepped out into the
fresh air. "I have my solicitor arriving from London today and then
Daddy may show up as soon as he gets the telegram, if the wicked
witch doesn't burn it first."

"Oh surely not," I said.

"You don't know my stepmother. She'll think with me out of the
way she'll get my inheritance, even though it will probably go to horrid Uncle Francis. In fact if she was anywhere within a hundred miles
of Cornwall she'd be my prime suspect. But the Highlands of Scotland are a wee bit far to come and commit a murder overnight." She
sighed. "So do you think I should stay on in Truro?"

"I think that's probably wise," I said. "You'll have to meet your solicitor from the London train, won't you?"

"Oh yes. Gosh, he's going to be annoyed that he's come all this way for nothing."

"Nonsense. He'll probably spend a couple of days at a nice Cornish hotel and put it on your bill," I said.

"So I should stay somewhere nearby, you think?"

I nodded. "Remember, the inspector will want to know where you are. We'll get you settled in but I have something I have to do back near Trewoma."

"You're not going to confront Rose?"

I laughed. "Oh, don't worry, I'm not going near the actual house but there is one thing I have to do." When she gave me a questioning look I went on, "I can't tell you what it is yet, but it may be helpful."

"You're being enigmatic. If it's something to do with the case, why can't you tell me?"

"I'll tell you later, I promise," I said. "Just trust me."

"So I suppose my hunch about Colin is now quite irrelevant? We shouldn't bother mentioning it to the police?"

"Let's hold off for the moment," I said. "If Rose confesses, then we don't need to go any further. So why don't we find you a hotel near the station? You can pop in and tell the police where to find you."

"You'll come back after you've done . . . what you said you wanted to do?"

"If necessary I'll stay at White Sails," I said.

"That is above the call of duty," she said.

"I'll survive."

"What if Jago decides to visit again in the middle of the night?"

"That could be interesting," I said and gave her a challenging smile.

"You're a married woman."

"That doesn't mean I don't appreciate the occasional middle-of-the-night visit."

"I'm getting worried about you, darling," she said. "I hope you're not turning into me. Poor Darcy."

"Don't worry. All is well, Belinda," I said. I had realized, on the way to Truro, that I could not tell her that Darcy was in the area, nor could I risk her seeing him. If I told her he was undercover, she'd probably forget or wave or say something like "nice disguise." I couldn't compromise his safety. I was just pondering these things as we walked down the steps from the county court when Belinda gave a little gasp—"Oh, look who's here"—and I looked up, expecting to see a distinguished lawyer or even her father. Instead, Jago was taking the steps two at a time toward us.

"They let you out," he said, beaming at her. "Have they decided you're not the guilty one?"

"It seems so," Belinda said. "So what brings you into town?"

"I had to drive one of the party to the station unexpectedly so I thought I'd pop by and see how you were doing and if there was anything I could do, as a local, you know."

"How very kind of you," she said. "As you can see, new evidence has come to light and I am free."

"So you'll be returning to London, I suppose, after all this unpleasantness," he said and I could hear the disappointment in his voice.

"No, I'm not allowed to leave the vicinity yet," she said. "And I'm still not sure that I want to abandon my plans for White Sails. It could be made into quite a charming little place, couldn't it? If I could shut off those stairs from the cave, that is."

He gave a cheeky grin. "Yes, you'd probably need to do that. I think the builder can do a good job for you. He's a reliable man. And I can keep an eye on things if you want to go back to London at some point."

"So you'll be staying down here?" she asked. "You don't have to go with your employer when he travels?"

"Some of the time," he said. "It depends where he's going and why.

But I like it down here. If you don't want White Sails, I'd be happy to buy it from you."

"Your own little smuggling retreat," she said.

He looked at her and laughed. "Is that what you've pegged me as? A smuggler?" He shook his head. "I have to admit my ancestors did very well from the trade. But I assure you I've chosen a more honorable route. So where are you heading now?"

"I have to find a hotel room so that I can meet my solicitor when he arrives. Somewhere near the station. Do you know Truro at all?"

"The Royal Hotel is probably the only choice for someone like you," he said. "Just down the hill from the station. Right in the center of town. Can I give you a lift? I have the boss's car."

"Oh, that's kind of you but I brought Belinda's car for her," I said and got a daggers look from Belinda.

"Well, you're all set up, then." He gave Belinda a friendly nod. "I'm really glad they got this sorted out so quickly for you."

I thought she might have said that her good pal Georgie helped get it sorted out, but she didn't. Jago gave a cheery wave and then sauntered off again. As soon as he was out of earshot she spun toward me. "He offered me a lift," she said, "and you had to say that I had my own car. What kind of friend are you?"

"Belinda, my darling," I said, "I had no idea that you were interested in him."

Of course I had realized, but I hadn't picked up that the offer of a ride was more than simple transportation. I was still clueless when it came to interactions and subtle hints between men and women. In fact it was a miracle that I had managed to snag one of my own. Actually quite a good one.

She sighed. "I suppose you're right. It's silly, isn't it? I mean, he's a little rough around the edges, absolutely NOCD. That has never worked, apart from Lady Chatterley, has it?"

(And in case you don't know, "NOCD" is upper-class shorthand meaning "not our class, dear.")

"I've never actually read *Lady Chatterley,*" I said.

"You haven't, darling? No wonder you are so naïve. I'll have to find you a copy. But anyway, Jago is regrettably quite unsuitable. Unless I'd like to settle at White Sails and learn how to gut fish."

I couldn't tell her that Jago really worked in the same kind of hush-hush activity as Darcy. But I did say, "He has a good job now, traveling the world, managing properties. . . ."

"For a shady millionaire. Not exactly stable. He'll probably be the scapegoat when the shady man is arrested and he'll wind up in an Argentinean jail."

"Anyway, as you've said, he's not suitable marriage material. Now let me escort you to your own motorcar and we'll find this Royal Hotel."

We located it easily enough. It wasn't exactly what I had been expecting. It was an old yellow stone building in the middle of town, but we were greeted with great deference, indicating that Belinda's arrest had not ever made it to the newspapers. She was so happy I had brought her suitcase of possessions with me in the motor. "My clothes," she sighed. "A long hot bath and clean clothes. Bliss. And you can take back Jonquil's cashmere dress. I never want to see it again."

I waited until she had changed and reluctantly took possession of the dress. I wasn't about to go to Trewoma to return it.

"I'll be back," I said. "You don't mind if I borrow Brutus, do you?"

"He seems to like you," Belinda said. "I'm sure you'll be nicer to him than I am. I seem to do horrible things to his gears."

"Well, I'll be on my way, then," I said, feeling suddenly awkward. Then she flung her arms around me. "You've been an absolute brick," she said. "The way you spoke to that inspector! Darling, you could be a barrister. If it wasn't for you, I'd still be languishing in there, living on bread and water. Shall we go and have a jolly good lunch somewhere?"

"I'm afraid I have to meet a person at a specific time," I said. "You enjoy your lunch. I'll see you later."

I watched her waving to me as I drove off, back to Rock. This time

I had to put my foot down and go rather faster as I had that assignment with Darcy to keep. I arrived back in the village at 11:45, left Brutus by the church and then sauntered across to the village shop. That was when, of course, I remembered that it was Sunday. The shop was closed. There were a couple of men heading for the pub but apart from that the village was empty and silent. It wasn't the kind of weather to be sitting outside or messing about in boats and I supposed everyone would be at home, preparing to eat Sunday lunch. This reminded me I was hungry. And no shop open to buy supplies if I spent the night at White Sails again. Then I reasoned I could do nothing more useful here after I had seen Darcy and I didn't want him risking his safety by taking the motorboat to see me in the middle of the night, however much I had appreciated his presence.

I looked around, then sat out of the wind on a bench beside the church and wrote a note, mentioning all the details on Colin and why he might have anything to do with two deaths. Then I sealed it and addressed it to Mr. O'Connor, just in case he was not able to be present himself. I strolled around, admiring the view, watching the ferry, then, as the clock on the church tower tolled twelve, I wandered back to stand outside the shop again. I was just in time to see Darcy heading toward the shop, stopping short as he too realized it was Sunday, and then looking around. I knew enough not to acknowledge him. I got up, walked behind him then called out, "Excuse me, sir. I think you dropped this?"

He turned and I handed him the envelope I had prepared.

"Much obliged, ma'am," he said in his distinctive Irish brogue. "It looks like the weather might be turning nasty again, doesn't it?"

"It certainly does," I replied. "Can I give you a lift somewhere?"

"I'm staying at a house nearby. It's no distance at all, not for an Irishman like myself, used to inclement weather."

"It's no trouble," I said. "I'm driving out to a property on the coast myself."

"In that case I wouldn't say no," he replied. "I didn't think to bring an umbrella."

I walked over to Brutus and got in. He climbed into the passenger side and we drove off.

"That was quite smooth. I'm impressed," he said. "But where did you get the car?"

"Belinda's. It's called Brutus. It feels horribly powerful," I said.

"Is she still in jail?"

"No. They released her this morning. It seems the autopsy revealed that Tony had been partly drowned first. And since I pointed out to the inspector that if she wanted to kill Tony, she'd hardly have half drowned him, then dragged him the length of the hall to stab him where everyone would pin the crime on her, he reluctantly had to agree. But she's to stay in the area."

"And what's in the note?"

"It may have nothing to do with anything now," I replied. "Belinda had a sudden hunch, but it had to do with a boy's death years ago. Jonquil, Tony and Belinda were all with the boy when he died." And I told him as much as I knew.

"And you think this might be a motive for killing now, after all this time?"

"I don't. Belinda had all night to lie and brood and this was her idea. I said I'd look into it. Do you have anyone who could do some digging?"

"Of course. Are you going back to White Sails?"

"I'm not sure there is any point. I can't go near Trewoma and Belinda is staying at a hotel in Truro. It's called the Royal Hotel—not particularly royal, off the main square. Her solicitor is arriving."

"I'm not sure how much longer I'll be here," he said. "Some of the party have already left."

"I know. We saw Jago in town," I said.

"Ah yes. He seemed very concerned about Belinda. Is there something there I don't know?"

"There could be. He's definitely interested and so is she. It's the problem of class, isn't it?"

"It does seem to be. Silly, isn't it, but it really matters. Lucky we found each other and you didn't have to wind up with Prince Siegfried." He broke off, looking up. "Ah, here we are. This is where I leave you."

"Do you know when you are coming home?"

He made a face. "I don't, exactly. I'll be here at least another day. Then I may be heading over to Dublin." Then he covered my hand with his own. "Don't worry. It's nothing too dangerous. We might already have what we need on Panopolis and his friends. I'll probably be home shortly after you." He opened the car door. "And if I wanted to find you? The Royal Hotel with Belinda?"

"I suppose so. She's not allowed to leave yet and I'll have to keep her company."

He nodded. "Many thanks for the lift, ma'am. Nice to have met you."

And he took off down the driveway just as the raindrops started in earnest.

Chapter 31

SUNDAY, OCTOBER 20, AND THEN MONDAY, OCTOBER 21
THE ROYAL HOTEL, TRURO, AND OUT AND ABOUT

Feeling a bit at loose ends now that Belinda is off the hook, but I'd
 really love the police to solve this murder and thus clear Belinda's
 name completely.

After such frantic activity it felt strange to have nothing to do. I drove
on, up to the entrance to Trewoma. I had been warned to stay away,
but I was dying to know if the police might be there yet, searching the
grounds for the wagon or the wet towels on the bonfire. I didn't think
they would have burned completely. I was really tempted to try and
find one of these things for myself, but I reminded myself it was no
longer any of my business. Belinda was no longer suspected and it was
up to the police to solve the case. I drove through Rock, lamenting
that the bakery was closed and I was awfully hungry, suddenly feeling that I'd like to go home. Back to Eynsleigh, back to Queenie's
cooking—which shows you how low I was feeling.

Eventually I drove back to Truro in a nasty squall of rain to find

Belinda sitting in the hotel parlor having tea with a distinguished-looking white-haired man who looked so much like a solicitor that I didn't have to wonder who he was. Belinda looked up and saw me.

"Oh, Georgie, you're back," she said. "This is Mr. Haversham, my solicitor."

The man rose to his feet and extended a hand. "Delighted to meet you, my lady. I hear you have been instrumental in securing Miss Warburton-Stoke's release. A nasty business, and a perplexing one. Have they actually made an arrest yet?"

"Not that we know of," I said.

"In any case I plan to stay in the area, just in case the police wish to interview my client again," he said. "Not a bad little hotel. Quite comfortable."

"I should leave you to talk," I said, now not sure what I should be doing. Should I also get a room here for the night? I had told Darcy this was where he could find me. So I asked at reception and was given a minute single room, just enough space to get in and out of a narrow bed. At least it was better than White Sails. I was told I was too late for Sunday lunch when I presented myself at the restaurant but they did manage to produce some grilled cheese on toast, which was better than nothing.

I joined Belinda and her solicitor for dinner, which was a most satisfying roast beef and Yorkshire pudding. Still no sign of her father, but that was to be expected if he had to make his way from the Scottish Highlands.

∿

THE NEXT DAY we had a leisurely breakfast and the solicitor announced he was going to visit the police headquarters to ask that they permit Belinda to return to London. We waited in the hotel drawing room, idly reading local newspapers with fascinating snippets about the disappearance of a pair of combinations from a washing line and the Women's Institute making a record sale of their chutney. We had lunch and just after, the solicitor came back to say the police would like her to remain in the area a little longer. He was going to stay another night and planned on visiting an old friend who lived nearby.

Belinda suggested we go and see the builder again and persuade him to come out to White Sails. This time I let her drive so we sped through the lanes considerably faster, until we came upon a flock of sheep, just released from a field. Belinda managed to stop inches from the nearest sheep's backside. There was much baaing and cursing from the shepherd who waved his crook at her.

"Silly man," she grumbled. "Sheep have no right to be on a public highway."

"It's hardly a highway."

"It doesn't matter. It's still supposed to be for motorcars," she said, inching Brutus forward as the sheep progressed at a snail's pace. Eventually we were free and found the builder in the village of Rock. He was an amiable sort and said if we gave him half an hour he'd have time for us. "Not that I can guarantee when I could get to the work," he added. "It all depends on how much that foreign bloke wants done. My word. Talk about fancy. All those bathrooms!"

We left him and wandered down to the quayside. The tide was coming in and it was interesting to watch how quickly the sandbars were swallowed up and the boats suddenly bobbed at their moorings. The sun had come out and it transformed the view into a perfect picture-postcard scene.

"It's lovely here, isn't it?" I said when at the same time Belinda muttered, "Oh no. Not Uncle Francis again!"

And he was coming up the steps from the jetty toward us. There was no way to avoid him. He saw Belinda and reacted with surprise.

"You're not in jail. I heard you'd been arrested. You didn't escape, did you?"

"If I did, I'd hardly be waiting on a public dock for the police to find me," she said.

"You might be trying to get somebody to sail you across to the Continent," he replied. "So they let you out on bail. That's good of them, considering that you'd be a flight risk. But, my dear child, I have to shake your hand for doing the dirty deed for me. Getting rid of that blighter Tony Summers. What a coup! I'm sure the watermen of Cornwall will erect a statue to you after you are no more."

"I'm sorry to disappoint you, Uncle Francis," Belinda said calmly, "but I am no longer a suspect in the murder of Mr. Summers."

"You're not?" I could read the disappointment on his face. "But I thought you were caught red-handed, holding the knife over his body."

"Alas no," Belinda said. "The police jumped to the wrong conclusions."

"The police actually questioned me," he said. "Apparently you told them I had a good motive. Not very sporting of you, I thought."

"You did suggest that I might put poison in his tea, I remember," Belinda said.

"But, my dear girl, that was a joke. Simply a joke. My God, Belinda. If I hadn't drunk a little too much that night and stayed on at the pub, I might have found myself behind bars. Usually I'm all alone on my boat. But thank God, for once I got involved in a game of dominoes."

"I'm sorry if I wrongly suspected you," Belinda said, "but I did ask myself why you had shown up at the house that day. You'd seen the daggers displayed."

"Apology accepted," he said. "So I expect you'll be hightailing out of here as fast as you can?"

"Not at the moment," Belinda said. "I've a builder coming to see White Sails. I need to put in a proper bathroom with some privacy."

She put a hand on my arm. "Come, Georgie. Let's go and see if that builder is ready yet."

When we were out of earshot she turned to me. Her face was red with anger. "Did you see him. He was so disappointed I wasn't languishing in a jail cell. Odious man. I'm going to make sure the builder puts in good doors with good locks at White Sails. I can't believe I ever considered giving him the cottage."

As we came back to the road a large car was approaching. It was the Rolls-Royce with Jago driving. It slowed when it saw us and Jago wound down the window. "I was told to give you this note, my lady," he said and handed me a letter, before speeding off again. Belinda stared after the car. "Wasn't that Darcy in the backseat with another man?" she asked.

"Don't be silly," I said. "Darcy is abroad. I suppose all Irishmen look the same to you."

"What is the note, then?" she asked. "And since when has Jago been handing you notes?"

"I had someone looking into a few details for me," I said, "in case we needed them."

"Details about what?" She was truly curious now.

I opened the envelope, praying that Darcy had not signed the note. It simply said,

Colin Huckerbee. Easy to trace. Parents still in area. Both work at Cadbury's Bournville factory outside Birmingham. Colin was only child. Adopted at birth. They did not know birth mother but, since they are Catholics and the adoption was arranged through the Church, they understood the child came from St. Anne's Home for unwed mothers in Coventry.

The home cooperated, knowing this was a police investigation. The mother's name was Alice Mannering.

Our eyes met.

"Mrs. Mannering?" Belinda said. "Someone connected to Mrs. Mannering? Her daughter?"

I shook my head. "Housekeepers always call themselves "Mrs." even though they are not married. It's her. She was the only other person who could have pulled it off. Come on, let's go up to Trewoma and see if any members of the police are still there. We have to stop them from arresting Rose."

I ran ahead of her to Brutus. Belinda started the motor and we shot forward. I realized I should never have suggested that she drive fast. Screeching around corners on a lane with granite stone walls on either side. I held my breath, also wanting to get to Trewoma quickly—in one piece if possible. As we swung in between the gateposts another motorcar was coming at speed up the drive. I opened my mouth to scream. Belinda jammed on the brakes, swerved and missed a Scots pine tree by inches. The other car almost wound up in a ditch. It came to a stop and Detective Inspector Watt wound down his window.

"What the devil do you think you are doing?" he yelled. "Driving like a madman." Then he saw it was Belinda. "Madwoman," he corrected. "What in God's name are you doing here? I told you to stay away."

I got out. "We were looking for you, Inspector. We have new evidence that shows that Rose Summers is innocent. You don't need to question her."

That was when I peered into the backseat. Rose was seated there with the sergeant beside her. She was staring at me in a sort of horrified fascination as if I was an apparition.

"What is this nonsense?" DI Watt demanded. "What sort of evidence, pray?"

"Can you get out of the car and go somewhere where we can talk?"

"Back to the house?"

"No, not back to the house," I said. "Away from the house. Where we can't be seen from the house."

He frowned as he got out of his motorcar. "I hope you know what you are doing, young woman," he said.

"I do. Please trust me. I think we may finally have got to the bottom of this."

I looked back at Belinda who was about to get out of Brutus. "You stay where you are. I'll be back." She went to say something, then realized the benefit of my suggestion.

The inspector and I walked together into the Scots pine trees. The wind made the branches above us creak and groan, but here there was no breeze and the ground was soft underfoot with pine needles. Above our heads a squirrel clucked an angry warning.

"Well?" he asked me.

I told him the story of Colin. He listened with growing impatience.

"You're trying to say that a boy's death, a summer visiting boy, not even one who lived down here, twelve years ago, has anything to do with this murder?"

"Everything to do with it," I said. "I have contacts within the Home Office. It has just been confirmed to me that the boy's real mother's name was Alice Mannering."

"Mannering?" He paused, frowning. "The housekeeper?"

"Yes."

He considered this while the wind rustled above us.

"You think this is revenge for the death of her son? A son she gave up at birth? After all this time? But it doesn't make sense."

"What if something finally pushed her over the edge?" I asked. "What if blaming Tony and Jonquil and Belinda for Colin's death has festered all these years, but recently something happened—" I broke off. "Tony was talking about selling up the house, turning it into a hotel and he said 'She'll have to go.' She loved to snoop. What if she overheard this and having Belinda in the house was perfect for her?"

"This seems like a long shot to me, young lady."

"The house is her life. She rules the roost here. If she was really going to have to leave—" I broke off. It would be in her interest to keep Rose in residence or she'd have no job.

He stared long and hard at me. "I hope you're right about this, young woman."

"I hope so too," I said.

Chapter 32

October 21

Back at Trewoma, hopefully for the last time!

We walked back to the motorcars. "It's also possible that she killed the late Mrs. Summers," I said, "but that would be hard to prove."

"The one who fell over a cliff?"

"That's right."

"In revenge for letting her son die?"

I shrugged. "Partly. Maybe in revenge that she had had to give up her son and Jonquil had led the most privileged life with everything she wanted. Who knows what can fester in a lonely person's mind?"

He looked at me long and hard. "How old are you?"

"Twenty-five."

"A big reader of crime novels, then?"

"No, Inspector. A big observer of crime," I said. "And I do know what living in a dark and isolated house like this can do to the mind. I grew up in a castle in Scotland. Luckily I had a kind nanny."

We reached the cars. He instructed his driver to turn around and drive slowly toward the house and told Belinda to stay well back. We did as we were told.

"Did he accept your story?" Belinda asked.

"Let's just say he's skeptical," I replied. "But he's willing to pursue it."

The police car drew up outside the front steps. Inspector Watt got out. We parked farther away.

"Perhaps we should stay here, out of sight, until the inspector has questioned her," I said.

"Are you joking? If she's guilty she would have gladly let me go to the gallows. She's a vile woman and I want to hear what she's got to say for herself."

We walked slowly forward as the inspector reached the foot of the steps. He had hardly started to ascend when the front door opened and Mrs. Mannering herself came out.

"I am so glad you returned, Inspector," she said. "I took the liberty of packing a small overnight bag for Mrs. Summers. Her basic toiletries and nightwear." Then she noticed Rose who had emerged from the vehicle. "Mrs. Summers? You are back. What has happened?"

"You are Alice Mannering?" The inspector stepped up to intercept her.

She looked surprised. "Yes, Alice is my Christian name. Why do you ask?"

"Mother of Colin? Colin Hucklebee?"

Her face had always looked white and featureless to me. Now she had gone even whiter, if that was possible. "Who told you about . . . ? How could you possibly know? Nobody knew."

"We have our ways," he said smoothly. "Suffice it to say that we know everything."

"There is nothing to know." She tossed her head defiantly. "I had a child. I had to give him up. But there wasn't a day I didn't think about him, wonder what he was doing, how he looked."

"And then he came here. Right on your doorstep, so to speak," the inspector said calmly. "That must have been hard for you—to have him so close and not be able to speak to him."

The look she gave him was of pure defiance. "You have no idea what I have endured, Inspector. No idea at all."

"But how did you find out the names of his adoptive parents? They normally keep them from the mother."

"I hired a private detective," she said, staring at him coldly. "I saved my stupid, hard-earned wages and I paid for him to find out. I used to visit the area in my summer holidays, just to catch glimpses of Colin. He turned into a lovely young man. His adoptive parents were so proud of him. Scholarship to the grammar school and talk of university."

"Was it pure luck that he came down here?"

She looked at him with scorn. "Of course not. I sent his family the brochures. I quoted them a ridiculously low rate on a bungalow. I paid the rest myself. And they took the bait. They came."

"Why did you want him down here? Just to see him a bit more?"

"I had a plan, Inspector," she said. "If you know everything else, then you must know that his father was Mr. Trefusis, the master of this house." I heard a tiny gasp come from Belinda. "I was a young, innocent housemaid. He took advantage of me. One does not refuse the master of the house, and it struck me that if I was a special favorite, maybe I'd get special treatment. Foolish notion, of course, but as I said, I was young and naïve."

She paused. "Then I found I was in the family way. Mr. Trefusis arranged to send me away to have the baby. I was a Catholic so he found this Catholic home for unmarried mothers run by nuns near Coventry and sent me there. It was awful. Like the workhouse but worse. Like prison, but worse. We were tormented, worked to death, treated like vermin. And as soon as I had the baby it was taken from me. I was given a week to recover and then sent back to work. I never saw my little boy again."

"But you came back to work for the Trefusis family?"

"I had nowhere else to go," she replied. "Beside, Mrs. Trefusis was now pregnant. I was offered the post of nursemaid to the child. An offer of appeasement, wouldn't you say? And so Jonquil became mine. Her parents were often away traveling or in London and I raised her. Such a beautiful child." Her face had become soft and wistful and I could see for a moment that she might have been a pretty young girl once. Then the look was gone in a flash. "Then she went away to school, and she changed. She became reckless, daring, foolhardy and to be honest ruthless. I did not like what I was seeing and I told her so. That was when she told me I was a servant and thus not entitled to an opinion. And I realized the truth. She didn't care about me at all."

"So your thoughts turned to Colin?"

"They were never far from him, but it occurred to me that Mrs. Trefusis had not been able to produce an heir. If I introduced Mr. Trefusis to his son, and he saw what a fine boy he was, maybe he might adopt him and make him the heir. So I brought Colin here, hoping for a fortuitous meeting. But before I could set one up, he was dead."

"An accident, though?"

"Was it?" Her voice was hard now. "I learned later that Jonquil knew Colin couldn't swim. And she always did have a sneaky side to her nature. I had caught her once before reading my diary. Had I expressed any of my thoughts for her to read? Quite possibly. I had nobody else to discuss things with. And she saw Colin as a rival, to be snuffed out."

"Why did you wait so long to kill her?" I asked, before I realized I should have stayed silent.

She glanced across at me, as if she hadn't even realized I was there. "Old Harry told you, didn't he? I knew he could never stay silent. Stupid old fool. I was sure nobody had seen, but he was always skulking around in the woods. I threatened him and I thought that had done the trick. But apparently not."

"So you killed him too?" the inspector asked.

She nodded. "After the first death it's never so hard anymore. You can only go to hell once, can't you?" And she actually smiled. "The truth was, Inspector, that Jonquil grew into a horrible adult. Maybe I spoiled her, maybe she was born with a personality flaw. But she started bringing men down here, making love to them under her husband's nose. She loved the danger, you see. One of these men had a splendid sailing boat. I heard them talking together, down at the dock. She said that she was already bored with Tony Summers and told this man she'd get a divorce and they'd sail off together. Sell the properties, buy a lovely yacht on the Med. She was standing on the cliffs one evening, gazing down the estuary, waiting for him. I came up to her. She said, 'Isn't it a lovely sunset, Manny? I feel so happy this evening.' I wanted to ask her what would happen to me if she sold the property, but while I was plucking up the courage she said, 'Go inside. It's rather cold.' And I said, 'Very good, Mrs. Summers.' And the moment she turned to gaze out to sea I pushed her over the cliff."

She looked almost triumphant. "I don't regret it for an instant. An eye for an eye. Isn't that what the Bible says? And she had not turned into a person of whom I could be proud."

"And Tony Summers?" DI Watt asked. "Was he killed for the same reason?"

"I quite liked him," she said. "He was well brought up and willing to learn, I thought. Then he married her—a cook's daughter. He brought disgrace to this house."

"Well, of all the ungrateful . . ." Rose said.

"I stayed silent, but then he talked of becoming bored, of turning this house into a hotel, of selling it and then I heard him say that I'd have to go. To go. After I have given my life to this house. Cast me out as if I were last year's fashion. So I saw that the timing was perfect, with Miss Belinda here."

"What could you possibly have against me?" Belinda asked.

Mrs. Mannering gave her a look of utter dislike. "Your grandmother. The wonderful Lady Knott. When I found that they planned to send me to that home for unmarried mothers to have my baby, I went to her. I had always seen her as a kind person. I told her I'd work in any capacity for her if she let me stay and keep my child. And she told me that girls with my low morals got exactly what they deserved. And she had me shown to the door. And then I saw her granddaughter that night. Flirting with a married man. And Mr. Summers went to her bedroom. He came out soon after but I knew he'd be back, and she'd welcome him back."

"That's not true," Belinda said. "I turned him away."

"Women always give in. Such weak creatures." She gave a snort of contempt. "So you gave me the perfect alibi, Miss Warburton-Stoke."

"We know exactly how you did it," I said. "You took Jonquil's little cart."

She gave me a cold stare, making me feel so uncomfortable that I wanted to look away. It was like the gaze of a snake. "I already knew it could carry several small children. I thought it would hold up and the rubber wheels made no sound. I hid it in the linen closet outside Mr. Summers's bathroom. Then I looked through his keyhole until he was lying back in the bath, eyes closed. I came in silently. He opened his eyes just at the moment I grabbed his ankles and yanked upward. Too late. His head went underwater. He thrashed for a bit but it was no use, of course, as long as his feet were in the air, his head could not rise above the surface. When he was unconscious, I put towels all over the floor to mop up the water, dragged him out onto a towel and pulled him down the hall on the wagon. Then I put him on her bed and I stabbed him in the chest."

"Where did you get the dagger?" I asked, remembering that we couldn't find where that particular one had come from.

"I keep one by my bed, for self-defense," she said. "I selected such a pretty one." She looked at the inspector. "Now, if you will give me a moment I will pack myself a small suitcase, like the one I prepared for Mrs. Summers, then I shall be ready to come with you."

"Go with her, Smith," the inspector said.

She gave him a hostile look. "It is not seemly that a man should watch a woman selecting her undergarments. I shall return right away." She stalked into the house. The young policeman went after her, standing at a respectful distance at the bottom of the stairs.

"I'll go and keep an eye on her," Rose said, stepping forward. "It's my house. She is my employee."

I watched her with appreciation. It was the first time I had heard her speak with confidence. They went up the stairs. We stood and waited inside the foyer. And waited. Just when I felt that they had been gone for a long time DI Watt said, "What can the woman be doing? She doesn't strike me as the type who would spend a lot of time choosing her knickers." He glanced at the constable waiting in the doorway. "You don't suppose she's given us the slip, do you? Gone out through the back door?"

"She didn't come back down the hall, sir," the constable said.

"What floor is she on?"

"I think the first floor."

"Aren't servants' rooms usually on the top floor?" Belinda asked.

The inspector shot her a worried look. "Go and check she hasn't come out of any back door, Williams."

"Right you are, sir."

"And we'd better see she hasn't done herself any harm." He started up the stairs. "Mrs. Summers, are you up here?"

He stood at the end of the first hallway, listening. Then he shook his head and started up the next flight. "Mrs. Summers?"

I don't know what instinct drove me but I went down the hall toward Jonquil's rooms. As I got closer I could hear hammering on a door, a muffled voice yelling "Help. Somebody help me."

"Inspector!" I yelled. "This way."

I tried the door. It was locked and no sign of the key. What's more, I could smell smoke. I shouted again. The sergeant came running. He tried hurling himself into the door with his shoulder but it was good solid English oak and didn't budge. Then he ran back down the hall and returned with a brass statue. "Stand back," he shouted and rammed it against one of the panels. It splintered. Smoke poured out and Rose's frightened face appeared. "Quick. Save me," she begged.

It took several more blows with the statue before enough of the door was broken to drag her out. I saw then that Jonquil's beautiful dresses were ablaze. So were the lace curtains.

"Where is she?" the sergeant shouted.

"I don't know. I followed her in here. She was already holding the oil lamp. She threw it at the dresses and lit a match. Then she shoved me to the floor and ran out."

I put a soothing hand on her shoulder. "Where can she have gone? She didn't come back toward us. Are there stairs at the end of this hall?"

"The servants' staircase."

We both ran down the hall to the end, to be greeted by more smoke. "What has she done?" Rose gasped. "Oh no."

We emerged onto the minstrel gallery above the big hall. Fire was now burning up the tapestries and across the floor.

"She's not trying to escape. She's setting the whole house on fire," Rose exclaimed "There are so many little servants' corridors she can get through."

"Call the fire brigade and get the servants out to safety," I said. "There's nothing we can do from here."

"I must find my mother," Rose said, suddenly realizing. "Oh God. I hope she's all right." She darted away from me shouting, "Mummy, where are you? There's a fire."

I heard an answering voice and heaved a small sigh of relief as her mother emerged from her bedroom.

I ran back and found the inspector coming down from the floor above. "Nobody up there," he began, then smelled the smoke. "What the devil?"

"She's setting rooms on fire," I said "She locked up Mrs. Summers. We're going to call the fire brigade."

"Georgie, are you all right?" Belinda was coming up the stairs toward me.

"I'm fine. Look after Rose and her mother. I have to call the fire brigade."

Servants had begun to appear from various parts of the house. "There's a fire in the library," a maid was wailing. "All the books are burning. It's going up like a torch."

"Make sure everyone is safe and accounted for," Rose said.

The fire brigade promised to get to us as quickly as possible, but they were a good ten minutes away. The footman started trying to organize a bucket brigade but the store cupboards by the kitchen were on fire and we couldn't get at the water. Someone ran for an outside hose. But there were too many fires, in too many places. It seemed that wherever we went she was one step ahead of us, knocking over lamps, setting the oil on fire and then disappearing to the next location. We could hear crackling and roaring as the fire took hold. Eventually we all had to retreat outside and wait for the fire brigade to arrive. The servants were huddled together weeping. The outside staff had joined the footman and were trying to be useful but with little success. Two fire engines finally came, one of them a tanker of water, and firemen started to spray their hoses, but it was clearly too little, too late.

"I'd just like to know where the damned woman is," DI Watt growled. "I've got someone guarding the back of the house. She hasn't emerged yet. She'll be burned to a crisp if she doesn't come out soon."

"That's probably what she wants," Rose said. "To go down in a blaze of glory."

"Save us the expense of a trial, I suppose," the inspector muttered.

"Where was her room, Rose?" I asked.

"I don't really know. I didn't pry much into where the servants slept. She always took care of that side of things. She was so darned efficient."

Suddenly someone said, "Look!" and pointed upward to the top of one of the towers. Mrs. Mannering stood there, hands on hips, laughing at us. "This is my house," she shouted down. "If I can't have it, then nobody can."

"Come down here right now," the inspector shouted back up at her. "You'll only make things worse for yourself."

"Don't be silly. I'm already going to hang," she shouted back. "Besides I couldn't come down if I wanted. And you can't come up. The ground floor is on fire."

And we could see that was true. Flames were glowing through the tower windows. We heard the sound of exploding glass and the flames licked up the side of the tower. We stood watching in horrified fascination as they came nearer and nearer to Mrs. Mannering. Suddenly we heard the sound of a motorcar, coming fast up the driveway. It was the Rolls-Royce. Jago jumped out of one door, and Darcy from the other. Both raced toward us. Darcy headed for me while Jago made a beeline for Belinda.

"Are you all right?" Darcy swept me into his arms, holding me so tightly I could hardly breathe.

"I'm fine. The housekeeper. She's set the place on fire. She's up there." I pointed at the tower. "No, don't think of trying to save her." I held on to him tightly, knowing his tendency to do brave and stupidly heroic things. "The lower floors are on fire."

"Belinda, are you all right?" Jago asked. "You shouldn't have come back here, putting yourself in danger." Then, to my surprise, as well as Belinda's, he grabbed her arms, drew her to him and kissed her savagely. I noticed that she was not struggling to get away.

"Well," she said, when she could finally breathe. "Well, that was unexpected."

"I've been wanting to do that from the first moment I saw you," Jago said.

"I must say it was a lot better than the last time you kissed me, when I was fourteen."

"I have had some practice in the meantime," Jago said. "Come on. Get in the car. I'm taking you back to Truro where you'll be safe."

"Sorry, Jago, I can't go with you," she said.

"What you need is a man to take care of you. I'm driving you back."

"That would be nice, but I'm not leaving Brutus here."

"Who is Brutus?"

"My little sports car."

"Georgie and I can drive Brutus for you," Darcy said. "You go with Jago."

"Darcy, what are you doing here?" she asked.

"Long story. Some other time. Now you go with Jago and we'll drive your car for you."

"If you insist," she said.

"We're taking these young ladies away from here. It's not fitting they should see this," Jago said. "They've had enough distressing things happening to them recently. You'll find them back in Truro if you want a statement from them, Inspector," Jago said. "Royal Hotel."

He took Belinda firmly by the arm and steered her to the Rolls-Royce. "You're very bossy, aren't you?" Belinda demanded.

"When I want to be," Jago said and bundled her into the front seat.

Chapter 33

Darcy and I didn't speak at all until we were seated in Brutus and driving away. I kept thinking about Mrs. Mannering up in that tower, waiting for the flames to reach her. I didn't need to look back but I knew in my heart that she had fallen to her death just like Jonquil. Either way I was glad Darcy had prevented me from seeing that spectacle.

"Are you sure you're all right?" he asked. "You didn't do anything stupid this time like trying to apprehend that woman?"

"No, I didn't. I merely told the inspector what we had found out and in fact Mrs. Mannering was so taken aback that we knew about Colin she sort of capitulated. She killed Jonquil Trefusis and Tony Summers and poor old Harry."

"For revenge?"

"It's complicated," I said. "I'll tell you later. But weren't you taking a big risk being seen here?"

"Absolutely not. Jago had to run an errand and saw the fire engines, then decided to follow them in case we could be of help."

"So you'll be going back there?" I asked.

"Just for tonight. Mr. Panopolis is chartering a yacht and sailing for ports unknown after this."

"I thought you were going to Ireland."

"Change of plans. I have to go up to London right away. I might be home with you in a couple of days."

"I can't tell you how happy that makes me," I said. He reached across and squeezed my hand, then swore under his breath as a farm cart was coming toward us and he had to swerve into the hedge.

⁂

BELINDA AND I were left at the hotel in Truro while Darcy took the London train and Jago went back to Trengilly. We settled down for a quiet cup of coffee and a biscuit.

"Goodness." Belinda put down her cup. "It seems so long since one has had a meal that isn't fraught with danger."

I agreed. "And we thought this would be a nice little break from boredom," I said. "At least we were never bored."

"Imagine that it was Mrs. Mannering," Belinda said. "I always felt that she was spooky, didn't you?"

"I did. She was just too perfect. There was one other time when I came up against a too perfect servant. And she was also dangerous. So remind me that I never get rid of Queenie. At least she'd only kill me by accident."

Belinda smiled. "I suppose living cut off from the world in a dark and gloomy house like that can start to prey on one's mind. She might have been a bright and hopeful young girl once. Forced into a relationship with her master. Baby taken away from her and she gives all her love and affection to someone who betrayed her."

"You were betrayed and had to give up your baby," I said, "but I haven't noticed you planning to kill anyone."

"No, I'm not the violent sort." She paused. "I must say I was disappointed to hear that my grandmother refused to help her."

"I remember that you were desperate that your grandmother didn't find out about your own pregnancy," I reminded her.

"You're right. She always was a stickler for correctness, in fact she—" She broke off as we heard raised voices in the reception hall. "I would have to check whether Miss Warburton-Stoke is actually in residence, sir," the frosty reception clerk was saying.

"What do you mean, have to check?" said an aggressive male voice. "Either she's here or she's not. I'm her father, dammit."

Belinda jumped up. "Daddy!" she yelled and rushed toward him.

"My dear child! Are you all right? I thought I'd find you in a prison cell. Are you out on bail? Don't worry. We'll find you the best lawyer. It was self-defense."

"Daddy, don't worry. Someone else has confessed. I'm a free woman. But it was so good of you to come."

"Had to leave a dashed good shoot," he said. "We were out three days stalking such a fine stag, and I had to leave the others to it."

"I'm glad to know I'm more important than a stag," Belinda said.

"Well, there are other stags but only one daughter," he confessed. He still had his arm around her. "What an ordeal, but you look splendid. Look, why don't you come home to us for a while. Let Cook try to fatten you up like she used to." There was a wistful look on his face. "We haven't seen anything of you in quite a while."

"You know why that is, don't you?" Belinda said.

Her father made a face. "I know that you and Sylvia don't exactly get along."

"Get along? Daddy, she made it quite clear from the first moment that she couldn't stand the sight of me. And she certainly didn't want to share your affection. The first time she came to the house I heard her saying 'You are planning to send her away to school, I hope?'"

"And she's made me feel unwanted ever since."

Major Warburton-Stoke coughed awkwardly. "Yes, but now you're a grown woman with your own life. You'd be a welcome visitor. I'd welcome a visit from you. Why don't you come?"

Belinda reached up and stroked his cheek. "It's sweet of you, Daddy. Maybe a little later, but right now I still have to stay down here. There will be an inquest. We'll have to testify. And I have to sort out what I want done to my little cottage."

"Very well," he said. "At least let me take you somewhere decent and buy you a slap-up luncheon. And you can tell me all your news."

"All right," Belinda said.

"I'd better see if this place has a room for me. I don't fancy another long train journey today. So give me a few minutes, all right?"

Belinda watched him go, then came over to me. "I should have introduced you but there didn't seem to be a right moment. Will you come to lunch with us?"

"I think you two should enjoy some time alone," I replied. "Who knows, this may signal a new chapter in your relationship."

"Not unless he strangles the wicked witch." She grinned. "Do you think I'm doing the right thing, staying on down here?"

"It's all about Jago, isn't it?"

She had the grace to blush. "Do you think I'm being silly?"

"It depends what you have in mind."

"I mean, he was so sweet, so concerned about me. He really cares, Georgie. But it can't work, can it?"

"He's not exactly a peasant boy, Belinda. He did go to Oxford. He's an educated man."

"I mean the whole problem with class. Look at poor Rose. Never really accepted. Never felt she belonged. I wonder what she will do now. Do you think she'll rebuild?"

"I doubt it," I said. "She was lonely, even when Tony was alive. I'm sure now that Mrs. Mannering put the doubts into her head that Tony wanted to kill her. That way she'd have a motive for murder. No, I bet she moves back to Bath to be near her mum." I looked up as a bright idea struck me. "You could buy the property, build the house you want on it."

"No thank you. I always felt there was some kind of gloom hanging over that place, didn't you? Maybe it is cursed. And it's too remote."

"Not as remote as White Sails."

"No, that really is a bit much. I don't think I'm very good at roughing it."

"So you don't want a place down here?"

Again she blushed. "Jago reckons that his boss's charmed life is about to end. He thinks the government will take over the property and I'd be able to buy it for a song."

"Back where you belong." I smiled at her excited face. "And where does Jago fit into this scheme?"

"I'm not sure yet. Small steps, Georgie. I'm not about to make any more mistakes. Jago suggested we might turn Trengilly into a hotel—with all these bathrooms! Have a manager on-site . . ."

"Jago?"

"Maybe. But anyway, it's an exciting prospect, isn't it?"

"I'm happy for you," I said. "Look, there's your father. You'd better go to lunch."

🐚

THE NEXT DAY I caught the train up to London and then transferred to Waterloo to journey home. I had called my housekeeper to let her know I was coming and to have Phipps pick me up at the station, and I arrived at just about teatime.

"Welcome home, my lady," Mrs. Holbrook said. "Would you like your tea served in the drawing room? I've had a lovely big fire made up there. It's certainly nippy out today, isn't it?"

"Thank you, Mrs. Holbrook," I said. "I'll go on through."

The fire was blazing away, the room looked comfortable and welcoming. This is my house, I thought. My home. And I felt a great swell of pride and happiness. I had just settled into one of the armchairs when I heard the sound of approaching feet. I looked up, expecting tea, but instead Darcy came into the room.

"I beat you to it," he said, beaming at my astonished face. "Welcome home." He came over and kissed me. "I'm glad to have you back safe and sound."

"I'm glad to be back," I said. "Sit down. Tea is about to be served."

"Did Belinda come with you?" he asked.

"She decided to stay on down there."

"Jago, I presume?"

I nodded. "I'm not sure if that's a good idea or not."

"He's a good chap. Solid. He may be right for her."

"I hope so. She deserves some happiness at last," I said, then looked up as I heard the rattle of the tea trolley. In it came, pushed by Queenie herself. It was laden with every kind of cake and biscuit imaginable: chocolate éclairs, cream puffs, brandy snaps, maids of honor, meringues, a Victoria sponge, a large plum cake, shortbreads, sandwiches and scones.

"Wotcher, miss. When she told me you were coming home I got busy," she said.

"Queenie!" I exclaimed. "When I said enough cakes and pastries I never meant . . . Now you've gone too far in the other direction."

"Some people are never bloomin' satisfied," Queenie said. "I work me fingers to the bone making everything that you like and you're having a good old moan about it."

"I am not having a moan, I promise you," I said. "It's just that—how are we going to eat all these before they spoil?"

"Now we've no option. We'll just have to invite the neighbors to tea," Darcy said with a cheeky grin.

"Oh, very well," I replied, laughing myself now. "Go on, Queenie. You can pour the tea for us."

"Bob's yer uncle, miss," she said.